G.A.S.P.

G.A.S.P.

R. JILL MAXWELL

ARCHWAY
PUBLISHING

Archway Publishing books may be ordered through booksellers or by contacting:

Archway Publishing
1663 Liberty Drive
Bloomington, IN 47403
www.archwaypublishing.com
1 (888) 242-5904

Cover image: Carlos Avelenda

This is a work of fiction. All of the characters, names, incidents, organizations, and dialogue in this novel are either the products of the author's imagination or are used fictitiously.

ISBN: 978-1-4808-2695-3 (sc)
ISBN: 978-1-4808-2696-0 (e)

Library of Congress Control Number: 2016900984

Print information available on the last page.

Archway Publishing rev. date: 03/15/2016

DEDICATION

For Brandon, Jessica, Alexandra and Jack

In loving memory of Ivy Ames

EPIGRAPH

"Hidden in the glorious wildness like unmined gold… " - John Muir

CONTENTS

Prologue xi

CHAPTER 1   Armed Sweat Money 1

CHAPTER 2   How 3

CHAPTER 3   Julie 4

CHAPTER 4   Dane 6

CHAPTER 5   Rules Part A 8

CHAPTER 6   Missing 10

CHAPTER 7   Rules Part B 16

CHAPTER 8   Buy In 17

CHAPTER 9   Stereotypical Or … 18

CHAPTER 10   Giddy 23

CHAPTER 11   Family … And Stranger Danger 27

CHAPTER 12   Anxiety 34

CHAPTER 13   Tracking Armored Truck 40

CHAPTER 14   Parental Guidance 41

CHAPTER 15   Auto Plant 45

CHAPTER 16   Airport Run 46

CHAPTER 17   Meet Rachel 53

CHAPTER 18   Nemesis 55

CHAPTER 19   Reconnect 58

CHAPTER 20   Unloading 69

CHAPTER 21   Dane 70

CHAPTER 22   Morning Of Reunion 74

CHAPTER 23   High School 78

CHAPTER 24   Friend Aubrey 89

CHAPTER 25   Accomplished? 91

CHAPTER 26   Transfer 93

CHAPTER 27   High School Reunion 94

CHAPTER 28   Just Post Reunion 119

CHAPTER 29   College For Life 131

CHAPTER 30   Business … Partner 132

CHAPTER 31   On A Roll 145

CHAPTER 32   Legal Client 150

CHAPTER 33   Direction Change 155

CHAPTER 34   Fallout 159

CHAPTER 35   "Biz" Trip 167

CHAPTER 36   Turmoil 177

CHAPTER 37   Exes Meet 184

CHAPTER 38   Paint And Upholstery 190

CHAPTER 39   Admonish … Again 191

CHAPTER 40   Everyone Loves A Parade 195

CHAPTER 41   Upside Down 201

CHAPTER 42   Revenge 212

CHAPTER 43   Home Visit 213

CHAPTER 44   Gut Space 227

CHAPTER 45   Followed? 229

CHAPTER 46   Julie To Aubrey 237

CHAPTER 47   Deeper Concealments 242

CHAPTER 48   Plan/ Try 244

CHAPTER 49   Transfer Complete 251

CHAPTER 50   Unexpected Intros 252

CHAPTER 51   Next Step 258

CHAPTER 52   Post-Concert 262

CHAPTER 53   Untimely 270

CHAPTER 54   Tag Along 274

              Acknowledgements 283

              About the Author 287

PROLOGUE

She remembered loving yet fearing him. He was handsome, strong, brilliant, adoring—his intensity frightened her though. Dane was far more mature and complicated than even she was; *his* being so at 17 was very unusual.

She was keenly aware of something else unusual, however. What could his big-time corporate legal career in old-established Europe have in common with her mom-turned-emerging-author in the casual Desert Southwest? Their lives had been completely separate for decades, and now they seemed to be constantly intertwined. The real question was why.

CHAPTER 1

Armed Sweat Money

The contents of the unmarked pickup were loaded into an armored truck. Swift and noiseless, the efficient team of two moved with obvious precision. A heavily armed four-man team surrounded the barren zone, clearly intending to complete their assignment uninterrupted. Everyone seemed completely unaffected by the subarctic temperatures of the remote Yukon Territory; but there was always one chatty one in a group.

"Okay, people, we need to talk."

"*How* and *why* are your lips still fuckin' moving?" snarled a muffled teammate.

"If you'd *come* from where I was to be here—" the chatty guard bragged.

"Just get the job done."

"I *was* gettin' the job done."

"Sounds like a personal problem, pal."

"Jesus *H.* Christmas, ladies! I'm gonna shoot you both, if you don't shut the *fuck* up!" threatened the chief.

"Ordered to be quiet in the middle of the boonies? Really, sir? Holy shit! They weigh a *ton*! What's in these boxes anyway?" Mr. Chatty grumbled. "Deceiving little bastards."

"Who the *fuck* knows or *cares*?" The chief's patience clearly waned.

"Yea, they paid us a shit-ton of cash, so *shut up* before we're sent back to that Siberian freezer," barked Muffled. "Froze our shriveled nuts off over there."

"Listen, assholes. Stay focused on the mission, so we get out of this mother-fuckin' cold, pick up our bonuses, and thaw our frozen peckers," ordered the chief.

CHAPTER 2

How

In spite of the unusually bitter temperatures gripping most of the Northern Hemisphere, Dane Michaels awoke early sweating that cold, dark January morning. He searched for her, haunted, though he logically knew she'd never been there. He was alone. But he'd more than felt her presence; he'd made love to her. "How could that possibly be? Was I *only* dreaming?" he mumbled aloud to himself as he stumbled out of bed and headed for the shower.

CHAPTER 3

Julie

Julie Archer sat anxiously at her computer. She was under deadline trying to figure out how to make girls' high school basketball come alive for the weekly sports update. It'd been a slow and predictable week with rivals Saint Catherine's Prep and Solanus Christian winning early in their seasons against much less-developed school teams. *Frankly, when some of these schools play each other, it seems downright unfair,* Julie thought to herself. High school sports in general, but girls' basketball in particular, seemed to have soared out of control with year-round playing and training. Julie knew all about this, since her own daughter was a starter for Saint Cat's, as it was affectionately known.

Six-foot-two Katie was strong, smart, and slowly coming into her own. She was awaiting her college acceptance to the University of Denver after already committing to their version of a partial-ride offer to play—hopefully throughout college. For years, Katie had dreamt of playing for a Division 1 program while academically nailing her studies so completely that the FBI, Secret Service, or the NSA would recruit her out of college.

Julie and her husband, Gabe, had supported Katie's dreams. A huge family commitment of club training, travel teams, and tournament play—not to mention workout trainers, chiropractors, and a variety of other specialists—kept Katie healthy and strong to play. Additional costs for the family to travel to watch her added up mercilessly, and there were *still* three other children to follow!

Julie caught herself daydreaming about her eldest daughter's impending future when the phone rang, and her email chimed in with a new message. She let her phone system record the message and ignored the email in an attempt to meet the deadline. She was genuinely surprised at how she struggled to get this article written. She'd never had a problem making girls' basketball real or interesting in the past. Having enjoyed playing in her own high school years, Julie understood enough about today's game to write intelligently. The challenge wasn't the writing. The challenge was that Julie's heart was no longer in the game. She just couldn't decide which game: basketball or her current game of life.

CHAPTER 4

Dane

Almost halfway around the world, Dane sat in a weekly meeting unsettled and agitated. His life was filled with meetings—some important, some just meetings about meetings. He was a lawyer's lawyer, operating at tremendous levels of stress. Bankers depended on his cool demeanor. Frantic clients called constantly. Assistants, however, held the key to his life: his calendar. He knew that without his top aide, Isabella, his professional world would be in complete disarray. She was almost as intense as he was, but she managed to keep her personal life gloriously private. Dane had had enough drama with his divorce and really didn't want to live through anyone else's drama, even if vicariously.

Though he was in charge of financially structuring vast deals between companies and entire countries, staggering amounts of money, and the evolution of international finance, Dane had little control over his personal life anymore. Since recently taking over two huge clients from his boss, Dane's life seemed to be on a dangerous tilt, heading for disaster. The missing money would normally have been just an accounting issue, but it had somehow been wrongly linked to his personal life. He was becoming antagonistically aware that not only was his time not his own, his life was slipping through his fingers, too.

He loved and hated his job. His position in such an outstanding firm was unparalleled. He was highly respected, though not even a partner yet, and even awed those who worked closest to him for laser-like focus and uncanny, methodical dedication to both the client and the firm. Still, he wasn't in a position yet to sift through and pick and choose what he wanted to really do within the company—or his own life, really—*or am I?* he wondered.

He didn't have time to be lonely, though when he sat still, even for just a few moments, an overwhelming feeling of isolation settled in his soul. He didn't miss his ex-wife; after all, they'd been divorced for years. He missed what she represented: a reason to go home, a reason to take a vacation, a reason to smile and laugh.

Realizing that he'd actually been daydreaming, an unusual and rare non-work activity, he forced himself back to reality and the tasks at hand. He gathered the documents he needed for his trip that afternoon, checked in with one of his interns since Isabella was already on a mission for him, located the department assistant traveling with him, and headed for the elevator to the awaiting limo. ***My** life just has to wait a little longer,* Dane ordered himself.

CHAPTER 5

Rules Part A

As she reflected on her post-graduate years, the exercise was meant to analyze and evaluate her growth. Business gurus taught her that she couldn't improve what she hadn't tracked and measured. When she'd first started, she'd been frightened and anxious, even taking backseats to lesser counterparts. She believed keeping a low profile and submitting ideas through male higher-ups would get her acknowledged without "rocking the boat." Instead, those higher-ups took credit for her work. Their betrayal had done more than just sting; it was more like a sucker punch, knocking all of the air out of her lungs. Greater than a mere life lesson, as several had suggested, she'd immediately recognized her core burning. This was a pivotal transition—a catapult to grow up, be accountable, and take charge of her life as *she'd* wanted it. How else was she finally going to be seen by the one person who mattered most to her?

Now she fumed at herself. She'd allowed others' doubts about her abilities influence what she *knew* about herself, so she vowed that no one from her past would guess that she'd become a powerhouse—a powerhouse who also needed, *right now,* more time and money to make her points. Oh, she'd keep a similar low profile. Ostentatious was simply not her style. *Better they barely take notice*, she'd decided.

Then they'd never know or understand what had hit them. My influence will be known when absolutely necessary, if at all. Sometimes it's just better not to be the obvious sledgehammer. The squeaky wheel doesn't always get the oil. Sometimes the faster or more clever one does. Damn, I love this self-reflection exercise. Warms my heart. Actually, it fires me right—back—up.

CHAPTER 6

Missing

The money was indeed missing, and Dane was being framed for it. He had an idea who was behind it all, but he hadn't been able to prove his theories yet—or why. So far, at least the "bad guys" weren't aware that he'd made this discovery. Still, he only knew five facts about the missing money: (1) only one client was involved; (2) that same client owned two companies in two very different industries; (3) his boss, Victor Bosko, had been the lawyer for that one client for many years; (4) Dane knew little to nothing about either field, or that client, for that matter; and (5) he, Dane Michaels, rising law firm star, hoping to make partner by year's end, was now the lead legal counsel for that client — and the only person under suspicion.

He scratched his head, trying to figure out how there could've possibly been a connection between the gold mining industry and the business of renovating old cars beyond who owned them. He knew the link existed, and he knew it couldn't be legal.

* * *

With his suit jacket slung over the back of an ergonomic desk chair, the high-powered attorney sat back. His right leg stretched out across the corner of a dark mahogany desk as he stared out of his office window—thinking. The third-floor view offered a decent, though partially obstructed, perspective of the sky above Zurich, Switzerland. Still, it was acceptable for a deep thinker needing to gaze off to gain insight—sometimes to just regain peace. American-educated Dane had grown used to the early-morning activity in the skies since he began his Zurich assignment. With a blank, white legal pad under his right forearm and a simple silver pen in his hand, Dane hoped to draw or note *some* connections.

Why would Victor be willing to send him to Arizona to meet with a car renovator client (a trip normally Victor himself would only have taken) and piggyback it with Dane's new Canadian gold mining client, another account recently turned over to Dane by Victor? Coincidence? Dane knew there was no such thing as coincidences. He simply didn't believe in them. There was something about this sequence of events that was irritating him. He just didn't know why. He sat confused and mesmerized in thought, clicking his pen mindlessly, hoping to jar his brain.

"Morning, Boss." Isabella Breslaux jarred it for him. "You're here earlier than usual, because I'm here earlier than usual. What's up?" Dane's smartly-dressed assistant brightly started their morning, clearly grounding her boss.

"Hey. Good morning. Just trying to get organized before I go out of town again. So many details and so little time. What's your excuse?" Dane looked back at his empty pad.

"I knew you were going out of town; figured you'd throw a bunch of last-minute challenges at me and guessed there'd be no coffee made," Isabella smirked. "Besides, I couldn't sleep and realized I was bothered by something here at work. I was hoping to sort through that and get some of my own questions answered."

Looking up, but trying not to look too curious, Dane nudged, "Hmm. Like what?"

"Like, well, I don't want to be too forward, but why are you suddenly being assigned to that mining client? You and I are already stretched to the limits on our other clients. We barely have enough time to breathe." Isabella glanced at Dane and quickly scanned his reaction for agreement or disapproval before pressing on. "Victor's been managing that client for years. And how about that car guy in the U.S.? I know you've met him—done a little business with him even—but why turn *him* over to you, too? Both accounts? Simultaneously? No offense, but that doesn't make sense. What do you think?"

Dane kept his face calm and as expressionless as possible, nodding a bit of consent to encourage the diminutive assistant's thinking aloud to continue.

"I mean, are you angry in overwhelm, or resigned in agreement?"

Dane considered Isabella's question. "Neither, actually."

The young paralegal breathed a sigh of relief knowing that Dane wasn't about to fire her; however, she was experienced enough to be concerned about what he *was* about to say or do. Patient silence was the best option. *Give the boss time to make his usual brilliant and thoughtful contribution to the rare discussion*, she reminded herself.

"I'm curious more than angry," he stated thoughtfully. "There's definitely something going on here, but I just don't know what yet. Keep your ears open at the water cooler. Let me know what you hear. Just don't say anything to anyone about this little chat we just had. Not yet. Understand?" Dane waited for Isabella's head-consenting nod.

"For your safety as well as mine. Let me know if you hear any talk about car renovating or gold mines. Offer nothing to those who ask you about any of our cases. Use the excuse that we're overwhelmed and grumpier than usual just trying to cope with a larger workload and not very sociable."

"Ha! That's easy! Aren't you normally like that?" Another quick glance and—*oops*—*crossed a line that time*. "Sorry. Um … seriously though? You aren't known as the most cordial attorney in this firm, so that excuse won't be out of line."

"Ok, I can't disagree there. Then how about even less sociable than normal? I'm focused. You know that. I'm not going to apologize for that. I can't make partner this year if I can't manage a sizable client list. I can't manage all that without my focus or your help. I can't focus if I have to be sociable, too. Besides, how are *you* going to make more and afford *your* fabulous lifestyle if we don't focus? Hmm?" Dane tried to sound a little charming.

"See, that's where we differ a bit. I believe you can focus at work and still manage to have a social life."

"Clearly, I haven't been very good at that last part."

"Perhaps it wasn't that you were socializing." Isabella knew she needed to tread very cautiously with this topic. "Perhaps it was *who* you socialized *with*." Her boss was a very patient man, but his private life was very private—even, for the most part, from her—though her usual respectful distance allowed her a certain latitude in their professional relationship over the years.

She'd worked for the firm for only a few months when she'd been assigned to Dane as a legal research assistant. He was really hard to get to know, though really easy to work with. He was direct and patient with all topics work-related. The other side of him, however, was essentially off-limits.

He hadn't gone out after work to have a drink with anyone at the firm until recently, when the varied partners started taking turns wooing him selfishly for their divisions. Isabella had worked for Dane for almost a year before she'd figured out that he was miserable in his marriage to a gorgeous lingerie model. Eventually, his now-ex-wife came into the office accusing "that assistant," as Rachel had referred to Isabella in a seething moment, as the cause of their marital problems. Every person in the office knew that wasn't true, so her job was never truly threatened. After the divorce, Rachel apologized to Isabella, who graciously accepted it more to benefit her boss and keep the peace than because she forgave the standoffish woman.

Dane looked down, half smiled, and knew damned well that truer words were never spoken. "Perhaps. I'm not there yet. Maybe this trip is better timing than either of us realize." After a slow breath in and then steadily released, they returned to the previous subject. "Anyway, offer some juicy tidbit that I won't care is going around about me and my lack of social life, like 'he's not figured out how to go forward yet' or 'he's not ready,' ok? That might get someone talking who otherwise wouldn't initiate an information-swapping session. What'd ya think?"

"Got it. Leave it to me."

"Just remember one thing: we don't know who or

what we are exactly questioning or dealing with here. Be extreeeemely careful," Dane cautioned. He waited another moment, then continued, "We've finally figured out how to work well together, and we don't want to have to start all over again, right?" He tried to keep a straight face. Isabella just shook her head and laughed at him as she walked away. She didn't see that he was actually a little concerned but attempted to mask it with rare humor to not scare her.

The boss rarely shows his humor, she thought to herself. *Maybe he's closer to being ready than he realizes.*

Rules Part B

Like matters of the heart, money elicited many emotions. Right now, however, she fervently owned the emotion of urgency. No longer fearful but fearless, the thrill of winning was an intoxicating incentive. She knew she needed to play it cool to obtain money for the excavation that had to happen *now*—before anyone else got wind of the geological survey's results or the landman's report. Now that she was certain she was the only surviving family member who'd inherited the mineral rights, her lawyer was scrambling to extend the 50-year lease about to expire on the land she also owned. She knew that the Big Boys didn't play fair once they got all their inspections, licenses, permits, and logistics worked out; that's why she'd made "friends" with the mining engineer surveying the land. He'd shared information about what he'd expected to find with her before he even realized who she was.

Though the big companies had been going after that information for years and spending millions, she'd been quietly asking questions of key people and squirreling away funds over decades. She just needed to stake her claim and start digging— while she still had rights to the land—AND remain anonymous. Time was running out before the sale went through. After all, she knew that whoever had the gold got to call all the shots.

CHAPTER 8

Buy In

"So, what you're telling me is that while most of the gold in circulation today had been mined over a hundred years ago, and only about a third of *that* gets recycled and reused *now*, there's still a LOT to be unearthed? How much is a lot?"

"Well, according to the U.S. Geological Society …"

"Seriously? 'According to the …'"

"Let me finish. And yeah, according to them, of all the gold that we can get our hands on now, well, there's still about a third more in the ground. However—and this is where things get more interesting—according to some investment guy who died a few years ago, there's actually waaay more than that still in the ground. So somebody's holdin' out on us."

"Some guy who died," he snidely noted. "That's a pretty significant-sounding source, my dear."

"Ever hear of a guy by the name of Peter Bernstein? He was a major leaguer in the world of economics and finance. Do your own research, but let's just say finance was in his blood. Anyway, according to a book he wrote about a decade ago, there's *tons* more than 30-ish percent in the ground still, and we're primed and ready to go after it."

The skeptic's raised eyebrows and slightly enlarged pupils gave him away.

She knew he was in.

CHAPTER 9

Stereotypical Or …

Her life was chaotic. Julie knew that *all* moms' lives were often just managing bedlam. Kids. Schedules. Husbands. Work. Stay-at-home or work outside of the home. This was an inescapable fact worldwide. Some seemed to be more organized and even thrive in the constant upheaval. Others appeared overwhelmed and under-supported. Either way, women were essentially putting themselves, their true interests, and passions last or even on hold. Motherhood's responsibilities regularly hogged the spotlight—not unusual given the enviable ages of the cast of little characters —and clouded most adult thinking.

Gabe made a great living and had been an amazing provider all their married life. He was diligent, focused, and the best in his field. The troubling economy affected everyone, though. It galvanized creativity and ingenuity, then highlighted weaknesses within all businesses— including the business of marriage. Julie and Gabe weren't exceptions.

"You know what's so crazy?" Gabe had grumbled recently one night after coming home from work. "Just when you think you've got it figured out, the economy nosedives because of some greedy jerks!"

Compassionately, Julie ventured, "I gather today's

mortgage bubble news had a less than celebratory impact on our big event business?"

"That's an understatement," he growled back at her.

"Ouch," she winced.

Oblivious to her retreat, Gabe continued his detached venting, "The whole industry is hardly what one would call 'recession proof,' Julie. You know that. Come on. It might as well be the entertainment or party business. Concerts are being cancelled, and tickets are being refunded. Who wants to celebrate when they're losing jobs and homes—lucky to even be able to make ends meet at all?"

When he'd finally taken a breath, he simply stared at the television. Julie knew he was anxious and concerned not only about the survival of their business, but of them as a family. She waited for him to remember she was still in the room.

"I've been looking for a new career path ever since you'd asked me to return to help in our business." Julie's anxious and strained voice tried to reach her husband. *Hmmm. No response. No point in trying to talk about this sales position right now,* she sadly thought. *He's unreachable—again. This communication gap between us is becoming the norm. UGH!*

Gabe's annoyed look made it clear to his wife that he hadn't wanted to revisit that topic.

Their big event business had been his passion, not hers. She was too far removed from that business to return in any capacity. It had truly outgrown her abilities, relevance *and*, more importantly, her interests. She knew it was time to re-align herself with her own values and aspirations, but in what capacity?

Eventually, determined to make a difference during harsh economic times, Julie accepted, then shared, her new sales opportunity with her family and friends who were experiencing the same ugly fiscal realities. Usually alone, though Gabe had agreed to help her get it off the ground, Julie couldn't shake an uneasy feeling deep in her core about his minimal participation and hollow support. *Uh-oh. Something's up. I feel it.*

Often alone with her thoughts as she travelled to sales training meetings, Julie became aware of other concerns. *Wasn't this new opportunity allegedly to be explored and grown with Gabe?* Apparently, Gabe had assumed Julie would just move forward on the training alone—he already knew everything about the products *they* were representing—while *he* continued to focus on their main company. Now she struggled to reclaim her time and focus altogether. She felt trapped!

She tried to rationalize with herself. "This new sales commitment *isn't* what I really *want* to be doing with *my* spare time. WHY AM I DOING IT THEN!?!" she shouted at herself in the privacy of her car. "I know I need to stay focused on the kids to keep them on the right track. They're the first priority. On the other hand," Julie elucidated, "I know I'm not getting any younger; time's still marching forward, and I *need* to go after something that *I* want."

She suddenly fell silent for a moment. "I also want to feel respected as well as desired, not just needed by my family like a conscientious but adored nanny." *Hmmm. Just as I'd thought. I'm no longer just thinking about my new career, or any career, actually. Ouch.* "I sound like a stereotypical character in the movies feeling sorry for myself. A tall order for reality or typical midlife crisis issues?" Julie lamented. "Maybe this high school reunion will be a perfect excuse to compare notes with my classmates," she thought, recalling the recent email she'd received to "save the date."

"How pathetic! What the hell is the matter with me? This *must* be a mid-life crisis," she muttered, mortified even though alone. "This is not all on him. I've got to accept responsibility, too, right? There," she figured out, "I've averted another crabby, unsettled mood shift. All better!"

Stopped at a red light, Julie checked herself out in her rearview mirror, appeared confused, and clutched the steering wheel. *Crazy! I just took responsibility for all the challenges in our marriage as well as my entire life. Is it possible to discuss all marital challenges in the car AND resolve them? Alone?* "When does one partner realize they need to cut their losses and move on? That the other partner is just not going to get it? No wonder Gabe seems to be let off easy. I burden myself, as most women likely do excuse their spouse, then eventually I'll just explode with resentment. Once I've let off enough steam, I'll return to 'normal,' making excuses for Gabe all over again without even giving him the benefit of speaking for himself. WOW! I really *have* done this to myself. So, this lacking feeling may or may not be due to lack of attention by my spouse. Could this have been self-inflicted??" An outward groan escaped her throat.

As she'd done so many times before, Julie ordered herself, "O.K. Quit your whining. You know what you've got to do. Focus on today's schedule, then either get this new opportunity going, or dump out fast and move on to what I *actually* want." She knew that any fiscal relief would help on so many levels—not to mention properly refocus some of her attention to something positive instead of all this feel-sorry-for-herself garbage. Yawning in flickering states of awareness, however, Julie knew that this opportunity wasn't her life's mission, either. Regrettably, she felt obligated to give it a solid go, especially since her husband was disappointingly withdrawing his initial support … already.

CHAPTER 10

Giddy

A quick phone call was all it took once the survey stakes had been set, core sample test results compiled, geotechnical reports accounted for, and plans prepared. Then excavation would begin. She simply verified with the local court that she was the sole owner on record, having answered all of the necessary identifying questions, as per her lawyer, for the sale to fall through.

"YES!!! YES!!! YES!!!!" she shouted to her dogs victoriously. "I *wish* I could see their faces when they get this news. OH! MY! LORD!!!!! It's almost not enough to just know they're going to be pissed; I want those assholes to writhe. Damn! Outsmarted by a girl! I can hear them all now. HA! Gotta give that lawyer of mine a bonus. Literally worth his weight in *gold*!!"

Squealing and panting, she decided a run with her dogs would calm her down before the kids had to be picked up from school.

* * *

Dane was alone at night. His kids came for most extended or alternate weekends only. He didn't believe that a middle-of-the-week overnight was healthy or stable for them, unless they were off from school the next day. He also didn't believe that children ought to be forced into switching houses weekly. At first, his ex thought he was trying to abandon his parental duties until he made her an offer: how about he be the primary caregiver? Let the kids live with him, giving his likely-soon-to-be-ex-wife the space she believed she wanted from him, the kids, and responsibilities. Rachel took him up on it—both shocked and smug—assuming he'd call begging her to come back within days, then suspicious as to why he'd really offered to begin with. Instead, almost the reverse happened.

He'd had the kids for just two months when Rachel couldn't stand being away from their children nightly. It was Dane she'd needed space from. He never complained aloud when he had the kids, even though he had to completely rearrange his work calendar and cut back on the travel crucial to the law firm. He gave the firm every ounce of available energy and focus. It was life giving. The partners valued Dane's efforts, loyalties, and production. He pretty much missed nothing, in spite of his demanding personal challenges. They always believed he'd figure things out with the ex. They were right, but not in the ways they'd expected.

Dane wasn't surprised when Rachel came to him tearfully asking for the children back, no longer wanting to be without them, to figure out what was best for them, and to ask for a divorce. She understood firsthand that Dane wasn't trying to shirk his parenting duties at all. He genuinely had the best interests of their children above even his own needs—a rarity amongst their social peers, male and female alike.

He was morose about dismantling his family but knew Rachel was right about one thing. She'd believed he wasn't over someone else, someone long before her. Rachel had hoped she could help Dane move on: gifted children, fabulous career, and lingerie-runway model wife. In her eyes, as well as in the eyes of all who knew him, he had it all! Very rarely did his calm demeanor change, his patience waiver, or was he ever overwhelmed or impassioned—about anything. In fact, he was so level that he also never seemed genuinely happy. He smiled, though it never touched his eyes; he laughed, but it was only polite.

Everyone didn't know Dane, though. Rachel knew what no one knew (including Dane): he was still in love with someone else.

"You've been in denial all our years together," she tearfully charged him as he left that first night the children were back with her. "I feel like you'd chosen to *settle* by marrying me. I don't want to be anyone's second best—ever." Voicing her agonizing realizations helped Dane to stop and truly listen to Rachel. That highly- charged plea was atypical of any discussion between them. She'd clearly decided that she'd cared for him so deeply as a friend, she really wasn't in love with him, either.

Distant but awed by her candor, Dane softly replied, "You're an amazing woman and mom, Rachel, and I'm so sorry. You don't deserve to feel second to anyone." That was all he said.

After the children moved back in with their mother, they saw Dane whenever they wanted and believed their parents were finally friends. While not the ideal family situation any child wants, it was peaceful, trusting, kind, and caring. They'd soon watch their parents fall in love with other people and know what that part of life was truly about. Dane was always willing to cover for Rachel, within reason of his work commitments, never flaunted other women around her, the children, or his work, and even welcomed

Rachel's new mate when that time came. David Novak was great with the kids, adored Rachel the way she deserved to be adored, and respected Dane. As divorces go, it had been about the kids—civilized and classy. It was never about infidelity or money. Dane had heard from many colleagues how vicious they could be and wanted none of that.

He'd never regretted marrying Rachel. He'd always believed he could and would move on from his past. The problem, he knew all too logically from his legal practices, was that one couldn't move on from the past if one hasn't dealt with it. Rachel encouraged him to do what he needed to do to move through that time period and be happy, whatever that meant. She seemed to care for Dane as a friend, as well as the father of their children. There appeared to be a respect between them—just no passion, no connection.

Now, this past he needed to face was across an ocean, living a very different life from him. How would he ever reconcile this? Perhaps he couldn't. So, until he figured it out, he was alone.

Dane had been lying in bed with his laptop, sending off the last meeting's feedback to his partner on a project when another email came in. It was late at night in Zurich, an unusual time to receive even business mail. It wasn't work related, he noted. It wasn't junk, either. His computer filtered junk. It was personal from the U.S.—a "Save the Date" invitation for his 30th high school reunion from a former classmate, obviously saddled with the arduous task of orchestrating this event. *Has it really been that long?* He couldn't take his eyes off of it. His stomach suddenly felt strange. *Had that dream about her been a premonition? Perhaps my past does hold the key to my future after all.*

CHAPTER 11

Family ... And Stranger Danger

As she sat in her latest training session, Julie realized the many goals she had. She realized how much *she* needed to grow to be able to help those whom she cared about and even those she didn't know. These were very challenging economic times. People became more desperate every day. They needed the same hope Julie had in front of her. She knew this from an intellectual standpoint. Julie also knew, after months of training, attending seminars, and practicing her presentation, that this *wasn't* her passion. This wasn't how she was going to help herself or reach others. *WHAT am I DOING?!* she screamed to herself in her own head. *This isn't me!*

Her cell phone vibrated at that moment. *Saved by the bell,* she chuckled to herself. A quick look showed her mom's number. Julie knew that she'd just gotten off the phone with her mom and had told her about the training she'd been about to enter. This call must have been her leaving a message about some thought she'd forgotten during their conversation. It happened all the time. Julie would call her later.

She put the phone down and returned to listening to the trainer.

Not even two minutes later, her phone vibrated again.

Wanting to confirm it wasn't one of the kids, Julie again checked the caller ID. It was her mom again. *Hmm, that's odd*, Julie thought to herself again. As she debated about picking it up, the phone stopped. *Maybe Mom realized she'd misdialed?*

As Julie looked to put the phone down, it vibrated in her hand. This time, Julie knew it wasn't a reminder or a misdial. It had to be serious. There was no other reason for her mom to persist.

Julie quietly left her seat in the small auditorium to answer the call.

"I'm sorry to interrupt you, honey. I know you're in a training, but I've just spoken with your father." Julie waited, and then heard her mom take a deep breath. "If you want an opportunity to see him one more time or make any peace with him, now's the time."

"Wow, Mom, that's pretty dramatic. That's not like you. What's going on?"

"He sounded really bad, honey. I guess he fell while on a business trip in one of those Eastern European countries he and his *fourth* wife like to '*explore.*' " Her mom stopped briefly for effect. Julie could almost see her mom make quotation marks with her fingers during the pregnant pause.

"And what happened?" Julie nudged.

"Well, apparently the fall was hardly the worst of it. Why he fell is the real issue. He's had problems for months, apparently, and didn't say much to anyone, including his wife. Now he can't walk, get off the floor, or anything. The wife had to call the hotel desk to ask for help. They sent up two young men who called for four more once they saw what had occurred. I happened to call looking for him after they got him into his hotel room bed. He's waiting for the ambulance to take him to the local hospital—likely not a good thing. They *are* in a *challenged* part of the world. It sounded to me like he'd already been doped up, too, on pain medication."

"Have you called my siblings?" Julie felt panic rising deep inside herself.

"I just got off of the phone with your sister, since she'd called me while I was on the phone with your dad. After I spoke with you, I'd planned to call the others. I'm not sure how long he's going to make it. He has a ferocious fever, too."

"Wow," was all Julie could even whisper. Her mind went in a thousand directions. *How fast can I get to him? Does he want me to? Can I make it before anything happened?*

"Julie, as much as your father is one of my least favorite people on the planet, he *is* your father. The one thing we did do right were you kids. I also know that I never had a chance to say good-bye to my father, and I wouldn't want that for you, if it were at all possible. It's a long shot that he'll get through this one. His stubbornness may actually be the reason, too, if he does pull through. He admitted to me on the phone that he ought to have gotten help before they left for this trip. He just didn't want to be told that he shouldn't or couldn't go. Typical of him … so childish."

"Mom, listen. I've got to call Gabe. Will you please email me or call me back and leave the information to where he's being transported? Do you know where he's going?"

"I'll get you the details." Her mom paused again. "Julie?"

"I'm still here, Mom."

"Hurry."

* * *

Julie sat staring out of the tiny window of the 757-400 jet. A seat in the economy comfort section was all that was left after she and Gabe had tackled how to get her to hopefully see her father before anything further happened. "I swear they're making these seats smaller," she muttered aloud to herself as she buckled the seat belt. She felt comforted knowing that her siblings were scrambling to get there as well.

As she settled into her seat, another late arrival scrambled to buckle in. She was a plain-looking, light brunette with startled eyes. She seemed pleasant enough in her flurry of boarding activities, so Julie allowed her mind to turn back to consider the likely concerns facing her upon landing—the first being the location of her dad's hospital.

She awoke with goose bumps, sensing someone watching her. Julie hadn't realized she'd drifted off and mused if it was just her overactive imagination. She shifted in her seat in an attempt to return to her very peaceful reverie when she again felt like she was being watched. She glanced at her watch and saw her row-mate staring open-mouthed at her out of the corner of her eye. The woman quickly looked away when she realized she was about to be caught. Again, Julie ignored the warning signs in her gut—despite knowing who was doing the staring—and figured no harm could come to her on a plane by a curious, even if slightly-off person.

With a speed that surprised them both, Julie opened her eyes and grabbed the intrusive woman's hand as it was crossing between Julie and the seat pocket in front of her in one swift, fluid movement. The stranger gasped as Julie released her hand and pushed the overhead call button to summon the flight attendant.

"What do you think you were reaching for?" Julie determinedly questioned in her best quiet-but-unyielding mom voice.

"I'm so sorry," the other woman stuttered, clearly never expecting to be caught. "I—I—was reaching for the In-Flight magazine and …"

"May I help you?" the experienced flight attendant asked interrupting them.

Julie took another brief look at the woman next to her, who shook her head ever so slightly, hoping Julie wouldn't turn her in. She wasn't nearly as young as Julie had originally thought. In fact, the woman seated next to her was about the same age, but she was unquestionably trying to look younger in how she dressed. Julie noted to herself not to make such an assumption about people again. *Really look at their faces next time,* she scolded herself.

"I'm so sorry," Julie softly covered for the woman. "I thought I was going to need your help with my seat, but I've got it. Thank you, though. Sorry for the trouble."

"No trouble. Let me know if you change your mind." The flight attendant walked away.

"I'd have been right in turning you in. What do you think you were reaching for? And don't tell me it was some magazine that you have right there in your own seat pocket," Julie glared. She looked vaguely familiar, but Julie had no idea why.

No response. The strange woman stared impassively at her own hands.

"Who are you? What's your name?" Julie decided on another approach.

Again nothing. "Listen, we've got a long flight ahead of

us still. I'm sure that flight attendant would have no problem helping me …"

"My name is Je–Jen, and I was reaching for your … book." The woman lied poorly. Julie knew it, too. Julie's kids referred to that "Mom" ability to catch on to any lie as her "Spidey Sense." Julie's "Spidey Sense" was in high gear. "I'm bored just sitting here without one. I left mine at the gate, so I thought I'd just take a peek at yours while you dozed."

Julie didn't miss a beat when she smoothly, firmly, and shockingly quiet stated, "And I'm supposed to believe that line of bullshit? I'll ask you one more time who you are and what you were reaching for; then I'll start to cause a scene and more problems than you're probably equipped to handle." She smiled in such a way that didn't quite reach her eyes. Julie was in the window seat. Jen knew that even though she was on the aisle, she was the one trapped.

A man sitting across the aisle from them had been subtly interested in the hushed conversations of his row and intervened, "I'm so sorry to have bothered you and to have caused an issue. I asked this young lady to reach for your book—very rude on my part."

He apologized again to Jen, and, quite abruptly, ended the conversation by putting his headphones back on and closing his eyes. The ponytailed man spoke with an accent Julie couldn't quite place. Again, she knew she'd been lied to, but she hadn't a clue as to why. She also tried to figure out why this woman looked familiar. Her instincts were talking loudly to her, but the message was unclear. Her probing side urged her to not let it go; her mom side urged her to find a safer route to the questions' answers. Though she didn't believe in accidents or coincidences, she'd no other reason to think the bizarre incident was much more than a lesson to listen to her instincts and look at people's faces more carefully. She knew, again instinctively, that this wasn't the case here. There was definitely something else going on.

She looked at Jen, whose averted attention was completely uncomfortable, eyed Mr. Ponytail (who was he in this scenario?), and decided to let it all go—for now.

CHAPTER 12

Anxiety

Gabe was anxious about Julie's second goodbye in only a few weeks. He'd understood the first trip as necessary. Her dad was dying; thankfully, he'd pulled through, though he faced many months of physical therapy. Gabe rationally understood that a spontaneous trip to an ailing parent didn't mean the need to cancel a long-awaited fun trip, but he still wanted his wife to, in spite of his unreasonable and flawed thinking. He hated when she left. Worse yet, he was embarrassed with *himself* when he realized how needy and bratty he behaved. His awareness didn't stop his nasty comments or senseless demands, though. Gabe was spoiled, and he liked it like that. Julie was always home, there for everyone. She was the one constant in their busy lives.

He knew it'd be better for her to go alone to her high school reunion to see her old pals, share silly stories without having to explain them to him, and remember inside jokes. They were great people, but business was too volatile during these challenging economic times to leave. He had to be there in Phoenix right now. *Besides, I know her closest high school friends, and I'm really not all that interested in getting to know people Julie seems to barely remember, let alone stay in touch with—except for one—who may not even attend,* he rationalized and hoped.

As calm and cool about her going as he was trying and failing to be, he also had this irritating feeling that gnawed at him. Something about this trip made him want to cling to her more than normal. Was he jealous of her going without him? Couldn't be that, could it—even after all these years? What did he have to be worried about? They'd always been committed to each other. He was outrageously attracted to her; life just got in the way, as it was sometimes said, too often. Kids' sports' schedules, musical involvements, school events, work functions, social commitments, and exhaustion, to name a few. Everybody had to deal with this stuff, right?

After all of these years, he wanted her now more than ever before. He just didn't show it as often as he wanted, maybe not as often as they both needed. He knew he didn't tell her very often how much he really loved her, how sexy she looked, or even how beautiful she was. He justified himself to her by saying she always looked amazing. She bought that line—once.

Her retort the last times he used it was: "What a cop out! Lazy, too."

Most mornings, he would just kiss her and leave. But *this* morning, he felt differently.

As he was leaving for an early appointment, Gabe approached Julie in her office to kiss her goodbye and confirm when he'd return to take her to the airport. Julie was just standing there, reviewing her calendar—naked.

"Okay, then I'll see you in a bit. Just needed to check my calendar fast before jumping in the shower," she explained her delayed response to his advance. He saw her standing there, completely nude and oblivious to his admiring stares.

This morning, though, a quick glance at his watch reassured him that she was worth his being late for his meeting—especially *this* morning. His deep need to be with her charged seemingly out of nowhere—*the perfect way to start the day. The perfect way to make sure Julie thinks of me the whole weekend: her scent, her taste, her touch mixed with my own. She's all I've ever wanted, and she's mine. Perfect time to show her.*

He lowered his admiring gaze, murmured approvingly at her current "outfit," and promised her that he was going to get a few things done at the office before he needed to scramble home to pick her up. He marveled as he took in her slim, sexy figure, her hair just casually pulled up in a big clip, and felt that familiar confinement grow against his pant's zipper. She was so easily appealing at that moment, completely available to him, and leaving for a long weekend—without him.

He quickly went to the garage, put his briefcase in his car, and returned to the house. Gabe saw his undressed wife rounding the corner toward their master bathroom and started to unbutton his shirt as he closed the door behind them. He was so spontaneous, almost frantic in his need. It was really more lusting than loving, he noted to himself. She turned, slightly startled to see him undressing, wondering why he'd returned.

"I'm too early." Gabe softly turned toward Julie and guided her to their bed. "The kids are still asleep, there's no school today, and you're leaving me for three long nights."

That was all that needed to be said. She felt as if this must be what having an affair was like—only better because it was with her husband. Their pull was unusually intense and sweet, impulsive and passionate. After she eagerly helped him out of his pants, his hands backed up his earlier appreciative comments and stares. Holding both sides of her face, noting the softness of her skin, he devoured her lips with his own, inhaling and absorbing her morning scent. His hands quickly moved to her neck and shoulders, down her back, noting she was perfectly sized to his liking, and he pulled her flush against him. They made love before he left for work, knowing they'd spend the rest of the day glowing.

In spite of that glow, disturbingly, Gabe felt only slightly more peaceful about his wife's imminent departure.

* * *

Julie knew she needed to leave things very organized, or Gabe would call her decidedly testy, unappreciative, and aggravated. She fully expected him to be testy as it was anyway. *At least one thing weighed positively in our favor this time: we'd certainly shared some appreciation of each other before Gabe left for work,* Julie chortled to herself. *He seemed almost desperate to make sure I left with our lovemaking as a parting thought. Right now, however, appreciating being on time for the plane is what I need to focus on.* Gabe was taking her to the airport shortly, and she still needed to finish scheduling the dogs' meds, the kids' various practices, coverage for her new business' meetings, and a date with her dad when she got to New York. She could hardly believe that she was actually going to attend her high school reunion!

She hadn't been to any of them since the five-year celebration. Julie actually wasn't even sure why she hadn't gone since then. Attending that gathering five years ago turned out to have been a good idea. Gabe's was the same weekend in the same state. There were a few people she enjoyed seeing at that five-year mark, but the one she'd really wanted to see again wasn't there. She wondered who'd be at this one—her thirtieth! It really didn't seem like *that* amount of time had actually passed since high school had ended! She certainly didn't feel old enough for thirty years to have passed! She didn't think she looked like it too much, either, except for those few stool-pigeon wrinkles around her eyes. Julie liked to think of them as character lines, that they perhaps betrayed a few secrets for those paying attention. They proved that she smiled, laughed, frowned, and that she was expressive, not dead or plastic for that matter.

When they'd attended Gabe's five-year event that was fun, too. Julie knew more of Gabe's friends than he knew of hers, so she vowed then that she'd attend her own alone next time. As it turned out, it was what was meant to be. The kids had too many things going on, and Julie had been sad that she'd missed the last few. She'd been too pregnant to travel one year or recovering from a birth another, traveling to basketball tournaments, or attending business events with her husband. *This* time, she was ready to go!

At 5'10" she carried her almost-medium build gracefully. Julie was athletic, yet feminine. She was active, ate well, and kept herself healthy overall: besides physically, there was spiritually, emotionally, and mentally (*though being married a long time and having four children certainly tested all of those areas,* she laughed at herself). All her years of dance training softened her athleticism without compromising her strength. She could sweat with the best of them, run circles around most, and outlast practically anyone with her boundless energy. When she finally sat still, she was statue-like, needing to completely recharge like a fine-tuned car sitting in the driveway with a dead battery.

She especially needed the recharging to attend this reunion. Her new writing assignment had already demanded more research from her than she'd attempted in years, so a brief respite would likely provide the much-needed mental boost that only time away can provide. She did have one other ulterior motive: she just wanted to bring some closure to her past with a few former classmates. *Was that why Gabe acted so possessively as I'd approached the shower this morning? Was he worried about who may be there? Possessiveness wasn't one of his usual personality traits. A glimpse of it and, boy, am I thankful it isn't!*

Tracking Armored Truck

The sophisticated tracking system allowed the helicopter to follow the armored truck from miles away. Those guarding the truck on board were unaware of the tracking device. For all concerned, it was a grave, but necessary, precaution. The contents of the loaded boxes were so valuable, it was wisest to have multiple checkpoints and to essentially trust no one until it reached its final destination.

Unlike the last crew, this one knew silence was the only option.

The tracking system also recorded everything.

CHAPTER 14

Parental Guidance

In his preparations for his U.S. trip and high school reunion, Dane made a point of calling his parents with his plans. As they'd aged, he became more considerate of them and their concerns. Being a parent himself had certainly helped that thoughtfulness develop. After all, how would he want his own children to treat him one day?

He'd moved them from the U.S. to Europe with him when he realized how much time he was spending there on business and how often they traveled there anyway to see relatives. As his time away from New York and the States in general increased, he worried about them being without him and traveling more and more. Then he met and decided to marry Rachel. She was from Switzerland, had been partially educated in the U.S. but finished in Europe, travelled in similar circles of friends, and would be a solid addition to the family. She was beautiful, enjoyed travel, and would be a good mom, he reasoned. So he informed his parents of his future plans.

Dane knew his parents liked Rachel, but, when asked, they also tried to talk him out of marrying her. They knew he wasn't in love with her and that this marriage was more of a well-thought-out business venture. They knew that he'd never gotten over Julie. After trying to convince him that he needed to give Julie at least a quick call during college, they finally succeeded during law school. He'd asked around and had heard that she'd moved on. He was too late.

So, when Dane had let them know that he was actually likely going to his thirtieth high school reunion, they were stunned. He'd missed the five-year when she was there. She'd missed the 20-year that he'd attended. He knew from research that she was most likely going to be at this one. His parents cautioned him. Though he'd been divorced for quite awhile and was on great terms with Rachel, he'd no idea what was happening in Julie's world.

"You'd be very wrong to think that she's going to drop her life for you if she's still married and raising children," his mother made clear.

"Mother, she does have children, and she's still married. I'm already aware of this," Dane tried to reassure her.

"Then why do you want to go? What's your point in doing so? You didn't even like most of the kids from that class. Neither had Julie. Perhaps that's why neither of you have made it to any of those other reunions. Why would you want to make a point to go now?" his father questioned him.

"My point is I need to know. Is she still *happily* married, or staying in a marriage because she feels obligated? Perhaps she's going for the same reason: to find out about me. I know she wouldn't, nor does she need to, bother otherwise. She sees those whom she really wants to see from high school periodically. I've checked." He smiled with that wry look on his face.

His mother nudged him, though, saying, "Dane, you know we've always loved Julie. We'd wanted you to work things out with her, to give her a little time back then, but you wouldn't listen. You had your own ideas and were stubborn and confused, thinking that you'd been rejected. Your pride got in the way then.

"You knew she was someone special, as did we. Your grandmother knew. She told you to be patient with this one. She was worth it. You knew we hadn't wanted you to even worry about a companion until after graduate or law school, yet Julie was different. How you didn't take your cue from that … that … well, that support and encouragement, we'll never know."

Dane had been looking at a picture of them as they spoke, but now he stared at the floor, feeling almost as if he was back in high school looking at them face to face. Only this time, he was a grown man, standing in his own home —alone. He knew they were spot on.

His mom continued. "Now, she has a family of her own and a life of her own. Are you really willing to let your pride get in the way again and possibly destroy not just her life but also her entire family? Would you have wanted that? Would you want a woman who was capable of that?"

"Mom, I'm not seeking to destroy or hurt her. I guess I just believe that this may be my last shot at taking that look back that I never did. I need to know if she's who she wants to be. If she's happy, I promise I'll leave her alone. OK? What if she isn't, though? What if she's that private that no one knows? Besides, I might not even make it to the reunion. I have several meetings scheduled. One's in Canada, and the other is in Hawaii with a stopover in Los Angeles en route to New York where the reunion will be. Depending on how those go, like I said, I may not even *make* the reunion. So, now you've something to pray for, huh?" Dane loved and respected his parents. Smiling, he hoped to set their minds at ease.

"Son, we've been married a long time. So we've seen and experienced many things together, your mother and I. Rachel is a lovely gal; we still care for her. She's our grandchildren's mother, after all, no matter what has passed between the two of you. She's generous with them, and she understood emotional challenges existed for you mostly instinctively long ago when you did *not*. Still, she cared for you, accepted what she *couldn't* change about you, and has moved on. You've been very lucky. I don't know if this has all happened at the perfect time for you, or if your reawakened love for Julie is ill-fated and poorly timed." Dane's father took a breath and continued.

"I know we don't normally speak of these things, you and I. I leave matters of the heart to your mother. She's, well, better at them than I am; but I feel very strongly that I must caution you. I *do* know that the only way *to* know is to go to this reunion. But be *very* careful, son, to know this as well: you may be opening yourself up to the most heartbreaking experience of your life—more pain than you experienced in high school, more pain than you've ever known—because now you're more aware. You fully understand life in ways you were still too young to in high school."

CHAPTER 15

Auto Plant

Activity rocked inside the immaculate 160,000 square foot auto plant. Speakers blared AC/DC's "Iron Man 2" album. Everyone knew his or her job and responsibilities without hesitation. Their focus deepened, and their productivity soared the louder and more intense the music—almost like a football or baseball team warming up for a championship game. These weren't ordinary factory workers, however; they were highly-skilled and trained old-car renovators with specialties in a variety of areas, such as upholstery, body restoration, color design, and mechanics, specializing in everything found under a hood.

Nobody asked any questions of the odd factory location, what was so special about these cars being renovated, or who was on the client list. They'd been warned during training not to ask any questions but to just do the job asked of them. They'd been chosen not only for their skillset, but also for their reputation of discretion.

They were all exceptionally well paid.

CHAPTER 16

Airport Run

Gabe had places to be after getting Julie to the airport.

"I love you." He gave her a quick kiss. As they shared a big hug, he rationalized his hasty drop-off in her ear, "You were delicious this morning." Julie grinned.

"You were the perfect going away gift."

"I'm sorry again for not going with you, but I'm sure you'll have a great time. Call me when you land, then when you get in the cab heading for the hotel."

"I'd have a better time if you were with me, and yes, I promise to call you—but after I track down my dad and have gotten situated at the hotel. You know how challenging he can be to get on the phone these days. Dad and I have dinner plans. Ok, this *is* my dad I'm talking about, so maybe I need to rephrase that as we are *supposed* to have plans." She laughed and shook her head. She was anxious to check on her dad after his rough recent hospital experience. Another quick hug and kiss were her final send-off.

Julie couldn't quite decide if Gabe was concerned with her safety or a little jealous about her going without him. Not usually a jealous guy, she brushed off his over-the-top concerns with just being protective.

Gabe, however, had nagging feelings about this trip

from the beginning.

* * *

Security lines were always a challenge at Sky Harbor Airport in Phoenix. Once through, Julie redressed. *I really need to come nearly undressed*, she snickered to herself. She smiled, knowing that next time she would probably say the same thing.

She gathered her belongings and found the gate. *A quick trip to the ladies' room, then I'll settle into the article I need to complete, call my dad, and be ready to board.* Julie struggled to concentrate, however. Her mind wandered as she stared into the throngs of people hurrying to make their flights. It was a busy fall, for a change, in the desert. Then she heard the announcement for a flight in from L.A. to report to her gate at Southwest. They'd been re-routed. *Oh, boy,* she thought. *So much for the extra seat on the plane. I might actually be lucky to even have one!* The oversold flight was destined to be a challenge. Julie wasn't aware how much of one … yet.

* * *

Private jet travel is THE way to go for any business executive who travels incessantly. Nothing is more liberating and convenient in the world of travel. It's also very spoiling, really indulgent, Dane silently recognized. His job had its perks, no doubt. So, when recent mechanical trouble of the firm's private jet forced him back to the "common" commercial flights, Dane was at first angry. Eventually realizing what a spoiled brat he sounded like, he resigned his bad attitude and sighed. It'd been so long since he'd flown first or even business class. *Poor baby*, he secretly marveled at himself. *Guess I'll have to suffer in first-class.* A chuckle, a bit of redirection of his assistants by phone, and a ride to the commercial airport were the priorities. Getting to Los Angeles International Airport, though, was always a nightmare. He'd always hated his layovers at LAX prior to the travel perk extended to him. Thick smog, horrific traffic, women dressed like hookers, men not acting like men. L.A. was NOT his scene. No class.

Once he'd finally made it to the airport, had gotten through security, and eventually to his gate, Dane made a few more phone calls. After being teased by several co-workers about his rejoining the rest of them in the "real world," the boarding process started. He was always disgusted by how many people had no idea how to travel—even in the business and first-class sections. The boarding process was just another example.

Shortly after takeoff, Dane's flight was caught in the middle of a late desert storm. Lightening flashed, and thunder clapped brutally close to the plane. It was followed by a jolt. Dane knew instantly that something wasn't right.

Just minutes later, the pilot's calm voice on the microphone explained that an immediate landing was necessary.

"Flight attendants, please prepare the cabin quickly for an immediate landing. Folks, please cooperate as instructed. Sorry for this delay. We, of course, have no control over what Mother Nature designs. We'll get you down on the ground as quickly and safely as possible. Thank you."

Dane shuddered, thinking that they'd end up in the middle of nowhere without cell service! Somehow he wasn't concerned about a safe landing. He knew these pilots were very experienced. *Guess you have to be careful for what you wish. Too much peace and quiet wouldn't be right at this moment*, he sarcastically spoke to himself in his head.

The young couple across the aisle from him was nervous but calm. *That* was reassuring. The family behind him was quiet. That was positive. The heavy man in front of him kept coughing—annoying, but unchanging since the flight began. All in all, the flight could have been worse. It could have been better, too, though. If he'd had someone next to him, someone who meant something to him or to go home to, he might have actually been concerned about the landing. He was, as he often found himself these days when he returned home, alone. He'd happily had the two-seat row to himself when he'd boarded the plane (his assistant sat in the row behind him). He needed the two seats to work, but he wasn't finding any comfort in it now.

The brief remainder of the flight was not nearly as dramatic as it could have been. They safely landed in Phoenix, Arizona. He'd always wanted to see the Grand Canyon and the gorgeous red rocks of Sedona. *I just hadn't made any plans to see them so soon*, he rationalized.

* * *

Dane wondered how long he was going to be stuck in Phoenix. He needed to take care of some business in New York if he was going to actually make it to his high school reunion. He'd been to only one reunion since graduation, and he really wasn't sure he even wanted to go to this one. Somehow, when he'd received the email reminder to "save the date," it just stayed in his email box. Eventually, one of his assistants asked what he wanted to do about the invitation and reminder. His instruction was to put it on the calendar and look to schedule New York business around it. He needed to get back there anyway for a small gathering of fellow law school graduates—a mini reunion for their class as well—and his Morgan Stanley client based there was in need of some attention. The timing for the reunion was actually pretty good.

The real problem was that he didn't care about anyone from his high school class with the exception of one person. Without being too obvious, he asked his long-time assistant, Kim, to get hold of an attendee list and to update him again the morning of the event with the agenda and attendee acceptance list. He'd make the final decision on whether or not to attend once in New York.

Obediently, Kim took care to make sure Dane had all the information he'd requested. She was anxious, though. She'd been in charge of his travel arrangements long enough to know when he was excited versus anxious about a client meeting or court event. This time, however, he was different. He actually seemed nervous—a new emotion for her boss to show.

Kim knew that Dane had been divorced, but he'd seemed only mildly saddened by it. She instinctively knew there must've been another reason for his wanting to attend this reunion. She just didn't feel it was her place to ask, regardless of the number of years she'd worked with him. As far as Kim knew, virtually no one ever asked Dane about his private life. He'd made that clear at the beginning of any new employees' orientation with him.

"I expect you to give me 100% when you are here. You are here to work. This is not a place for your private life.

What you do on *your* time outside of this office is *your* business. Don't bring it here. In turn, I will give you the same courtesy. Lastly, I won't ask you about your private business (unless it may be affected by what I may need from you time-wise here), and I won't answer questions about mine," he'd laid out clearly but with a warning tone. He was definitely a taskmaster to work for, but he was always fair and sheltered a kind heart.

Kim suspected Dane was nervous about meeting someone who may have been important to him in high school at this reunion. Work didn't make Dane Michaels nervous. Perhaps there was "unfinished" business to settle? She guessed it must have been an old girlfriend, because she'd never seen him unsettled by any man or woman— ever. She just hoped that whomever seemed to have a hold on Dane's heart managed it kindly. Though she could say nothing, she didn't want to see her boss hurt.

Dane had attended one high school reunion just as Kim had started working for him. She hadn't known him long enough to understand the subtleties in his varied moods then. But after a decade of working for him, watching him go through a divorce, and listening to Isabella's inroads with him, Kim detected a similar uneasiness in her boss's deportment. As she watched him distractedly deplane, she decided it was a perfect moment to delay her own departure, giving her boss some space from his clearly embarrassed state.

Dane had believed Julie would be at their class's 20th gathering, and then she'd never made it. He never asked anyone why. He hadn't wanted rumors to start or information to get back to her. He didn't know what her status was, nor did he want to compromise it due to his prying. He wondered if she'd taken the same steps about him. Did she ever think about him? Did she ever wonder why he'd never responded back that night he'd sprung their premature breakup on her? Did she care any more?

Dane had no way of knowing that he'd soon be able to have those questions answered. He had no idea that she was entering the busy airport terminal and his life once more.

CHAPTER 17

Meet Rachel

Rachel knew from the day she'd met Dane that he was in love with somebody else. He could deny it all he wanted, but as a woman, she knew better. Rachel, though, had tremendous confidence in herself. Her 5'6" waif-like figure, frosted blonde hair, and light blue eyes turned many heads. She knew she was a beautiful woman with a great education and the right family upbringing and connections. She was athletic and smart, a quality that had appealed to Dane when they first met —even more so than her good looks. In fact, she was shrewd enough to have had a very successful career as a lingerie model and convert those earnings into wise investments. She knew that she was a complete package.

Rachel also knew that it was going to take more than her just being the complete package to get Dane to forget this other woman—the one about whom he never spoke— the one he denied even existed for him. Working out daily, Rachel took great care of herself, gave him two beautiful children, and supported whatever it was that he needed to do for the advancement of his burgeoning legal career. Somehow, she just knew it wasn't enough. Dane never told her such a thing; she just felt it … a woman's intuition. When she tried to gently point out the fact that he'd seemed so distracted at various dinners or events, Dane admitted that he was distracted, yet blamed it on a case he'd been working on, or some other work-related issue. He apologized, then tried to make it up to her over the course of a few weeks. Nonetheless, life would lapse back to the status quo.

Rachel tried to speak with girlfriends about it, and they all echoed the same inattentiveness about their husbands. Yet, they all seemed much happier, even okay, with the lack of passion in their relationships. Rachel wasn't happy or satisfied. She grew increasingly restless with her husband's denials. In fact, he flipped everything around and blamed Rachel for being obsessed.

"Rachel, you're driving a wedge between us. If you want out of our marriage, then just say so. I can't keep discussing something that has no bearing on our relationship now. You're apparently obsessed with somebody who hasn't been in my life for over two decades. I don't even know what you're talking about," Dane defended himself. But the words were hollow, even to his own ears; he just didn't know why.

CHAPTER 18

Nemesis

"**B**ob, it's been a pleasure. We're going to do a great deal of business together. You will be more than fairly compensated for your prompt attention to my business needs." The tall, well-dressed man's smile didn't make it past his mouth. His eyes were a calculating and cool brown, the opposite tone of the warm, dark-brown Jaguar XK he'd rented. "Do we need to worry about your neighbors?" he gestured toward the house sharing an oleander screen.

Bob Couvey shook his head no firmly but kept an impassive expression. He knew this man wasn't to be trusted, though he'd no clue why. "They're too busy working and raising their kids," Bob stated frankly, hoping to be dismissive. He wanted to finish his business with this new client and return to what he preferred to be doing— renovating old cars.

Tate Parker seemed satisfied with the answer, especially as the neighbor's car rolled into its garage. The kids' flying backpacks and the mom's focus on their activities verified Bob's response. "How often do you speak with her?" Tate observed her through his sunglasses while he appeared to look at Bob; the mom paid no attention to the two men at all.

"Couldn't tell you."

"I'm sorry?" Tate didn't care for such flip responses.

Sensing a potentially dangerous change in the atmosphere, Bob levelly replied, "I couldn't even tell you the *last* time we spoke—that's how often. It might be a year? Two years? In this neighborhood, people pretty much keep to themselves. Does that answer your question? What's the worry, Mr. Parker?"

Bob had had to be firm about how and when he expected to be paid. While he wasn't attached to any of his neighbors, the nice, young family next door never bothered anyone— least of all Bob and his wife. He especially didn't want any involvement with neighbors in his business.

"I just like a certain level of privacy with my business transactions."

"As do I. We don't bother anyone and expect the same in return. In fact, we chose this neighborhood years ago to be away from prying eyes. It's worked out very well to date. We intend to keep it that way," Bob almost scowled at Tate. "I hope we understand each other now." Without waiting for Tate's response, Bob walked away from the younger man as he stated firmly over his shoulder, "I'll look for your first order tomorrow. I've got work to finish …"

Tate had been warned to give the older, eccentric man his space. "The Tate Intimidation Factor will backfire otherwise," his lawyer, another car collector, had counseled Tate regarding his dealings with Bob. "He's shrewd and will do right by you, unless he feels like something will cause him regret. Bob—let's just say—doesn't do regret."

Perfect. Tate took mental note. *Then with his age comes the wisdom to know to keep private matters private. He's definitely not much of a talker. That's a plus.*

* * *

Bob had been restoring old sports cars for decades. His clients came from all over the world, including his lawyer, who currently was also a client. In fact, the bulk of his clients came from referrals, and his lawyer sent him many. They were all uncomplicated and pleasant people—until Tate knocked on his door after the two men had been introduced at the Barrett-Jackson Car Collector Show in Phoenix a year prior.

Bob usually welcomed business to his garage with open arms. After meeting Tate, he wasn't so sure that accepting this client was a good idea. He'd no idea what Tate was up to; he just knew he didn't want to know. What did his lawyer know?

Bob left the driveway meeting heading to the phone in his work garage. A quick call to his lawyer both thanking him and warning him to screen future clients more carefully left both men uneasy—but for different reasons.

C H A P T E R   1 9

Reconnect

He couldn't believe his ears. Not only was his flight being re-routed, he was going to have to fly on *Southwest Airlines?!* His usually unflappable demeanor began to unravel. To be stuck in Phoenix was one thing, but to have to be shuffled onto an airline that didn't even have assigned seating was almost unthinkable! So he quickly got to the new gate and stood in line. Ugh! It was his next least favorite thing to do, and something he didn't have to do any more. Kim had to run to the bathroom, so he couldn't even pawn off the time-consuming task.

As he stood there checking his smartphone voice messages, he barely noticed out of the corner of his eye a woman coming over to stand next to him. Her papers seemed disorganized, and she promptly dropped most of them. Being the gentleman that he was, he leaned down to help her, as she knew he would.

* * *

As she was reading her article notes, Julie glanced up, less than thrilled with her topic, looking for inspiration in the throngs of busy people before her. Her daydreaming suddenly snapped into focus. She sat stunned, watching him head over to the ticket counter, briefcase in hand. It was as if their imminent high school reunion had re-opened the doors of chance meetings. She casually closed her laptop, grabbed her sweater, purse, and papers, and made her way to where he stood in line. She deliberately bumbled her handling of various items in her arms, dropping several and prompting him to lean down next to her to help.

Quietly, Julie chuckled, "Do they let everyone in a nice place like this?"

"Do you always say that to strangers?" he politely challenged, glancing at her sideways but without really looking at her.

Still looking at her fallen belongings, she briefly pondered how to deliver her next line and murmured with a smile in her voice, "You're not a stranger, Dane."

She could feel his head snap to attention while his eyes searched her profile. Uncertain as to what his reaction would be, she slowly turned to face him. His facial expression gave nothing away. It was clear from his soft, brown eyes, however, that he knew her. She gave him an out, nonetheless, in case she was being presumptive.

"Either it was completely unremarkable, or you've chosen to forget our senior prom completely," she quietly teased.

He looked shocked. He couldn't *ever* forget her. Was it really her after all this time? They'd parted after prom and graduation on less-than-friendly terms, and he knew then that she'd never stay in touch. Now she'd reappeared AND was talking with him—as if she wanted to still be in touch—really almost as if they'd never lost touch.

"Julie?"

"I was starting to think that you'd forgotten me altogether! I know a few years have passed, but do I look

THAT different?" She cringed, wondering how many wrinkles were revealing how much time had changed her.

"I'm so sorry to have been so rude. I just can't believe you're actually standing here in front of me. That's all." He seemed breathless. "No, you look amazing. I mean, you were beautiful then, but look at you now! I can't believe what I'm saying … I mean, wow, you look great, and how are you, and please jump in anytime to help save me from myself here, and …"

"OK, I guess I could help you out, but I'm actually having fun watching the awakening and the fumbling all in one fell swoop, so carry on," she playfully taunted.

"Thanks a lot." He shook his head, snickering at himself. "I was scared of you in high school, and here I am clearly still scared of you. How embarrassing," he confessed, dropping her papers again. He couldn't help wondering what his problem was. *I'm Mr. Self-Assured, Mr. Big-Time Lawyer, Mr. Now I Know Why I Divorced My Wife of Four Years Years Ago And Haven't Remarried Since; and the reason is standing right in front of me: Live, not Memorex, as the TV ads used to say.*

Julie was an issue between Dane and his ex-wife, Rachel, throughout most of their six-year relationship; only neither he nor Julie had had any awareness of this. His ex had, though. She'd tired quickly of living in the shadow of another woman she'd never met, or whose name she'd never known. So, she and their young son and daughter had moved out, living close enough that Dane could see them regularly.

"YOU were scared of ME? I think you took too many spills on your head when water-skiing and have memory issues—no offense meant. I was scared of YOU in high school!" She laughed and shook her head.

Feeling like the wind had been knocked out of him again in the two minutes since she'd walked over, his jaw dropped open, "What did you say?"

Her humor was still the same; her smile was more confident; her tone just as easy and fun as he'd always remembered. He was still kneeling down trying to pick up the dropped papers, not taking his eyes off of hers. She could feel his intensity burn right through her as if they were still 17. Only now, she knew this feeling, and it was wrong to have it with him. That feeling was reserved only for her husband. He was just as intense as Dane. In high school, she couldn't handle it, but after college, she recognized it as a mandatory quality in a future partner. Knowing that she'd blown it with Dane years ago, she'd never tried to stay in touch with him during college. He'd made it clear that they were over that evening at his house when he'd decided to enter an early water-skiing competition in California.

On the flip side, he'd never contacted her, either. She'd heard that he'd gone to school in California, become a lawyer, and that maybe was working in New York. She figured she'd really messed up when he no-showed their five-year class reunion. So, when she'd replied that she'd attend the 20-year event and then decided to pull out, she had no idea that Dane had actually decided to show up. After his five-year no-show, Julie hadn't wanted to attend another since—until now. *Has it really been 30 years since we've seen each other?*

It was now Dane's turn at the ticket counter. "Sir? May I help you?" the Southwest counter attendant politely repeated. She'd apparently asked him once already, so her tone was a little less patient sounding. Dane almost robotically handed the airline employee the two boarding passes, hardly taking his eyes off of Julie.

She realized he was still waiting for her to repeat herself. Staring at him, hesitating, she repeated, "I said I was scared of you in high school …"

He cut her off. "I really don't mean to be rude again by interrupting now," he gaped wide-eyed, "but I think you're not clearly remembering post-prom night and the beach celebration the next morning."

Her stomach lurched, and, deep in the entangled forest of her thoughts, her memories were slowly sorting themselves out. The announcement for their flight stated that boarding would begin shortly. The counter attendant quickly took care of Dane's tickets and smiled tightly at him as she handed them back.

"Ah … um … excuse me. I need to run to the ladies' room before we board. I'll be right back, ok? Here, let me relieve you of these. Thanks for the hand." Julie collected her papers, shoved them back into her folder, and dashed across the hall. She'd organize them on the plane.

As Julie headed for the bathroom, Kim walked unknowingly past her. Dane had been staring at Julie as Kim approached. Kim looked at her boss, smiled, but then realized he wasn't even looking at her. He wore a bizarre expression on his face. What or who had he seen? Kim looked back in the direction she'd just come from. What had she missed? "Boss?" She tried getting his attention. "Dane? Dane?"

Dane snapped out of his trance again and finally recognized that now Kim was standing next to him—speaking to him. *Shit*, he thought to himself, *that's twice in mere minutes that I hadn't heard someone speaking with me. What is with me?*

"Kim, oh, um, sorry. I was just thinking about … never mind." He knew he needed to get a quick handle on himself, where he was, and what he needed to do. "There wasn't enough room on this flight for us both. I've booked you on the next one out in about one hour. Head over to that gate now—Gate C6. We're standing at Gate D2. Here's your changed boarding pass. Sorry about that. We'll meet in the hotel lobby tomorrow morning at 9. We can grab coffee and game plan the day then. Ok?"

Kim nodded her agreement.

"Good. Now you better hurry before you miss that flight." He dismissed her, before Julie might return. He didn't want work and personal mixing—yet.

In the bathroom, Julie knew to always "try to empty out," as she'd told her kids. But she also knew she needed this time to regroup—regroup her feelings, regroup her emotions, and regroup her thoughts, not to mention her lipstick. *I'm dry-mouthed, for Pete's sake. Grab the water, check my teeth—good GOD! What am I thinking? Hold it. Stop right here. What ARE you thinking?* she thought to herself. *You're a married woman of over 20 years to a man you're crazy about; you have FOUR children with him, thriving businesses, and a new writing career. Get a grip on reality here, sweetheart,* she silently chastised herself.

Once Kim left, Dane nervously waited for Julie to emerge from the bathroom. While Julie virtually sprinted to the ladies' room, Dane stood there in awe—until Kim brought him back to reality. *Oh, crap*, he thought. *Did Kim see Julie? She respectfully hadn't asked why he'd been so distracted. Of course, she knew better,* he reassured himself. *We've never had that kind of employee-boss relationship.*

Julie had just managed to slip away from him *again*, and he hadn't said a word…*again! I really am still completely intimidated by her. How could that be? What is it about her?* he wondered as he continued to look toward the ladies' room. *She was beautiful the last time I'd seen her. She's even more beautiful now—not in a plastic, fake kind of way, but in a real way, a tangible way that makes me want her all over again.*

The plane started boarding. He tried waiting for her until almost the last call. He was actually worried that she wasn't going to make it. Would he miss this opportunity to talk with her? Catch up on her life? He'd heard that she was married, had kids, and lived somewhere out West. Was it here in Phoenix? He was just connecting through from L.A. He had business that would allow him to travel back here to Phoenix—possibly to wherever she might live even. He needed to check into that. *Whoa.* Dane caught himself thinking too many steps ahead, when Julie hadn't even emerged from across the hall yet. He told the gate attendant that she was still in the bathroom, and then he boarded the plane. He was startled by how much her presence had affected him in those few minutes.

The ex had been right all along. How've I never seen that before?

Julie had waited for the very last call to board her flight, looked to see if Dane had left the boarding gate area, and then quickly slipped into her middle seat at the front of the plane, cursing herself for checking luggage. She knew she would likely meet Dane there, and she wasn't sure that was a good idea. She'd wondered on and off for years what he'd been up to. Now, here he was, right in front of her, alive and well and looking as amazing as she'd imagined, and she was virtually running away from him. *Where are your manners?* she wondered to herself. *Grow up, Julie. He wasn't going to bite. He's married, has kids, no doubt, and is happy.*

After takeoff, the "fasten seat belt" sign had been switched off; Julie got out of her seat and found Dane just a few rows back.

"I was starting to wonder if you were going to make it," he joked.

"Thanks for letting the attendant know. There was a line in the ladies' room that I hadn't anticipated," she lied. "I checked a bag. Did you?"

"Yes. I don't normally," he simply stated, "yet I had a feeling I needed to this time. I'll walk with you there."

"Deal." She smiled and made her way back to her seat. The four-hour, non-stop flight allowed Julie to reorganize her dropped papers as well as take a nap. She knew roaming to the back half of the plane again to talk with Dane just wasn't an appropriate option.

She also realized that bolting and disappearing again was not an option, either, so she casually waited for Dane in the jet way. As he grabbed his belongings, he absentmindedly left his cell phone in his seat. The nice, older gentleman sitting next to him stopped him by tapping his arm with it.

As he handed it to Dane, he winked. "A little preoccupied, eh?" the older man teased.

"More than I'd realized." Dane shook his head somberly. "I travel for business all the time. In all the years of traveling,

I've never left anything anywhere."

"Happens. Maybe that's a sign to take a breath," offered the kind senior citizen.

Dane smiled, thanked him, and turned toward the front of the plane feeling unsettled. He was preoccupied and concerned that he'd said something to frighten Julie and decided to immediately apologize when he saw her—if she actually waited for him in the jet way.

He felt a strange wave of relief when he saw her standing there waiting for him.

"Hey, I didn't mean to offend you back in Phoenix. I'm sorry if I was rude. Would it be ok for me to walk with you to the baggage area?"

"Of course. That's why I waited. You did catch me off guard, I will admit, but you weren't rude. I appreciate the apology, though it's completely unnecessary. I'd love it if you'd accompany me."

As they made their way to collect luggage, very light conversation turned to catching up on parents, siblings, and grandparents. It was the ease of an old friendship settling in as the shock of the initial meeting slowly wore off. They laughed when they realized they were staying in the same hotel and shared a Super Shuttle to it.

After checking in, they agreed to meet for a drink before heading to dinner appointments. In spite of this being a business trip, they'd made sure that they were taking some time off work to be human—an unusual step for each of them.

Julie phoned her dad to see if they were still on for dinner, then she checked in with Gabe and the kids to let them know that she was safely in the hotel. Dane confirmed the details of his impending dinner meeting with his Morgan Stanley clients and called Kim to make sure she'd landed at LaGuardia Airport.

As they'd dressed, they both did so with more care and attention than usual. Dane knew he was a handsome man and rarely worried about his appearance. It just wasn't that important to him normally. Yet, tonight, he wanted Julie to notice him—really notice him. He wondered crazy things, things that he'd have teased a buddy unmercifully about. Like would Julie still talk with him at the reunion, or would she be too involved with catching up with everyone else there? *I can't believe I'm already feeling a little jealous of our time there. How can that be? I've only been with her, what, collectively maybe 45 minutes, and I'm already anxious to see her, anxious to clasp her hand, to dance with her, hold her, the entire time. THAT will NOT be cool. Besides, we've not even had time to talk about our home lives.*

Dane tried to shake off the anticipation of their upcoming cocktail. Instead, he found he couldn't wait and left the room—ten minutes early.

Julie had just gotten on the elegant elevator, also with much eagerness. She felt almost puerile at the prospect of a quick cocktail. No dinner to prepare, no homework to help with, no lunch money to dole out. She wasn't doing anything wrong. *Then why the unsettled feeling?* When she'd called Gabe to check in, she'd also shared whom she'd run into and whom she was expecting to see yet since check-in. She'd nothing to hide. Gabe was supposed to attend this event with her but had major work functions and kids to cover. He'd insisted on Julie going. Still, she sensed a strain in his voice, and he clipped the phone call shorter than usual. A wave of guilt roiled through her internally, though Julie couldn't determine why.

As the elevator doors opened, each emerged and turned to look for the hotel's bar. They stood surprised and started laughing at not only each other, but also themselves. Thirty years ago, they might have felt out of place. Now, they appreciated the excitement, the enthusiasm, and the anticipation—not to mention the promptness. Gabe was always bugging Julie about being on time or aware of how long it took to get somewhere. Though she was almost always on time for set appointments, she *did* struggle with the concept in general—an annoying, yet endearing, quality of whimsy she possessed. Dane also hated being late or being kept waiting, so he smiled at the idea that she was already there.

A quick drink at the swanky hotel lobby bar caught them up just enough on more old family news to be a great prelude to the reunion the next evening. They'd both made plans before they'd arrived in New York, so there simply wasn't enough time for anything more. Having kept their conversation fairly superficial, they parted easily, though the chemistry between them was undeniable to those around them at the bar. They seemed to be the only ones who were oblivious.

CHAPTER 20

Unloading

The armored truck unloading process was equally as efficient, quiet, and heavily guarded. The guard shift change also happened in silence immediately upon arriving at the compound. There was no cross training or upward movement of any kind in this organization. One was hired to do a specific job and only that job. The simplified reason for this policy: it was for the employee's safety, both within the organization as well as outside of it. The legal term was plausible deniability.

Vegas was well known for its use of, but didn't have a stranglehold on, a particular slogan recently adopted deep in the Yukon. What happened within the compound stayed within the *compound*. Equally important: what happened *prior* to the compound stayed away from the compound.

CHAPTER 21

Dane

Dane wasn't a big man physically by today's standards; regardless, he carried his 6' frame big. He exuded a core strength and stature towering him over many others more vertically blessed. His broad shoulders tapered down to a perfectly- proportioned waist supported by strong, muscular legs. He had mogul-skier's knees, but he walked with a smooth, confident gait. His dark hair was closely, but tastefully, shorn (he trimmed it every three to four weeks). He didn't care for his hair touching his suit jacket's collar. His athletic frame invited admiring eyes, yet he carried himself with a quiet, understated confidence—a man who'd travelled, spoke several languages, and could still fit in anywhere. His warm, milk chocolate eyes concealed an intensity and focus that had always acquired, analyzed, and processed information rapidly. While appearing relaxed and almost laid back, Dane was anything but.

He led a very structured, scheduled, and safe life. From his soft, well-groomed, rich-brown hair and carefully-regulated diet to his consistently-scheduled racquetball outings in the company of the usual partners (and select clients with just a certain amount of sweat to indicate a decent workout), to his tailored suits, high-end leather lace-ups, and monogrammed cufflink shirts, there was little about him that indicated an unmanaged breath or free moment. Even his exceptionally rare (and eventually firm-required) "breaks" and "vacations" were scheduled and planned—right down to exactly when he would wake up, work out, eat breakfast, sit by the pool, reply to emails, and confirm dinner reservations made by the concierge—in advance, of course. After all, there wasn't anyone he wanted to take with him (taking the kids while so young was more of a family activity than just a dad one), so he decided he might as well make good use of his time away from the usual daily interruptions.

His typical lawyer life wasn't the glamorous one that may have attracted him to the field. He knew that the first years would mean being overworked to the point of abuse. He accepted that. What he wasn't even aware of was that he'd come to need that pace, that singular existence. When he wasn't at work, he thought about work, called into work, and even woke up having dreamt about a case. He was a firm's dream hire: fit, healthy, and work-obsessed. His family life suffered—a typical casualty of almost every young, new, big-firm lawyer.

As a single man, his private life appeared to go from gloomy divorcé to exciting, successful bachelor. While he dated some of the world's most beautiful women, and his married colleagues lived through him vicariously, he was utterly lonely. After awhile, he dreaded being set up, disliked most of the women he was introduced to—even in relaxed group settings by well-meaning friends—and rarely took the lead on any names shared. Of the dates he initiated, all were superficial or pathetically transparent in their intentions or easily detected after a date or two. None were even remotely worthy of knowing he had children, let alone actually meeting them.

He decided if he was meant to be married or be happy in a relationship, then it would eventually happen. He had no concept of *how* it would happen, so he stopped trying or even thinking about dating, focused on his children, his work, his good health, and the infrequent time he took off, usually spent water-skiing in the warmer months alone. A pretty uncomplicated and boring reality, but one he was resigned to for now. Deep within, Dane was vaguely resigned to the idea that he was settling for little, if any, happiness, and there was nothing pressing him to consider otherwise. Consequently, he seemed to almost accept his solo life (other than his two children whom he adored) and simply exist.

It wasn't until Dane had had children and Rachel divorced him that he'd realized how he had and hadn't developed as a human being emotionally. During the divorce proceedings, his ex-wife had made sure to point out examples of his aloofness and coldness in their marital relations. Dane had been so shocked listening; yet, he sat there impassively. He didn't even have to keep his anger in check the way he'd heard so many men had because he really didn't see any point in arguing with her. She was right; he wasn't in love with her.

He was ordered by the court to go through some psychological assessments, as was his ex-wife, to determine the dynamics between the couple as parents, as well as with their children, to validate even their ability to parent, and to hopefully confirm competency. The information Dane got from the testing was far more revealing to him than it was to anybody who knew him. In fact, he was downright shocked to learn some things about himself, so detached and stunted had his emotional growth been after he and Julie had broken up.

The court-appointed testing had been incredibly revealing *to* Dane *about* Dane. One of the revelations answered an unspoken question he recalled having had in his childhood. Dane had difficulty truly emotionally and intimately connecting with friends and family, except for his parents and maternal grandmother. That was the way he'd always been—until he'd met Julie in high school.

CHAPTER 22

Morning Of Reunion

Early the next morning, in spite of the three-hour time difference, Julie was already in high gear; the gym had beckoned. It was a good thing that Julie's dad hated to be up late in his advancing years. It gave her the opportunity to turn in early, then get up primed to workout—something she loved to do. After thirty minutes on the elliptical, she stretched, knowing there was about another fifteen minutes before the spin class would begin. She headed back to the dark spin-cycle room, thankful that she'd already reserved her bike with a place card before hitting the cardio machines. Already feeling calmer from the much-needed physical release, Julie considered all that she needed to accomplish before the exciting late afternoon and evening events erupted. There was an underlying tension she couldn't deny and knew the workout would help her manage it.

Dane walked into the spin room as Julie was at the end of her bike warm-up; the energizing music in her headphones drowned out any chance for her mind to change. As she closed her eyes and let the music play with her imagination, Dane watched, marveling at her lithe figure and great energy. *Thank God some things never changed,* he thought. He could see she was transfixed and didn't want to disturb her, so he just watched—until someone else entered the room. When he realized he looked like a stalker, he dropped his towel on the bike he'd chosen and walked over to her.

"You're an early bird," he said.

Startled, she looked up and pulled one headphone out of her ear. Dane repeated his comment. Regaining her composure quickly, Julie smiled gently in response, "Looks like you are, too."

"I have to get in the gym early before I even show up to stop myself," Dane self-deprecatingly shared.

"I used to be a night owl until my first child was born. Then I realized that the only time of day I might get for myself would be in the hours prior to her getting up. So, I taught myself to seize this time. I have to admit, there are some days when I slip into staying up late for the same reasons, but I hate to miss out on anything in the morning."

"I get that. I get my best work done before my staff shows up, before the phones start ringing," he scoffed.

"Every so often, I crash and burn, though, by 'burning the candle at both ends' and need to restart my body's time clock with an early-to-bed-set-an-early-alarm approach. But I usually love this hour for the serenity or the intimacy of it. How about you?"

Dane swallowed at her use of the word intimacy but caught himself quickly. "Sometimes it's hard with the clients I have. Some are from other parts of the world, so they're already up and anxious to get to me first thing in the morning, hoping to monopolize my time before another client does. I've had to draw some boundaries about their needs on a few occasions, because I know that getting exercise first thing in the morning helps my brain work better and energizes me for the rest of the day."

Julie smiled, knowing someone else out there agreed with her, and nodded. "I could *not* agree with you more. Early morning workouts wire me! Speaking of that, I need to quick finish stretching. We obviously have a class to take, and then I have weights to finish. So, I'll look forward to seeing you this evening at the reunion?"

"Absolutely. Have a good ride." *Crap! I don't want to stop talking with her. I've so many more questions to ask her. Our quick drink last night had only barely touched on topics*, then his cell buzzed. He guessed fate had just stepped in to save him. "That's one of those clients. I better get going. See you tonight." Sheepishly, Dane smiled at Julie, crossed the small dark room, and got onto his bike. *Must remember to thank that client for his timing.* He'd saved Dane from himself.

The teacher walked in, flipped on the black light, and settled on a very random music playlist. Jason Aldean's song, "Burnin' It Down", came on to warm up the class. *Appropriate lyrics,* Dane chuckled inwardly, though country wasn't his preference.

"OK, gang," the spin class instructor gently guided through her microphone, "find your heart rates, just get those legs moving; no resistance. I suspect many of you may have been doin' just that last night or you're gonna tonight, so let's start nice and easy…"

Still, Dane couldn't help but watch Julie as she finished stretching, though he really tried hard not to be obvious. She was the whole package.

Julie knew Dane was watching her, though he struggled to be more nonchalant. She chuckled at him as well as herself for even noticing. She didn't change a thing she usually did—though she did think about it—not wanting to show off. Hurting herself was not an option. Missing tonight was not an option.

"OK, let's stay with Jason and kick it up a few notches." She cranked "Sweet Little Somethin'." Now, it was Julie's turn to laugh at herself. *Country isn't my first choice in music, but clearly this class is gonna be fun … .*

CHAPTER 23

High School

It took Dane months to gather the courage he felt he needed to reply to her when she spoke with him after English class at school. It took even longer for him to ask her to go on a date. Julie actually had thought he didn't like her and was so surprised once he started speaking with her at school.

Always amused by her comicalness, she brought out his fun and humorous sides. In fact, he was so powerfully attracted to her that she was like a bright, life- giving light with a warm, sheltering glow. As silly as it sounded even in just his mind (and particularly since they'd just had a class discussion about Shakespeare's *The Merchant of Venice*), Dane hoped Julie wasn't anything like the character of Portia. That character compared potential paramours to moths drawn to them singed by candles' flames. Because he was genuinely happy around her, Dane believed he was more like a plant drawn to Julie's sun.

He'd always felt like he was on slightly uncertain ground with people in general. But with Julie, he always felt confident, safe, revered. They just enjoyed each other's company—even the few times they'd had unchaperoned dates outside of school. His family adored her, and he knew that hers felt the same way about him. Deep down, despite their state of happiness, he'd always had this foreboding feeling it was temporary.

Regardless, he asked her to their senior prom, and they had an incredible evening. He thought Julie was the most beautiful girl he'd ever seen, and that was when she wore tee shirts and jeans. But in the prom dress, her ability to pull herself together for such an event blew his mind. She really could fit into any circumstance or situation with any person and be at ease. It didn't matter how elegant, how snobby, or how high-end, nor did it matter how down and dirty, gritty, or earthy. She fit in anywhere.

She did stand out, however, in every situation, because she was that light, that energy to which people were simply drawn. It didn't matter how much she downplayed her presence or how often she spoke; she simply stood out from the rest—particularly for Dane. He loved that about her. It was one of many reasons why he loved her; he just hadn't a clue what that translated to in reality for him.

After the prom, however, they knew it was time to face the reality of college. Neither had wanted to break up with the other, yet they both knew they needed the freedom to explore unencumbered. They'd accepted the philosophy that if they were meant to be together, they'd find their way back to each other. Julie was attending college in Florida; Dane was going to California, then to law school. He knew Julie had ambitions as well. Her journalistic ambitions were arduous, another point of fascination, respect, and love for her he felt, despite their looming ending. They weren't likely going to be close to each other—except during holidays or summer break—so there was no point trying to stay together when their experiences were going to be so different, they'd rationalized. *And really*, he thought at the time, *it makes no sense to get involved emotionally any further, or sexually at all, when we're going to be apart anyway.*

They'd planned on hanging out during the summer prior to their splitting up and saying 'hope to see you over the holidays,' when Dane had heard rumors after the prom. Those rumors were about why Julie had actually planned to break up with him; college distances between them were allegedly not the actual issue for her.

That was the first time he'd learned the word *allegedly*. She was allegedly planning on breaking up with him after the prom because he was short and had big ears. When a buddy of his shared this nasty rumor, Dane didn't ask where he'd gotten that information. He'd always trusted this guy. They'd been friends all through high school. Dane had no reason to mistrust ... or so he thought. Genuinely shocked and intensely wounded, instead of questioning Julie and confronting the situation, he decided it was just easier to let her go without fanfare. He recalled that conversation of more than twenty years ago as if it had just happened…

"Hey, we need to talk about something." Dane had started the conversation as casually as possible for him.

He remembered that with almost no physical motion, Julie had just raised her eyes to look at him. "That tone sounds ominous."

He tried to remain nonchalant, but he suddenly had zero confidence. "I was just invited to compete in a small water-skiing competition series this summer."

She breathed a small sigh and attempted a lighter attitude. "Awesome! When are they?" She tried on a little smile.

Dane continued, "They begin this weekend." Julie's jaw dropped, her eyes filled with tears, and her breathing seemed to stop. Dane immediately regretted doing what he was about to do. He was committed at this point, though. He silently questioned Tommy in his mind.

"Oh. Wow." She struggled to regain her composure but seemed determined to do so. Julie knew how important the sport was to Dane, so she'd never question his intentions. She respected and admired all of Dane's varied ambitions.

"That soon, huh?"

Dane remained quiet. What could he say? He just nodded his head slowly as he stared at the floor. Julie tried to will him to look at her.

"Well, that sounds like quite an honor. I knew you were planning on going, but did I forget when those dates were?"

"No," he quietly interrupted, "this came up suddenly and really was too good to pass up. I knew you'd understand." He drifted to silence again, looked down at his feet, and breathed very deeply and slowly.

"Ah. Ok. Well, you know I'd never question your need to go and fulfill those ambitions. I'm really happy for you." Julie swallowed hard and continued, "I'm just— well—um—I better go, since you probably have packing to do and ... ." Silently, through her tears, she frantically rifled around her purse for her car keys.

Dane was really taken aback. Julie was so sincerely tearful and upset that they were officially breaking up so early in the summer. He now knew that the rumors had been just that—rumors— and that again this breakup was wrong, but he was too late to stop it.

Sure, he'd initiated the conversation, much to Julie's surprise. She really thought they were going to have this conversation later in July prior to freshman orientation. She couldn't understand why he was saying nothing further to her. This conversation didn't seem to affect him at all.

"I'm searching for rapid closure here, Dane, and you're giving me nothing," she tearfully pleaded with him. "We've gotten so amazing at communicating with each other that your sudden aloofness is making this whole experience nauseatingly difficult." They made brief eye contact. It was just long enough to convey her intense pain and confusion. She read little on his face to her disappointment.

"Oh, my gosh. This has been your plan the whole time, hasn't it? This way, the good-bye was shorter, less painful, right?" Dane couldn't look at her. "Dane? Please," she implored, "look at me, talk to me. I mean, there's no drawn out closure needed for this quick break. That's what this is about, right?" She watched him as tears streaked down her cheeks.

"Well, ok then." She paused and realized she just needed to get out of there. "Good luck," she whispered, walked over to him, as his gaze bore a hole in his own shoes, leaned up to kiss his cheek, and walked out of his home. She knew she'd just walked out of his life. She just had no idea why he'd pushed her out. No good-bye or good luck to her. No last hug or kiss. Nothing. He hadn't even tried to walk her to her car— the way he always did.

She'd never pictured it this way at all. He heard her cry all the way back to her car.

After they broke up that evening, Dane was left completely confused and heartbroken. He regretted not confronting Julie about the rumors he'd heard. While he knew that the breakup was inevitable, he also felt complete dread in his gut that he'd been wrong in why he'd done it, when he'd done it, and how it had ended. He hadn't said good-bye or even hugged her. He'd envisioned a very different parting.

There could've been no way that she'd said those things with the way she'd reacted just now. Why didn't I at least give her a chance to clear the air between us? Dane silently berated himself. *Though I'd initiated the discussion prematurely and never argued with her conclusions, I hadn't wanted it any more than she had. She'll never know any of that, though. Maybe it's better this way. Maybe she'll just hate me, get over me fast, and move on. I'll never be over her, though; I'll never be over what an asshole I just was. Her tears— and then her accusations— crushed me, and I didn't say a damn word. Shit.*

He suspected Julie knew something else was up; she was too smart and knew him too well to not have picked up on even Dane's subtle shift. He called his buddy, Tommy, the same one who'd shared the ugly gossip. Dane knew better than to have listened to rumors or gossip. He never did during high school. He was never sucked into that stuff. That was for all the drama "kings and queens," not for Dane, who'd kept himself separate from—even above—such a waste of time. However, the conversation he'd had with his buddy after the breakup revealed information that Dane knew was more like the truth.

"Dude, I'm so sorry," Tommy had responded. "I know how much you cared about her. I thought you were going to wait until July to break things off with her, though."

"I was until you told me about the fact that she was going to break up with me for reasons other than college distance," Dane begrudgingly admitted.

"What are you talking about? I left you a message and told you who said it to me. You broke up with her because of what that jealous slut said? Dude, seriously? Come on; you know where comments like that come from. They always come from jealousy. That bitch never says anything nice about another girl if she thinks for even a second she could have a chance with that guy. Oh, man, seriously?"

"What message are you talking about? You left me a message? When?" Dane's look was one of horror. He'd just made the biggest mistake of his life! He was really relieved that his friend couldn't see the expression on his face right now, though he knew his voice had given him away.

"I'm sorry, man. I should've guessed when I hadn't heard back from you that you hadn't gotten the message. I found out that it was a vicious rumor. Leslie wanted to hurt Julie because that meant that every guy wasn't fawning all over her. Really sorry, man."

"It had to end anyway, Tommy. Don't worry about it," Dane offered dejectedly. "Thanks, though, because at least I know she didn't say those things. I couldn't imagine that she would've. It all makes sense to me now."

"What does?"

"Why she was so upset when I broke things off earlier than originally planned. I was a total asshole. I don't know why I didn't at least *ask* you more about that drama bullshit when she'd never *ever* given me *any* reason to believe she'd be so nasty. She was never like that. Shit, I should've at least asked her." Dane ran his free hand through his hair despondently.

When Dane and Tommy hung up, Dane just sat there in his family's dining room staring down at his hands. Every curse word he knew ran through his mind, yet he sat there completely impassive. *What the hell did I just do* was all he kept screaming silently in his brain. *She'll never want to talk to me again.*

When his mom found him there shortly after coming home from the store, she immediately knew what had happened.

"Dane? How about helping me unload the rest of the groceries?" she asked gently.

Silently, Dane rose and numbly made his way to the garage to help his mom. He moved almost soundlessly as he unpacked broccoli and steak; the sight of his favorite foods turned his stomach. He looked at his mom and felt her concern brewing.

"I broke her heart today, Mom," he lamented.

Tenderly, she reminded him, "It was going to happen in a few more weeks anyway, right?"

"I didn't do it for the right reasons, Mom. I did it sooner rather than later in the summer as we'd agreed, and I did it based on nasty rumors."

His mom just looked at him puzzled.

After a long exhale, Dane continued, "Tommy heard

something nasty said about me. Being my best friend, of course he was going to tell me about it right away. That nasty rumor about me was supposedly why Julie had really wanted to break up with me. Not only wasn't it true, but it was meant to hurt Julie. I found all this out after I'd already broken Julie's heart this evening. I was … ."

Dane's head dropped down, his eyes closed, and he breathed in and out very slowly.

"Mom, I broke a cardinal rule I've had forever: never listen to rumors; always seek confirmation and/or the truth, and then confront the situation for clarity. I rarely have to ever do all that, because I've remained completely outside of those emotional traps. I just don't get involved with that crap—until now! I'm so embarrassed, ashamed that high school's actually over, and I fell into it. I really thought I'd escaped most of it. Guess they got the last laugh. Shit. Of course, that sounds like this is more about me and my fucking ego than about hurting the most important person in my life outside of you and Babcia."

Dane's mom started toward him to offer comfort, but his look made her stop.

"I'm not the one who needs comforting, Mom. Julie does. I also completely lied to her and told her it was for a mini-series of water-skiing competitions out in California."

His mom's eyes grew wider with understanding. Dane dropped his gaze to his toes. He just didn't lie. No wonder he felt so horrible. He hadn't confronted Julie with the rumors; he'd failed to give her the opportunity to share any truths, and then he'd compounded the premature breakup with lies, feeling that the early ending would be softened with something that Julie knew was so important to him. Julie had always said she'd never get in his way of pursuing interests important to him and expected him to respect hers in return. His mom knew this. It was one of so many endearing qualities about Julie. She wasn't a clingy girl, but rather an independent, yet inclusive, soul. Charming—the type of girl his family had always believed would be perfect for their son. Her son was actually the clingy one, but Julie managed those personality challenges well with him. It was too bad that they'd met in high school.

"And you won't call her because you were going to break things off anyway, so why muddle it with more words? Is that what you are thinking?" She waited.

He slowly shook his head yes. "Do you think she'll understand if I explain it all to her at Christmas? I think we might see each other then, you know, if she'll even talk to me, when we all get together for the first time since graduation, compare first semesters at college … ." Dane stopped as he looked at his mom.

"How was your parting when she left?"

"She cried all the way to her car," he confessed. "I watched her from the window."

"You didn't even walk her to her car? Say a final goodbye? Nothing?" His mom's disapproval of his handling of the sad situation was clear in her expression. She'd raised him to be more respectful than that.

"Dane, let her go until you know what you want. Do *not* lead her on. She respected you enough to not question your change of heart no matter how much it may have hurt her."

"But I love her, Mom, and I really didn't want to end it—ever. Besides, you and Babcia love her, too. Babcia said Julie was THE girl for me."

"She was exactly perfect for you AFTER you'd both gone through your college experiences, had your fun," his mom winked playfully at him, "and enjoyed being single. Both of you! She loves you, too. I know this. Her mother and I had spoken before the prom." With a gleam in her eye, she continued, "I hope you find your way back to each other one day. For now, let her go and grow to become a man she would want even more—successful, strong, and desiring her for all she becomes. That's when you can apologize."

Dane soulfully smiled and finished helping his mom. He'd never known how much she'd loved Julie. *He'd* never shared with anyone that *he'd* loved her. He hadn't actually even admitted those feelings to himself —until it was too late.

He'd held on to those feelings all these years and had hoped that one day he'd have the opportunity to share them with her.

CHAPTER 24

Friend Aubrey

They'd met during summer orientation before the start of their freshman year at the University of Florida in Gainesville and soon discovered they'd been randomly paired as roommates. Though from such different parts of the country, the girls had similar upbringings and found they had much in common. A mutual love and appreciation of physical activity to manage stress was one discovered accidentally.

Julie always knew she'd needed some sort of workout almost daily to burn off nervous energy and decided to give a vaguely familiar intramural sport a try. Turned out Portlander Aubrey Pulaski had the same idea. While attending the first intramural ultimate Frisbee practice of the season, the two tall, athletic, and attractive brunettes arrived on the practice field at different times and were assigned to the instructional group. Thankfully, though laughing through the entire practice, the gregarious roommates learned quickly enough to be invited to compete on the travel team. They'd made a splash in their home opener, but soon found the travel commitment too large for their schedules to handle.

* * *

Thousands of tons of earth had to be cleared first. The

thawing ground slowed the "*overburden*" removal process, but the strip ratio considerably favored the existing gold that tested present over the amount of dirt necessary to be removed. She'd debated which type of mining to pursue. Based on the extensive core sample findings, the decision was to go with placer mining. It was expected to be the least permanently invasive of the options with the easiest recovery plan to move into place, and, hopefully, yielding the fastest gold harvesting. Though she'd been ecstatic with each step that positioned her ahead of the big boys, she knew time was actually a finite thing—a very finite thing. There was only so much of it left before the lease ran out.

CHAPTER 25

Accomplished?

Julie hadn't wanted to attend the reunion as "just a mom." While she was proud of being one (she'd taken that job seriously), she also knew that to be respected in this world, as inadequate as it may have sounded to her, she knew that she needed to humbly bring *other* accomplishments to the reunion table. What was more troubling was that she used to feel that she'd so little to share, or that she had to go through others to validate herself, having allowed her *own* passions to take a back seat.

She wondered how many other women felt like this. Perhaps *they* were able to see that being a parent was the most difficult job and honor it. Julie knew from raising children that she'd wanted more in life for them, so she'd decided to be more for herself first to set an example for them. She'd wanted them to know that they could be or do almost anything, *if* they wanted it badly enough, got not just a good academic education but a financial one, too, actually *decided* to work determinedly, and then went for it.

It took friend and professional therapy, private prayer, and time soul-searching to realize all that she *had* accomplished. Having gotten past that highly insecure point, she smiled at herself now with a less judgmental heart. Julie went from defensive and prideful to confident and humble—*a little therapy went a long way.*

She stepped into the shower more at peace about the imminent reunion chitchat, but she'd a feeling there would be little of that with most of the attendees. As the hot water warmed her and she found the hotel's travel-sized shampoo, Julie sensed an inner turmoil she thought she'd managed with her morning workout. That strong, deep-seeded confusion had returned. Julie knew she was about to find out why, then cope with it like any other challenge—head on.

CHAPTER 26

Transfer

The new team of twelve armed guards completed the highly sophisticated transfer of the armored truck's contents into the small sports cars' interiors. The process was a painstakingly slow and detailed one. Even the tiniest movement might cause a nick or mark undetectable to the naked eye but traceable by authorities. This was the step that potentially caused mayhem on the scheduling department, and all teams to follow were strictly on an on-call basis.

These biathletes' abilities to control breathing and calm nerves were rewarded at premiums unknown to all of the other project personnel. From unflappable marksmen to precision specialists in the spacious, immaculate white room, each interchangeable team member moved to different areas with a highly specialized and developed skill set. Under cool LEDs emitting 5,000-10,000 lux, knowingly being videotaped from both inside the sports car as well as outside of it, members seemed virtually absent of nerves.

One member of the videotaping viewing audience stood in the back of the room in shadows. He watched the process finally get underway—live. The collectable car's return from the U.S. was easier than the last one had been. He *must* remember to reward his new associate.

CHAPTER 27

High School Reunion

Julie arrived at the trendy Midtown Manhattan restaurant/ dance club alone and a little anxious. She hadn't been to a reunion in 25 years and wondered, shamelessly at first, about all of the typical (and insignificant) things—would she stack up to her classmates in maintaining herself physically? Would the men all be typically fat and the women all typically fabulous? Was the food going to be something she might eat (her eating habits had changed), or would she be so nervous that food was the last thing she'd want?

She knew she'd taken a small step into the past. Though she'd never lived in the past a day in her life, here she was. *Why am I here again? Oh, that's right,* she tried to mollify herself. *This is about friends and closure.* She wanted a glass of wine to further quiet her nerves even to just a normal place. A relaxed state just was not going to happen—that was obvious. *Let's just not make an idiot of ourselves by being too anxious,* she thought to herself. Then she spotted some old friends she'd stayed in touch with over the years, and she slowly felt a little of her breath return. She hadn't realized that she'd been holding it. *How silly after all of this time. Old habits… .*

The contemporary music was amazing, the buffet food was average, the wine served was well below standard, and regardless, the many old faces that had returned for the function could have cared less. Some of those who did show were predictable, while others, like Julie, were shocking. It was classic people watching—highly entertaining.

While the entering attendees fascinated her, Julie had just started wondering if Dane would even make it, actually worried that he might not, when he arrived … *searching for me? Was that my imagination? He looked relieved as we made eye contact. I feel relieved that he's here. Uh-oh.* Warning bells sounded silently, yet she couldn't help but enjoy watching him cross the room. He strode toward her as if no one else was even in the restaurant. Julie wasn't the only one who'd noticed both Dane's entrance as well as her reaction to it; she could have cared less at that moment.

* * *

Dane *had* debated about attending. An urgent issue had legitimately come up at the start of spin class that morning, yet he chose to handle it with the help of technology and feigning unavailability to return. *I'd never done that for my ex, yet I couldn't bear to miss Julie tonight. After running into her in the gym this morning, nothing was going to keep me from seeing her this evening. Why'd I debate then? Fear. Fear of what? What am I worried about?* He decided he needed to know. *I've never been good at running away, so why start now. I wonder if Julie's been thinking the same way.*

He said many obligatory hellos, shocking most of the attendees by being social. Just before he'd reached her, he veered toward chatting clusters of familiar faces, very calculated about not going directly to Julie. He knew how years had passed, but people were still people—and they talked. He didn't want to cast Julie in the wrong light. *Better I should look like a cad than have her polished image tainted.* Even in these more "open" times, the double standard still existed: it was always easier for men to make bad choices and just look "stupid," unless they were really drunk; women were still branded desperate, pathetic, or simply as cheaters. He instinctively knew to be very careful.

When the DJ played the right song at exactly the right time and synced the light pattern to it, Dane asked Julie to dance, whisking her away from a group of old friends. At last, after all this time, he was holding her again—publicly— legitimately. His entire being was a rush of emotions. No one who knew him now would recognize him. *Shit, I don't even recognize myself,* he silently acknowledged. *I'm a basket case, as my grandmother used to say.* He tried very hard to control his heart rate, which he knew would give away his insane nervousness. His heart beat so anxiously, he might as well have run to get here.

He decided to hold Julie with a little more than the normal distance so she couldn't feel his heart thumping in his chest. *Besides, that was what a gentleman should do anyway, right? He shouldn't press himself up against a lady from the start, especially a married one. After all, what if that's not what she wanted? I'm finally this close to her again, so let's not blow it by being presumptuous now*, he thought as she warmly clasped his hand and followed him to the dance floor. Others followed.

They each took varied partners to be more socially correct than anything. Dane spent more time by the bar talking with several old classmates; he couldn't bear to dance with anyone else again. Thankfully, Julie, too, had tired of her former contemporaries. So many were completely loaded. Again the lights changed, and the sultriness of the moment was an irresistible lure to the dance floor. The DJ's seduction ensnared even the most timid. As the music took a very sensuous turn, Dane glanced down at Julie where she was seated. He decisively reached for her hand, then looked her directly in the eyes.

"May I?" he barely whispered. Julie smiled a small, sweet, almost honored smile and let him lead her to the dance floor again. He gently turned her once, then pulled her firmly all the way to him. She gasped, as there was no space between them, his lips a breath away from hers. Her ears were suddenly and acutely aware of her heart's rapid, strong beats against his chest. She knew he could feel it when his small, content smirk could barely be concealed. That was when she felt his as well.

He closed his eyes briefly, gently grazed their cheeks as he held her tightly, securely, then slowly pulled his head back just enough and gazed at her as the music seemed to fade everything around them to black. The chemistry smoldering between them was so evident to those on the dance floor near them that they felt the need to fade away from the enchanted couple. So entranced by them, the DJ replayed the same song. It was clear no one wanted to break the heady spell. Only a few knew that this undeniable chemistry was really amiss. Only the couple creating it had any idea that old business left undone was drawing them together—though that wasn't on their minds at that moment. They'd been so completely overtaken themselves by what was happening between them, they noticed no one and nothing near them.

Dane willed himself to break their gaze and quietly

moaned into Julie's ear as his cheek again brushed hers. She was mesmerized by his enchanted hold on her, his clean smell, his firm touch, his calm control, and his undeniable warmth. Mentally, for a brief moment, she tried to stop this dance from evolving. She tried to slow things down saying Dane's name. Instead, it came out breathlessly. She knew it sounded wrong—and right.

Wait. What? Wrong AND right? What's going on? She even asked God for guidance, though it was virtually impossible to hear Him while in Dane's secure arms. Their bodies melded together as one with the music moving them, completely attune with each other. Her trust in God to quickly sort these conflicting thoughts was muddied in the musical passion that was palpable between them. *Is this the Devil's work? I'm married! Divine intervention? I've lost him once, and now he's back in my arms.* Her moan of confusion mixed with one of passion, weakening her every thought seeking clarity. *Is God agreeing with the lack of passion and direction in my life? Perhaps so much so that He put me on this path so I don't waste another moment of my capacity to love and be loved? Or, is He testing my marital commitment?*

The music changed. The mood shifted. Julie led Dane to the bar, needing to think, which she simply couldn't do while he was holding her.

"What just happened?" She barely was regaining her composure, her knees strangely unstable by his letting go of her. It was clear how much energy they fed each other.

"What do you think just happened?" His gaze just melted her, weakening her legs to the point of needing to sit—quickly. He caught this, worried, and flashed a look at the bartender that said where they would be sitting in an instant. Faster than she even realized, they were sitting on a small, comforting loveseat near the bar.

"Guess I'm not the first to swoon after dancing so closely, huh? They even provide couches." She laughed at herself.

Dane grinned, slid his arm around behind her, then under her neck so her head didn't just collapse backwards. He'd marked her. Of this, she was breathlessly certain. *How, or in what way exactly, I'm not sure yet. Had he slipped something into my drink? I'm that unclear. It couldn't actually be that he's like a drug to me, could it?*

"Does this happen with all of the women you dance with? If it is, that's not very nice."

"Only the ones who can hold me the way you just did. Since no one else can hold me the way you do, then I guess my answer is that this is a first for me, too," he chuckled almost sadly. *I can't believe I've missed out on this feeling with her all these years.*

"Me? Hold you? I believe you held me up! I mean literally! Did you drug me? Seriously! You held me up as you just turned me into mush! I don't turn into mush," she softly made clear. "I do the mushing. Oh, boy, that just didn't come out right. What I'm trying to say rather unsuccessfully is that …"

Dane saved her, "You're speechless—a rarity? You're weak-kneed, and I had an effect on you that was completely unexpected; thus, you're unprepared and without your usual walls put up and in place."

He's now marked me inside permanently with such simple insights, too. I can't tell him this, though. That wouldn't be appropriate. In fact, this whole scenario isn't appropriate, she thought to herself. *I'm married.* Though the marriage was troubled, and they were likely about to separate, she was still married. These thoughts were almost more than she could handle. Dane took in her silence apprehensively.

"I'm not being clear here. How one-sided. It's just that you seemed stuck. The truth is," and he moved off the couch to kneel on one knee beside her, "*you* caught *me* off guard, too. As I led you to the dance floor, I thought we would just take another spin and talk. We've spoken about children, careers, and our latest interests. We've shared how I got interested in old sports cars, and that you've run marathons. Then the music shifted, and it was as if I was being told to pull you closely to me. It was as if *you* had the hold on *me*."

Their server brought their drinks, acknowledging them both with an almost reverent, admiring bowing of her head, signaling she'd just been witness to something remarkable. *WHAT is going ON?* Julie shouted in her head. *Was it so obvious to everyone that we just had a storybook romantic chemistry on the dance floor, or is it just my out-of-control imagination? How could this be?* She knew she hadn't had almost any alcohol to drink. A few sips of one glass of wine hardly constituted drinking.

All that time, Dane was impatient to know what Julie was thinking. *What's happening in her head RIGHT at this moment? What's happening in general? What have I done?!* Anxious, concerned warmth radiated from him. He shifted his body just enough off the floor to sit next to her to cause her brain cells to go haywire—again. His mere physical presence both strengthened and depleted her. When he spoke, she was completely captivated. Then Dane actually took Julie's hand and looked her in the eyes so deeply, so intimately, she almost believed he could read her mind.

"Talk to me," he quietly urged.

"This isn't real, is it?" she asked.

"What isn't real?"

"This whole evening…the way you held me, the way you looked at me while we were dancing, the way you're looking at me right now, what you've said to me. ALL of it! It's all reunion-provoked; then we'll go back to our lives, and this will all just be a dream, right? This was merely closure to our high school experience, right? What we didn't get that night I left your house? I know I sound both hesitant and almost sad. For a married, strong woman, my pitiable demeanor *dumbfounds* me. Yep. I'm sure that's how I look— dumbfounded." She shook her head slightly but kept her gaze firmly fixed on Dane's face and his body language. She looked for any clue he offered her in clarification.

Dane seemed as sad as Julie was, though. She took heart in the kindness that such a cool, successful businessman could share. He normally seemed so calm, so cool, and so unemotional that she was besotted by his obvious display of raw sensitivity.

"A dream? I—am—beyond—flattered. I thought I'd be passably fortunate to see you and share a dance with you. For *this* to have happened was unplanned— entirely impetuous. I *am* as bowled over as you—maybe more! How this happened, I couldn't even begin to fathom." He sounded and seemed genuinely perplexed, off balance, elated, and distressed simultaneously. Then, thankfully, the celebrity DJ/mixologist took a brief break, so the volume of the music dipped enough to allow the couple to communicate more effectively without yelling.

OK, should I have been insulted or pleased just now? Her

internal skeptic cautioned the validity of what had happened. Meanwhile, her inner spirit reveled and basked in their reconnecting. He read her thought as soon as it appeared in her head, or was it on her face? Was he a mind reader, or did she so generously wear her every emotion?

"Please *don't* be offended. That's not what I mean. My life is very neat, simple, orderly. My attention is on my work and my kids. That's where I'm safe. Going to this reunion was simply a way to tie up old, loose ends, bringing closure even to a little of the past. Isn't that why you're here? Then *this* happened."

"Help me here—please define *this*." Julie invited him to intellectualize and even analyze *this* for her, since his sheer proximity disallowed her brain to function clearly. At that moment, she had to move away from him slightly.

"Please don't," he gently pleaded. "Please don't shift away from me."

Wow, she thought. *He doesn't miss much, does he?*

"I have to. I can't think clearly with you so close." She smiled and dipped her head almost shyly. "I can't believe I just admitted that out loud." His gracious sigh and soft temperament agreed with her, though.

"You've a point there. Maybe that's all we need—a little distance back—a little thinking room."

"You're not getting out of the diagnosis, doc," Julie reminded him. "Please define *this*."

"*This*? Well, *this* is, um, this… ." He waved his arms in an almost tossing action toward them both.

"Well, that really nailed it down for me. Clear as mud," she smiled broadly.

"You still have a great sense of humor. You've always

found a way to put a smile on my face, even when I'm at my most serious—well, almost always." A small defeated sigh barely perceivable escaped from his face.

"That sigh. Hmmm. OK. I'll bite. Almost always?" She didn't see it coming.

"Until we broke up that night in early summer, which, of course, wouldn't have put a smile on my face. Agreed?"

"Agreed," Julie reluctantly acquiesced. She let a beat pass, then added, "But you seemed pretty re-directed and didn't exactly stop me. You didn't appear to be really broken up by it, either, since you knew you were leaving the state— this side of the country, actually. You were off to compete and then to college and, undoubtedly, wanted your freedom to explore and not be stuck to some female at home, right?"

"Right," he grudgingly agreed.

"Nor did you track me down or show up at a reunion or call me, so the almost part of that is a hard guilt trip to press. Agreed?"

"Yes and no," Dane countered. *Typical lawyer*, she thought to herself.

"Are you *really* going to make me drag *everything* out of you? Really?"

He smiled, obviously debating with himself about how far he needed to go in explaining his answer. Though his internal deliberation nearly made her nuts, her patience paid off.

"Yes, it's a hard guilt trip, because you're right about us both having needed our freedom to become the people whom we've become. For all of our good and bad experiences, those experiences have helped shape us to be the people we are at this moment. People who have travelled, are intelligent, forward-thinking, passionate," he hesitated. Dane moved a little closer again, and then continued, "… determined, believing in more than what we just see. So, no, it's not too much of a guilt trip, because, while you're right about me not showing up at a reunion you attended, I *did* track you down and think about calling you—you just didn't know about it. Believe it or not, I was even engaged at that point. I wanted to talk with you about it before I went through with the wedding. I'm sure you're thinking why, aren't you?"

She smiled. She *was* thinking why, though she *was* having grave difficulty thinking or even breathing, since he had gotten closer to her on the couch again. *No wonder he's so successful in what he does. He's persuasive just with his physical existence. Now we're on to the hardest topic of the evening, the hardest topic of all of our conversations—our marriages—and I'm having a problem thinking. Perfect.*

"I'd grown in many ways and wanted to see if you had. I wondered that if we'd been a little older, at least through college, if we might have, well, made it. So, I thought a conversation was necessary—I guess to make sure I wasn't missing out on someone amazing. Crazy thinking, huh? Very self-centered, I know. That type of thinking *alone now* would have stopped me from marrying anyone.

"I never told my parents. In fact, I've never told anyone that story. I've been too embarrassed to admit it. It was shitty. I know. I was really thankful I hadn't shared such thinking with anyone, because when I'd finally found out where you were, you were already married. I was embarrassed that I'd missed my opportunity.

"Then a rough realization had set in: *you'd* never called

me about *your* engagement. I knew, at that moment, I wasn't going to turn back."

Julie listened quietly as Dane spoke of how long it had taken to marry and then how briefly it had lasted. Though she wanted to slap him for how he'd processed the entire sequence, her compassionate side knew he'd finally grown up. Instead, she gently asked what had happened; Dane carefully sidestepped the answer.

"We didn't see eye-to-eye on many things, and she decided that life was too short to waste it on counseling to try to find middle ground with someone who wasn't willing."

"You weren't willing? What about your kids, though? Wasn't the marriage worth trying to save for their sake?"

"Julie, sometimes the best thing for kids to see is their parents agreeing to disagree, cutting their losses, acting like adults in solving problems, and moving on. We both did things to hurt each other, but I was really the wrong one. I was selfish, arrogant, and evasive and often didn't recognize any of it until she'd called me on it. We get along great now. No regrets by either of us for moving on. She's married to a great guy who is terrific with my kids. I've no worries of him replacing me, either. He's a solid addition to the family and respects that their dad is still very involved and around. I'm actually more involved now since we divorced. It's no longer complicated, thankfully."

"So, if you know what happened and you grew to love her then," Julie pushed, "why not fix it and get back together?"

"Sometimes people just grow apart and are better off apart rather than together. Now, I've hogged the spotlight for too long. Let's get to you and your relationship."

"So, you're not going to answer me? Just that fast.

Change of subject."

"No, I'll answer you, after you give some. This is an exchange, a dialogue, not a monologue. Not where you listen and I monopolize. That doesn't seem very fair to me. So, it's your turn. Please. Tell me about you. Are you still married?"

Why had Julie felt that lurch in her stomach again? *Oh, boy,* she thought. "Yes, I'm still married. Over 20 years to the same great guy. So, now about answering my question?"

"Hold on there; not so fast."

"What? I answered your question, and now we go back to you." She smiled.

"That's all you have to say? Twenty plus years and yes still married. Do you love this guy? What does he do? What makes you stay? Come on. Play fair."

"Hold on. You didn't answer all of those questions."

"I've answered more than you have. Come on."

"Why do you want to know? Twenty-three years probably answers the questions. Yes, I love him. We're in the event promotion business; it's a grueling but growing industry, and what else do you need to know? I want to know why you haven't remarried? What really happened? Hmmm. Maybe I've had enough wine, and I'm getting too familiar. I apologize. A bit pushy and none of my business. Please forgive me."

"Don't apologize. You have *every* right and *no* right to know." He paused and then took a leap. "You asked why not fix it if we knew what was wrong and we loved each other." The waiting made Julie's stomach clench. She knew she needed to be quiet, patient. "I didn't love her."

"You fell out of love?" Julie tried to understand.

"I thought I loved her enough to marry her, have kids," he

spoke softly but resolutely. He sighed because he knew Julie was looking at him. He could feel her intense and almost forceful urging that he finish his thoughts. "I never loved her."

Dane took a long, deep breath. "In retrospect, I can't help but wonder if I subjected that lovely woman, the mother of my two children, to marrying me out of a little sadness and a lot of rebellion. I wanted you to find out and feel the pain that I, too, didn't need to look back."

Dane looked down at his hands. Julie sat so still she seemed to not breathe at all. "So, I doubt I married for the right reasons. Hold on, that's not true. I KNOW I didn't marry for the right reasons. After she and I split up, she found someone else, and I've never remarried. She's a great lady. She wasn't a great lady for me."

He looked her straight in the eye. "It was because of you." Silence. "Oh, shit. Maybe I'm the one who's had too much to drink."

He turned away, not sure he was ready for the backlash or rejection he dreaded could happen. He really didn't believe it would, but he knew women could be very unpredictable. Just when he thought he might have gotten a clear read on a female, he discovered he was totally wrong. This one was the exception to almost any rule he'd ever encountered. She might as well have written the damned handbook on how to shock a guy!

Holy sh … don't say it. Julie, she cautioned herself in her mind, *don't even think it*. She must have looked as wordless as she felt. Dane's next words were simply, "Breathe. Please breathe."

She stared at him with wonder and love and fear and then horror as each emotion registered.

She could barely breathe or move or think. So, Julie just felt the tears fall. She'd no idea what else to do. Then, she decided she had to get up and find a bathroom. She had to separate herself from this situation to regain self-control. Julie was also horribly embarrassed about her tearful response. She just hated when women were so damned emotional. *Be soft but so emotional? Ugh. Not coping here.*

Dane, though, wouldn't let her leave his side. He pulled her firmly, yet tenderly, to him. He held her and murmured gentle sounds and gracious smiles. He kissed the top of her head and then just held her. His kindness and honesty had blown her composure. *Am I being played? Is this for real? Was it really just a smart breakup at the end of high school gone astray due to lack of communication? Was it really just not meant to be until now? How could it be meant to be now, though, if I'm going to hurt someone else in the process? Or worse, hurt my whole family?!*

"I need to find a ladies' room," she sniffled.

"Sure, just please…come back. I'll wait here, ok?"

Julie looked directly in his eyes and softly smiled saying, "I'll be back. I just need a minute."

In the bathroom, as Julie pulled herself together, she realized they'd danced and talked for hours as the DJ played his final songs. They were about to close the place down. Neither had imagined that they'd had so much to cover, so much to talk about. She didn't realize that Dane was sitting there thinking the same thoughts.

* * *

Dane sat dreading every minute Julie was gone. He knew the longer she was gone, the stronger she would become—the more this incredible, dream-like moment would recede back into his imagination. *Did I really just admit all of that past to her? Did I really utter those words aloud? Does she believe me or just think I was trying to hit on her? She's gotta know that I'd never admit being such a jerk before, and I'd never settle for anyone ever again. I'll never want anyone but her. Crazy that we had to lead half of our lives for me to figure that out and actually have the courage to tell her, AND now at what cost? She's got kids, too. Unlike me, she's still married. Still and all, her marriage must not be so great if she spent all this time alone with me. Right? Or was THAT the kind of foolish thinking that would get me/us in trouble? Pretty brazen. We haven't even spoken of that. Not very nice of me. She must think I'm really a selfish asshole now.*

Dane moaned in confusion and sunk his head in his hands while his elbows dug anxiously into his knees. He continued the debate in his head. *WHAT have you done? WHAT a mess. My parents warned me. Why didn't I listen? What was the point of telling her all of that? Just to make her feel guilty? One-up-man-ship? No. It was to let her know how much I'd missed her, how I've always thought of her. It was to give us a chance. What a selfish jerk. Typical lawyer, she's probably thinking. Fuck, I've screwed this up—again.*

Julie had finally emerged from the bathroom and saw Dane with his head in his hands. She saw the answer to many questions she'd been forming in the bathroom. This actually was for real. This wasn't him playing her or telling her a bunch of nonsense. His agony was obvious. Unfortunately, they weren't going to get to clarify anything—yet.

"I knew I shouldn't have asked. One must always be careful what one wishes for," she murmured, trying not to startle him.

"What did you just say?" Dane knew he'd taken a huge chance by telling her, but he figured what the hell. *I'd probably never get the chance again, and I didn't want to go to my grave with any regrets. She didn't slap me, so that's a good sign,* he thought. *But were my ears just playing tricks on me?* The night had been incredible. He loved every second of holding her. The ease of their movements drew them closer together, especially when most of the crowd had left. He knew he was no longer being presumptuous when there were no gaps between them. Their conversing was the way he'd always imagined it could be, unlike with his ex when it was always a challenge between too much properness and too little casual realness.

"What did you just say? Just repeat what you said." He held his breath and held her gaze as he stood to gain clarity.

"I said that I knew I *shouldn't* have asked that question, and that I should be careful what I wished for." Then Julie just stood quietly, staring at Dane, not having any idea what to do next.

The bartender helped them both, explaining that it was time to leave. All of the cleaning up had happened around the entranced couple, and it was time to go. Neither Dane nor Julie even acknowledged the tired, disheveled bartender. They were in another place and time not wanting to change the mood for even a moment.

The bartender flicked the lights on, walked over to the stunned couple, and said, "I see this all the time with reunions. Old friends or former couples reuniting and BAM—what a story, blah blah blah. Just for the record, and I know I'm alone in my thinking, but why didn't you two just stay together? 'Course, I'm sure you both see that now. Pretty obvious. Anyway, sorry folks for the reality check, but

I really have to get home. Hope you had a good time and thanks for coming."

"Guess that's our cue," Dane murmured, dazed by the bartender's words.

Dane helped Julie find her coat and slip into it, though all he really wanted to do was slip her out of everything she had on. He'd never ever considered moving in on another man's relationship. In fact, the friends he had who'd done such a thing he saw as pathetic and distasteful. *Find your own lady* were Dane's thoughts on the matter. *There are plenty in this world to go around. Men don't need to covet another man's lady* is what he'd always thought. Yet, as he stood there getting his own coat on and watching Julie tie her scarf around her neck, he was thinking the same wrong thoughts. His brain screamed at him: *say good night and walk away, no RUN away!* Instead, he said, "Silly to take two cars. Why don't we send one away and take one together."

"I don't think that's a good idea." Julie tried to catch her own breath, still reeling from the DJ's outsider observations, too. "I'm not sure being alone with you right now is a good idea at all. I'm not sure I would be making appropriate choices, even if you did." As she said those words, she felt her insides clench down low—a sensual warning that she'd spoken the truth.

"OK," Dane smiled, small but gratified at Julie's admission, his incredible intensity never wavering.

"Dane, please *don't* make this more difficult than it already is. I've never cheated on my husband a day in our marriage, and I'm not going to now. It's bad enough that I'm having thoughts about you that I *shouldn't* be having. I wondered for years what your wife was like and then prayed you didn't have one. I'd hoped you'd wanted me enough to find me and then prayed for amnesia to hit me to forget you. I was incapable of handling a man with your intensity and focus in high school, and yet, all of the others paled in comparison. It wouldn't be until college that I'd realized that your intensity was exactly what was so incredibly sexy and magnetic to me until I dated a Marine with the same quality.

"That didn't last because he was almost twenty years older, had served two tours of duty overseas, was divorced with kids, and had had a lifetime of experiences I could never relate to. I knew I'd never fit into his world, and it'd be wrong to take that away from someone closer to his own age and world. I knew at that moment that I wanted to grow that with you, so I moved back to New York."

"Stay right here. Please don't move. I'll take care of this driver; we'll go back together, and nothing will happen except talking, ok? Deal?"

Julie barely nodded her agreement, afraid of herself, afraid of not ever seeing Dane again, afraid of hurting Gabe, afraid of screwing everything up. *What am I doing? How is this going to end? Had I really heard him right? Perhaps it was just the wine? Perhaps it was my creative writing mind out of control?*

Dane walked back over to where they were standing on the sidewalk outside of the closed restaurant. Silently, he opened the only remaining unmarked cab's door for Julie to climb into, then crawled in behind her. He purposefully sat with space between them, though he could feel himself drawn to her warmth. Julie shook with anticipation, but appreciated the distance between them to think. The driver had the decency not to ask but to just close the privacy window.

"OK. So, I believe we left off with you moving back to New York because of me, right?"

On high alert, and slightly embarrassed at her confession, she forged ahead, expecting to feel better for finally getting this out of her system. "I was courageous until I'd started to ask around about where you were and what you were doing. After all, we'd only graduated from college the prior year. I felt foolish, though, about how I might get back in touch with you.

"I then started to realize that you weren't tracking me down. I started to think that you were probably still in California or had met someone, and that I needed to move on. I dated and took a job with a jeweler spontaneously instead of at one of the networks where I had been interviewing. Then I dated a guy who *looked* a lot like you, but he was shallow, stupid, and self-centered—*nothing* like you—and that was the end of that. Then, as I was standing with fellow employees who'd become friends at a bar one evening after work, a deep, gentle voice started speaking to me with some of the most clever pickup lines I'd heard. I was tickled. I fell in love with him, and we married. The rest, as they say, is history.

"Now, here you stand before me, even better than I remember you, as if that could've really been possible, ready to take me home. I'm sure I must be dreaming, or you've got a one-track mind, or I'm so naïve there's something I've missed. I could've sworn what you said to me back there was that it was because of me that you haven't remarried. 'Help me, Rhonda, help, help me, Rhonda,'" she giggled to break the tension.

"Confirming what you thought I said before: you heard

right. I haven't remarried because no one is like you," he stated simply. A rare moment, but Julie was actually stunned, speechless. She sat there staring at him, her green eyes wide and mouth tongue-tied. *Truth or cliché!*

"Say something. Please."

"I'm stunned," she whispered.

"Good stunned or bad stunned?"

"I'm afraid to answer, actually." Her voice was barely audible—even to herself. "I must be dreaming. I know that there's NO way YOU would be interested in me like that. There's NO way. I really had only wanted to set the record straight and let you know how much I have appreciated who you were then and what you brought to the table then, and that I GET you, and that you set the standard for me."

"That's why you came here? To thank me?"

"I never dreamed you'd be so direct so fast. You're a lawyer. They aren't always known for their directness." Julie smiled, more to herself than to him. She didn't *see* the complete dismay on his face. She blinked after having stared at Dane. His features really hadn't changed much at all over the years. His hair was shorter, but his warm, brown, intelligent eyes were just as intense.

"You came to thank me? NOT be interested in you? Why wouldn't I still be interested in you?" he questioned her, completely confused.

"Well, first of all, I assumed you were still married. Secondly, I'm still married, so I was _never_ _looking_ to complicate anyone's life, especially my own! I also lead a very provincial life in comparison to yours, I'm sure. Kids, activities, local clients. Look at you! Big-time, worldly lawyer taking Europe by storm and who knows where else?!

My life is very busy but almost boring in comparison. My travels include basketball tournaments, swimming meets, and golf matches—sometimes out-of-state, though mostly in state. I harbor no regrets, mind you. I love and worship my kids and support them in all they do, much like our own parents did for us. But seriously, I'm well-read, concerned, and quick to learn but—in the U.S.!"

"You haven't mentioned another word about your writing, so you're completely undervaluing yourself. Such modesty is a sexy and powerful aphrodisiac, but you've got to throw that in here. You're not as—what did you say?—provincial?—as you're trying to make yourself sound. You've travelled and are interested in the world around you. You've never been provincial a day since I've known you!" Dane laughed at her attempt to minimize herself. He noticed her squirming under his gaze.

"Dane, I really appreciate your belief in me. Sincerely, I wasn't coming to this reunion, or *any* reunion actually, until I realized that this was a chapter in my personal history book that had never really been completed. I'd been thinking about you and wondering about you for so many years. I couldn't be certain that you'd show up. I just hoped. I'd hoped someone would somehow get the idea of attending across to you enough to make you curious about me. I haven't looked back almost since graduation from college. Looking back is just not what I do when I can run with my future ... ." She stopped herself at that point. She was suddenly crazy aware of what she was saying, but WHAT was she actually saying?

She looked up at him to see him studying her. An appreciative smile, coupled with the warmth in his eyes, found their way to her core. *Mmmm. I love how he's looking at me—ah! WHAT am I thinking?!* She'd been cold waiting outside of the restaurant for the car to take back to the hotel until now. She hadn't realized that she'd been shaking. Cold car? Nerves? She mentally acknowledged his very few wrinkles and suddenly became very self-conscience of her own. She became aware of his similar assessments of her.

Dane smiled almost slyly, realizing they were making the same observations. *How could she think,* he wondered, *that I wouldn't be interested in her? She's warm and intelligent, totally unaffected, and real! Most of my world is the exact opposite.*

"What?" she pressed her knees together anxious. She'd always been so hard on herself about her looks and intelligence, not realizing how she made men's heads turn in admiration and women's turn in jealousy and fear. Her graciousness was disarming, and her humor was charming. She knew she was bright and that her energy was good, but she was unaware of how Dane was soaking up her light, her brightness. In their engaging conversations, even in her hushed tones, she had something that captivated him. She always had. It was to the point of his feeling entranced by her.

Julie, though, being ever the self-effacing soul, believed he was staring almost down at her, perhaps even appalled at how small-town she'd actually become! She couldn't stand the silence and observing any more.

"OK, why are you staring at me like that? Maybe I don't want to know," she mumbled at the end.

"I'm in awe."

She laughed, not sure how to interpret his comment. "I'm afraid to ask, but I'll take the bait. In awe of what?" She shrunk back in the car's seat a little.

"You. You really haven't changed at all." Julie again laughed aloud. Dane understood the vagueness of his statement and clarified, "I mean you're still slim, strong, tall, but soft and thoughtful—just with a few lines," he taunted and laughed with her. "Obviously, you're happy!"

Though he stated this simply, he felt envy and sadness at his own words. *The simplicity of my feelings is in those two words: envy and sadness.* Dane envied the man she'd married, that *he* could reach over, pull her close to him, and hold her. He recognized an old emotion resurfacing. He was more than just sad, and more deeply than he'd realized; he was heartbroken by his own doing! *Why did I come to the reunion? Perhaps my parents had been right: I've opened up a deeper pain than I'd even recognized existed. Narcissistic thinking is what got me here. I guess I WAS hoping she'd come looking for me without attachments. To make it even crazier, she is here. Why? Worse yet, THANKING me!? He yelled silently.* He was jealous of anyone she'd known all these years; he unexpectedly resented anyone whom she'd smiled with or laughed at or cried for. He was suddenly more intense and morose about missing her and doing nothing about it.

His tone and expression, though subtle, was not lost on Julie. She sensed pain and despondency, but, of course, she'd no clear idea why. He seemingly had everything: an ex-wife who worked things out regularly with him for their children, supportive family to assist them both, and the freedom to do what he needed to do for himself—not to mention his skyrocketing career. While not wanting to be assumptive, she also didn't want to be obtuse, either.

She'd heard him say that he hadn't remarried because of

her. That couldn't be the real reason. He would have tracked her down if that had been the case, right? Perhaps that was the excuse he'd given himself for always having been a man on a mission? If he really wanted something, he went after it. Julie didn't doubt that she hadn't been in his plans, so why tell her these things now? Gut check! She feared her naiveté and ego were out of control. Thankfully, they'd just arrived back at the hotel.

It was time to cover that issue, too. No sense in living in a fantasyland. *That* would be cruel.

CHAPTER 28

Just Post Reunion

Once back at the hotel, they decided a nightcap was in order; they'd just started to get to the hard topics. Though jet-lagged and clueless about where they realistically stood, Dane offered his arm to Julie as she gathered her belongings to leave the cab—both highly aware of the other's touch. She smiled and graciously took it. Though clothing separated them, their sheer proximity seemed cause for concern. Their attraction to one another was palpable. They both knew they were headed into a place they'd never anticipated being.

Silently, they walked into the lobby bar and instantly knew they'd become the talk of the evening—bad thing! Several of their mutual high school friends were staying there. Talk would get around. These people weren't trustworthy in high school; virtually nothing had changed since then for most of them, either, as Dane and Julie discovered during the more social portions of the evening. Both Dane and Julie instantly recalled why they'd never missed the rest of their classmates. They hadn't done anything wrong, yet they both felt otherwise.

A roar from the already-loaded friends as Julie and Dane entered the bar signaled their need to join the loud crew. Dane felt Julie clench his arm with anxiety. "What can I get you from the bar?"

"Um, a seltzer water with lime? No, wait, how about a glass of champagne? I think my nerves need that right now."

"You got it." As she withdrew her arm, Dane felt a warmth go with her. *Time to put on my most social side,* Dane cringed inwardly. Sitting apart from her, Dane knew he needed to share some of his attention elsewhere. He'd do it only for Julie's sake, since he could've cared less what any of them thought of him—never had. He struggled to concentrate on whomever was speaking with him, preferring eye contact with Julie at every opportunity. *I can't believe I'm willing her to look at me. I'm a grown man, long out of high school, and I'm heartbreakingly thankful for her every glance and suppressed smile. I can hardly keep my eyes off her. This is foolish. Glad I've opted out of alcohol for the rest of the night. When are these people going to leave? On second thought, maybe I need a nightcap.*

A few drinks, a round of good nights, and the gang dissipated. "Finally," Dane sighed relieved. "I can't believe we've managed to outstay everyone."

"I've no idea how, either. I'm wiped out." She shook her head and softly giggled at herself.

"What are you giggling at?"

"Myself. Us. If I were a bettin' gal, I'd bet we're both unwilling to let the evening end." She laughed aloud, "OH, MY GOSH! That sounded like *such* a come-on line!"

Dane grinned, agreeing, "Maybe we're just marveling at our great fortune to be here—together—at this moment. We'd both hoped the other would show up at this reunion; neither of us had known with certainty about the other's attendance—never mind all that's transpired between us."

Julie shared, "I know I may be sending you mixed signals

when I say this, but I likely won't get too many chances ever again, so I might as well just leave it all out there, right? If I wasn't happily married, I'd lean over and kiss you right now. I want to know if I've remembered our last kiss after the prom night/beach celebration as clearly as I think I have. I, uh-oh. I can-*not* believe I just told you that. Crap. I need to go to bed…I mean…sleep right now. *Please* forgive my forwardness. I hope to see you in the gym in the morning." She began to amass her belongings.

"Wait. Julie. I forgive you. I just need to know the same thing. I know, though, that you've never been a cheater. You'd never hurt anyone, and especially not your husband. I respect that. I want you to know that I'm curious, too. Does that make you feel a little better?"

"Yes…and no!"

"OK, wait. I have to ask you this. I may never get the chance again, so here goes, ok? Dang, now I'm using that excuse over and over! Anyway, two questions. Here's the first one: What did you believe was the reason as to why we were breaking up?"

"You told me you had an opportunity to go early to some big competitions, but I knew that wasn't true." Julie looked down at her belongings.

"You knew that wasn't true?"

She just nodded without looking up at Dane.

"Why didn't you question me? Challenge me the way you always did?"

"Dane," she met his gaze directly and calmly, "you were final in your demeanor. I knew on the rare occasions when you were like that there was no discussion—at least not for a short period. Forlornly, I knew this wasn't going to be a short period, given the timing of your announcement. Will you please tell me the truth now?"

"Remember right before the prom how you told me that I was too intense and needy for you, and that you couldn't handle someone who seemingly could know more about you than you knew about yourself? Seemed fair and mature as statements went.

"I still stand by that statement, from that perspective then, of course. *Now?* Totally different! Too late, though. What did that statement have to do with your breaking up with me two months early? I'd thought we'd gotten past that." She looked as dumbfounded at that moment as she had the night he'd broken up with her and stood coldly watching her leave. *FUCK, am I a self-absorbed dumbass sometimes!!* Dane chastised himself.

"Shit, this is going to sound really stupid." He struggled to spit it out, clearly and sincerely embarrassed. He knew what she was going to say, and he knew he deserved it. She waited. "I'd gotten a phone call earlier that day and, well, let's just cut to the facts: you allegedly said some nasty things about me and why you were really about to break up with me." Dane shot it all out of his mouth as fast as he could, then looked into Julie's stunned and hurt eyes. *SHIT! She doesn't even have to say a word! The look in her eyes is killing me! Fuck.*

"You broke up with me because of a rumor? *You?!* Mr. I'm Immune to That Drama? *Really?!*" She waivered between wanting to laugh or cry or even hit him. "All this time wasted—over a stupid rumor? What was it? Did you ever figure out if it was true or false?"

"I knew that night, right after you'd left, that it wasn't

true. Later that night, I got another call confirming I was such an asshole for even thinking it might be true. I so doubted myself at that moment that I believed anything that might have pitted us against each other. After all, how could you really care about me long term? We were so young. I figured you were better off anyway, though I knew I wasn't.

"It was my ex who couldn't take it any more. She knew from our start that she wasn't the one. She'd just believed that I'd get over whomever I hadn't let go of, that she could help me forget. In the end, there was no forgetting or comparing anyone to you." Dane looked ashamed, but relieved, he'd finally told her the truth.

"And you really believed with as much as I liked your family and how much they had liked me that a fair and mature reason like a rumor was enough to keep you away for good? Without ever giving it another shot? I knew that we were going to college and moving on—for at least that time—but we never talked again," she pointed out.

"Julie, I was … ."

"Very final about it. I respected what you had to say. I knew what I was like: emotional, passionate, and demonstrative. You were the most calm, mature person I knew; you were turned off by it at various points."

"Julie, that had nothing to do with the bullshit I put you through that night! Listen, you know me. I'd never force myself on anyone. I still don't. Not even in business," he pressed. "If I'd had even a clue or a whisper of a hint that you'd forgiven me, that I was on your mind, I would've been on the phone at least to get in your life. I never heard a word."

"I *don't* know what to say to you. I'm stunned and

grateful for your honesty—as well as the lack of it." Then she quietly gathered her things.

"What? Wait. That's it?" he tested uneasily. "That's all you want to say? Or ask? Or share? Or accuse?"

"Please tell me what you need me to say and need me to know. Do NOT wait for me this time. Take charge of what you want and what you want us both to know — respectfully," she smiled, clearly putting the ball in Dane's court. "You're actually trying to make our not reconnecting *my* fault now. Stunning and unacceptable." She wistfully re-gathered her belongings, which she'd absently placed back on the barstool as they'd come clean about their feelings.

"I was afraid."

Julie froze. "You? Afraid of what? Or who? Me?"

"I was afraid of your rejecting me."

"You'd have deserved it."

"I know. That's why I was afraid. I'm not afraid of really anything—not in my entire life—as you know. Then you came along."

"Oh, please, Dane, please don't make me feel stupid here," Julie begged.

"Why on earth would *you* feel stupid right now?"

"Crap, I guess it's my turn. I guess because I'd really *like* to believe that what you're saying is all true, that I'm not being played, you're not just saying shit to get me into bed, that you're finally coming clean after all these years. I guess my heart *needs* those words and feelings to be true to finally heal."

He then leaned over and kissed her cheek slowly, taking in her perfume, heady in the experience. He knew he smelled life and love. He knew that he needed to figure out how to have her in his life again permanently. He needed to be a part of her life and she a part of his. How?

As if she was afraid to move at all, she stood mesmerized waiting for him to lean away from her. The electrical current between them was unquestionable. Julie knew it wasn't the alcohol. Other than the one glass of champagne when they'd first returned to the hotel, she'd been drinking water most of the evening, not wanting to regret any of her actions or words. She wanted to remember everything in case it was the last time they'd ever speak.

Dane had consumed very little for apparently all the same reasons. The rest of their classmates had gotten loaded and all but passed out in the elevators. That's usually how reunions went—an excuse to act like 17-year-olds again. Dane and Julie had noticed that about each other. Both were acutely present in this moment.

"I need you to tell me that you wished I'd contacted you on a college break. I need … ."

Julie interrupted Dane, ever the skeptic that she was. "Wait. You come from just as old-fashioned and traditional a background as I do. Boys pursued girls. Girls didn't pursue boys. If you were interested, you'd have asked around. You've already admitted it was your old male pride. Now, *you* need to tell *me* that *you* wish *you'd* just called me. You're forgetting one other factor; you'd also had a new squeeze in California, right? So, here's the second question: Come on, why the turn around now? Maybe I'm just being naïve here, my ego is getting in the way, and you've actually been playing me for a complete fool or what?"

"Hold on a minute. Do you *really* think I'm here to burn you? Have you ever known me to be the guy willing to share deep feelings, or any kind of emotional intensity, easily? Of course I had a girlfriend in California. You told me you dated in Florida. Was I supposed to live like a monk?" he half joked. He was suddenly completely knocked off balance by her quick, potentially incriminating, concern. "With your shrewd sense of self-protection, *you* ought to have been a lawyer. I'm almost a little offended that you're thinking this way at all, though I guess I understand." He shook his head looking dazed and frustrated at how he could've given Julie such a wrong impression.

"Thanks. I think. My mother once told me that. Anyway, of course you weren't supposed to live like a monk. I'm just saying that if you'd been all that interested, though, you would've made a point of finding me, or keeping track of me. Please, don't flatter me with lawyer-eze. I've never known you to be full of it, but you're a *trained* lawyer now. I truly don't mean to be offensive; I'm already flattered to even just this point. Listen, I've genuinely meant every word I've said. You're an amazing person and," she straightened herself out a little, "… and I pray that you're happy. A man as bright and intense a light as you are ought to be happy. I'd know. Now, how about you escort me to the elevators and we say good night?" She smiled, a little sadly but serenely. At least she'd had a chance to share her thoughts and bring some closure to this part of her life. It was time to regain her composure, put a little distance between them, and take control of the remaining moments of the evening.

Dane smiled, grabbed his jacket, held her chair out of her way, and firmly—but gently—placed his hand on her lower back as she slowly maneuvered around the bar furniture. Exhausted, Julie decided she was better off getting some sleep than saying anything else that may not be appropriate. Dane escorted her to the elevators. Knowing that her reputation might be compromised, Dane offered anyway, "Would you be willing to allow me to escort you to your room?"

Shocked, Julie simply replied, "Let's go with just the elevator. OK?" They both got on the elevator, but only Julie pressed her floor's number. She didn't say anything.

Concerned that she'd really given him the wrong idea, she worried as he left the elevator with her. Thankfully, as if he'd heard her question out loud, he gently answered her, "I'm on the same floor."

She looked down at the floor, sighed, and smiled. Then suddenly he grabbed her, kissed her hard, and held her until she acquiesced, embracing him back. She'd never be able to say that she'd compromised her marriage. He'd always be the "bad guy" now—the one who'd forced himself on her—if she shared this evening with her husband. He could live with that. He couldn't have lived with himself if he hadn't at least made the attempt to know, after all these years, the answers he so irrationally sought. Did she still taste as good as she had? Feel as good in his arms when he held her? Was she still as good a kisser?

God help him; she was better.

* * *

Once Julie came up for air from Dane's breathtaking kiss, she slowly pulled back enough to take his scent in once more, brushed her nose softly past his and, almost unwillingly, let him go. Dropping her gaze to the floor, she backed away a few steps and somehow found herself in her room alone—in tears.

Julie sat in her room crying at first. She was numb and thrilled and stunned and frightened. *Words can be weak or powerful. It depends on what you actually do with them that makes them so. I, of all people, know this. What am I supposed to do now!?* She gasped for air, almost hyperventilating at what had just happened, realizing only now she'd been holding her breath!

"*WHAT the hell* has just *happened?* How would I feel if this had happened to Gabe? Well," she attempted to rationalize, "if *I'd* started it and grabbed Dane, that would've been unforgivable. I not only hadn't started this, I walked away. So, I can move on and never look back, and that would be that. Right? I didn't pull away immediately, though. Shit! After the initial shock, I actually really enjoyed what was happening! Shit. I need to try to sleep on this. SHIT!"

Oh, my GOD! I need to regain a clear perspective here. I'm starting to panic. One side of me had wanted to slap him; he knows I'm married! But, it wasn't the part of me that had prevailed; it was the part of me that's wanted him all these years—the part of me that had missed him deeply. I hadn't wanted to let him go. For a split second, I'd actually thought about disappearing with him to wherever he was going—as long as we went together. Soul mates. We're not, however, in high school or even college any more. It's not that simple.

* * *

Dane stood rooted in the hallway. He didn't follow after her at first. He was too stunned at their intensity, their connection, and their completeness. He hadn't felt anything like that since they last kissed almost 30 years ago! He felt immobilized initially by his audacity, then by her yielding to him. He knew she would've said no if he'd asked; and, he believed, she'd be too shocked at first to move, if he'd actually had the nerve to just kiss her. Then, he figured she'd just push him away. He was prepared for that—almost actually okay with the idea. It would keep things between them as simple as they'd been for all these years.

He finally returned to his room, confused and contemplative. *For the first time since high school, I'm actually uncertain of myself, uncertain about what I've done, uncertain about what I need to do next. Okay, Mr. Big-Time Lawyer, NOW what are you going to do? Look at the mess you've created.* Dane was actually nervous. He hadn't been nervous in so many years that the feeling was almost unrecognizable. He was completely unprepared to cope with it, too.

"I need to call Julie. No, wait. I need to see her. Wrong. No. That is *exactly* what I *DON'T* need to do. I'd kiss her again if I got within eyesight of her. I *know* that much. Holy shit, I'm talking to myself," Dane muttered aloud to himself as he paced back and forth in his hotel room. "I also know I'd never leave her room, or even let her go, if I got my hands on her—and *that* would REALLY not be right. So, seeing her is out of the question."

He found himself in front of the window, saw his reflection, and spoke to it, hoping to convince himself he hadn't lost his mind. "Call her. Apologize. Beg for forgiveness and…wait a minute. I don't *want* to apologize." He started to chuckle a little at himself. It was the first time in years he was being completely honest with himself about his own feelings. *I'm sorry AND not sorry for what I've done. I'd waited so many years for that opportunity! I am sorry for upsetting her, though. I know I have. I almost can't believe how I'm looking to rationalize this whole situation. I never rationalize anything. I mean, as a corporate lawyer, I deal with facts, numbers, and statistics. This is way outside of my reality. FUCK! What have I done to us both?* he lamented.

Her yielding, almost collapsing longingly, into my impulsive embrace was altogether unexpected—what an understatement—and it was everything I'd only imagined and wished for. And wrong! She's married!! What have I done? What has SHE done? What's going on? She seemed happy, fine, and SAFE to have done something so spontaneous with! Shit! What was THAT thought?? A wrong and selfish one. What am I going to do now? I know that kiss wasn't just a kiss. That was an authentic connection of spirits intertwined deeply in their souls.

Dane stood frozen in confusion in front of his hotel suite's window until dawn.

CHAPTER 29

College For Life

Opting to work out together twice weekly instead of attending Frisbee team practices allowed Julie and Aubrey to reconnect, considering their vigorous academic schedules surprisingly prevented much contact between them. The girls lived in the dorms together through their sophomore year, parted to share an off-campus apartment with different classmates for experience, and knew that was a mistake within the first few days. Wanting their senior year to be as drama-free as possible, the two took over Julie's apartment lease in a northeast neighborhood of Gainesville known to be full of yuppies, yet not too far from campus co-eds.

Senior year was hardly a cakewalk for either student with a full load to complete their majors and minors, paid internships for credit as well as club activities, and their requisite social life. They sighed on graduation day, feeling as if nothing in the real world would ever challenge them as much as their final collegiate year, enjoyed a dinner celebration with their families together on Main Street near campus, and vowed to be in each other's weddings. With jobs secured and post-grad lives to begin within mere weeks, the friends retreated to their hometowns for rest and regrouping.

CHAPTER 30

Business ... Partner

While Julie often felt isolated in her marriage emotionally, she wasn't alone in her feelings. Gabe knew something had changed upon her return from the reunion. She seemed to be leaving details out of her stories from the trip. She always answered his questions; she just didn't seem to share to the extent he'd grown accustomed.

She brushed his concerns aside by laughing and reminding him that he'd chosen not to attend. "You either have too much time on your hands to suddenly start worrying about my stories, or you've decided to start paying attention to me! Now which is it?" She'd stifle a smile, raise an eyebrow playfully, and await the answer to her challenge.

Gabe silently reasoned *I may have played rugby for years, but I still have most of my brains intact. It's pretty easy to figure I'm in a lose–lose position right now.* His business brain didn't work well around his wife. She was so distracting. Instead of telling her, though, and reveling in her charms, he just got angry, felt trapped by her words, and walked away. He knew he was disappointing her with his reaction, but he felt clueless about how to handle this side of her when it emerged.

Frustrated by that old school notion that men's honesty with their wives was a sign of weakness and loss of control, Gabe barked at his computer, "Control isn't the issue.

It's liberating to share the burdens and responsibilities—especially with someone I not only trust and know can handle me, but someone I love and whom I know loves me in return. To have to *always* seem at odds or combative is just *wrong and exhausting*." He shook his head and grimaced, "I just don't have any concept about how to shift, what to shift, or even that I ought to shift at this point in life. Is that weak, stupid, stubborn, or D—all of the above?"

Sometimes I've felt like I wasn't good enough for her, like I couldn't meet her needs and expectations. She's a sensual and romantic woman who hates being constantly dragged back into reality. "I can't blame her, really," Gabe admitted, completely smitten by her outlook on life. "Yet, I keep dragging her into my stark, cold 'real world.' I hate doing that to her, but I can't go it alone. Besides, she always seems willing to go along with me."

He knew she loved him. Frankly, he preferred her the way she was, the woman he'd married: sexy, alluring, and passionate. He hated feeling like he was forcing her to change, not being who she really was, or like he'd failed her in some way. She was passionate, all right. He used to allow himself to get lost in her, and she never failed to help him escape … .

"Gabe. Gabe? Gabe!" His partner, Ben, was trying to get his attention.

Gabe looked up startled.

"Hey, partner, where were you?" Ben chuckled. He marveled at his partner's ability to focus. Lately, it was a little scary, though. Ben wondered what was happening in Gabe's life that he literally seemed to disappear. Professional trouble he hadn't talked about yet? Personal? Julie? The kids?

"Sorry. What's up?"

"The crew's in the conference room … ." Gabe looked confused. "Event planning?"

"Right." *Damn it. Too much on my mind. Wish I could share it with Ben, but he tells his wife too much. She would DEFINITELY share it with Julie, too. That'd be bad.*

"Be right there. Thanks."

Gabe had married well. In fact, really too well. Julie was beautiful in spirit as well as looks. She liked all sports, including football and rugby; shopping was of little interest to her. His friends envied him; their wives loved shopping not sports. Though she preferred wine, she didn't mind a nice, icy-cold beer with him and his buddies. She was fiercely loyal and a true ally to him. He felt lucky to have such a vibrant woman by his side. Before Julie entered his life, Gabe's last girlfriend, Jennifer, cheated on him. Julie had helped him love and trust again.

Sadly, he'd a deeply seeded feeling that disconcerting days with Julie were still ahead. She was growing in varied directions, especially professionally, as she attended trainings and seminars, and her writing was published. Because of his recent as well as impending choices, those days may even be limited in existence at all. She'd likely soon figure out that he'd accepted a call from Jennifer recently. He knew Julie would be completely sideways when she found out— regardless of the circumstances.

He also believed Julie had altered some of who she really was because of his demands; once she figured *that* out, too, he believed she'd move away from their marriage. He felt that shift periodically. He felt powerless to know how to keep her. He didn't understand his own self-worth or importance to her. She'd even recommended a return to counseling to him, but he brushed it off trying to blame her for their problems. His kind, brown eyes watered at his looming loss. Though she hadn't gone anywhere yet, he knew he was pushing her away—she'd shared as much with him.

He pushed his large 6'5" frame away from his desk, out of his chair, cleared his throat, and steeled himself for this planning meeting. His marital concerns had no place in there.

* * *

After his planning meeting finished, Gabe phoned home looking for the scoop about dinner. No one answered. *Humph. She's not answering her cell—again. She knows I hate that. She doesn't answer the house phone, either. Where the HELL is she?* Gabe wondered in his head. *As her writing has shifted from high school sports to more in-depth topics, Julie's less and less available to me and the kids. We're all losing out on time with her, yet the kids seem happy and great with her. Is it just me?*

He tried one of the kids' cells—nothing. *Oh, that's right. Everybody had some practice or other activity. Where's my wife, though?* He speed dialed her cell number again, and "Hey," Gabe tried to sound casual. "Where've you been? I've been leaving messages and calling back a dozen times, but you never answer your phone."

"I *never* answer my phone? A *dozen* calls? Really? You're quite the exaggerator these days. If you weren't so grumpy, I'd laugh at you!" Julie chuckled quietly to herself as she sat in her car outside of the school's gym.

"Well?"

"I was on a hot date. Where'd'ya think I was?" *Ugh. Silence. He's so testy*, she grumbled to herself. "I was in that swim team parent meeting. Remember? The one I asked you to attend with me?" Silence was her best option right now. She wanted to shout: *Don't you ever listen or remember things I share?!* She knew that wouldn't do either of them any good, nevertheless.

Julie and Gabe hadn't been getting along very well for a while. However, even the kids noticed the increased bickering, the unsupportive attitudes, and shortness in patience. They'd called both parents out on it, too, not wanting to take sides. Suddenly, it didn't seem to matter what was going on, what was being communicated; their lives were in turmoil. Simply clueless, Julie grasped futilely by blaming it on her hormones or his business, kids' schedules, or just life stresses. The answers never pretended to be simple.

Something definitely appeared to be happening with Gabe, though. She started to pick up on his pushing her away. She just couldn't figure out why. *Another woman? Couldn't be...just not Gabe's style—was it? Money concerns? They were always there for Gabe, or were they worse than usual? Business booking or no sales? Bad logistics or poor follow-through?* Still, if Julie asked him, he typically just blamed her or he snapped, "What? That's absurd! How many times have I repeatedly stated that I'm just busy? I've no clue what you're talking about. Everything's fine with us, especially if you'd just quit asking stupid questions."

She'd walk away cringing at his hurtful response and knew those were all telltale signs—but of what?

This time, for now, Julie was very confident she knew what the current provocation was: her focus was no longer just her husband and their kids. She needed more support as she got serious about her emerging writing career. Regardless of her sensing Gabe's disconnecting for unknown reasons, it was more than time for Julie to consider her own future. She actually felt behind for not employing her education. *I went to college, too, and not to only be someone's mom and wife. It's time to live my other purposes in life. If not now, then when?* She recalled a quote from a book she'd read long ago, Ayn Rand's *The Fountainhead*: "*The question isn't who is going to let me; it's who is going to stop me.*"

"Oh, that's right." *Crap. She DID tell me that this morning. What's wrong with me? Why was I so suspicious? She's never done anything to warrant that attitude. Shit. That's on me! I better back off before... .*

"I have to finish an assignment, too, when I get home. Remember, I mentioned that this morning as well?" She tried to sound gentle.

Gabe knew he was out of line, but his tone grew defensive anyway. "See you shortly."

* * *

When Julie hadn't discussed her new writing assignment with the family and had just started to be consumed by it, there was excitement, confusion, and some resistance. Mostly, it came from Gabe. The kids were usually okay to go along with most anything, as long as their worlds were still fairly intact.

Gabe, on the other hand, felt like his world was falling apart if Julie didn't answer her phone in the first few rings or immediately complete undertakings they'd discussed. After years spent trying to figure out how to share his wife with their kids and fledgling business, "they" decided it was in their "family's" best interest to have her stay at home and not go to work. *Wasn't that supposed to be how it worked?*

Now, he'd a hard time figuring out what Julie's connection to this new project actually meant for him. "I just want to know when we're going back to 'normal'?"

Julie had tried to nail it down for him. "What does 'normal' mean? If normal means I'm available when you expect me to be, then 'normal' has been redefined. Gabe, here's a newsflash: YA GOTTA SHARE ME—just like I've always had to share you, your time, and attention with our business." Clearly far from appealing to his more traditional side, Julie clarified, "The kids' needs are because they're not able to completely fend for themselves. My dreams, our couple time, our family time…all that has to be attended to differently than it had been." In fact, it caused a serious and very heated discussion that evening when she broke from her writing.

"You mean, we have to get used to whatever it is that YOU want and screw us, right?"

"You *know* that's not what I'm saying. That's really unfair."

"You're basically changing our family dynamics by yourself! THAT'S what's unfair," Gabe accused. "I'm all for you wanting to work, but when push comes to shove … ."

"When push comes to shove, if it's not a conventional job that you can wrap your logical mind around, it must be bad and wrong and … and… *screwing* you! Always about you! UGH!" Julie exploded. She stopped her rant, took a deep breath, and changed her tack.

"This isn't about screwing *you* or hurting *you* or

short-changing *you*. In fact, it's not about *you* at all, just like starting this event company was never about me. It's always been *your* dream, *your* goal, and *your* passion. I've always helped you, but it was never *my* baby. Does this help you a little?"

"I hate when you compare our situation to work."

"That's all you understand!"

"I understand you like to compare what I do to … ."

"The comparisons are dead-on. Why not take something you understand, show the parallel with our emotional melee, and voila! You ought to have a grasp of what's happening."

"I struggle with not being able to reach you by phone when I need to get hold of you."

"Ah. You can call *me* back when it works for *you,* or put me off until you *feel* like replying, or even forget to call me back at all, and *that's* ok?"

"I'm *working*," he'd intoned. "Someone has to so you can play journalist."

"Really, Gabe? That was completely uncalled for. 'Play' journalist?"

"Well, it's inconsiderate. You're so consumed; I feel—unloved when you don't answer."

"Did you really say that? You feel unloved when I'm not immediately available to answer?"

Gabe just looked at Julie, unsure about how to respond. *Will she laugh at me, or take me seriously? I already feel like a fool, now that she rephrased my feelings that way.*

She looked down at her feet. *HOLY SHIT! I just became very aware of what Gabe has been doing to me all these years! He's masterfully been manipulating me! Unintentionally or not, it's been first-rate. If I put it that way, however, he'll have a complete meltdown.*

"So, I'm having this epiphany, an ah-ha moment, if you will. Ready to hear it?"

Gabe only nodded.

"For so many years, I thought you were disconnecting from me because you no longer cared about me, just like you're feeling about me right now. All along, however, it's really been your unintentional inability to manage your career and personal life, *and* I've allowed it! How do I know this? Well, now I'm doing the very same thing to you, and it's also unintentional—only you're putting your foot down right away, and I took much longer. I've come to this frustrating realization, just now, that this has been both of us all along, and we've not even known it!"

Julie felt the weight of the world slowly unburden itself from her shoulders. "At least there's been a logical reason for all the strife and discord we've been experiencing! Makes sense, doesn't it?!" She waited for Gabe to catch up to her logic.

"That's your rationalization for why you've been ignoring my phone calls?" Gabe was completely unaware of how mean he sounded until he watched Julie's hopeful eyes drop into a crestfallen expression.

Getting Gabe on the same page, having him be proud of me, as I'm proud of him, not intimidated or threatened, isn't going to be easy, if it happens at all, Julie concluded from his reaction.

As he offered her a glass of wine, he softened his approach. "I'm sorry. This is apparently going to take some time to get used to going forward. Off and on, it's likely to improve… ."

"And then, Gabe, we'll take ten steps backwards. You see, as my research and writing slowed down, things at home seemed to settle down. After this recent intense writing time, though, I've realized I'VE had to let my foot off the gas considerably. That's not going to work going forward, unless I'm at an appropriate stopping point. So, in an effort to prevent the ruffling of feathers at critical times in the future, we need to get this straight between us. I'll call for a family meeting, but I guarantee you the kids will be pretty open to anything—as long as it means Mom and Dad are ok." Julie stared at him, questioning and expectant.

"I don't want to fight with you any more," Gabe settled.

Julie felt the cold between them thaw a little; but she knew to be wary, since he'd said yes before. "I don't want to fight with you, either. I need to make it perfectly clear, though, that I'm going to be very busy in the next bunch of weeks with deadlines, and I really need your help and support even more than usual."

Gabe was trying to pay attention to his wife's words during their "family meeting" with the kids, but he found himself just getting swept up in the passion of them instead, in her. *She reminds me of what I sounded like when we started our business. I miss her being a part of it, although we're healthier in our marriage without that crazy level of involvement, aren't we? Or are we?*

"After all," she explained, "you're all perfectly capable! I'll do my best to work as hard as possible while you're all gone for the day and to *try* to be available to you when you first come home."

Julie knew Gabe had checked out but tried to draw him back in using his name. "Gabe, I mean Dad, is busy at work, too, and he'll be doing *his* best to help pick up Mom's slack. So I'm counting on you all."

Gabe didn't realize initially that he'd just been

volunteered. Julie was making it clear how busy *he* was opening a new aspect of their event business to a few new corporate clients. The reality of what Julie had been saying dawned on him: *I'm going to have to do more within the boundaries of the family AND still work my regular job?!* Gabe's relaxed position tensed, and his demeanor changed. *So much for changing the mood with that glass of wine.*

By the next morning, almost no matter what Julie said or did, she was wrong or thoughtless. *Didn't we all just talk about the challenges last night?* The kids clearly felt something was off, because *they'd* started to act rude and be argumentative with each other, then with their parents. *Time to adopt the old notion of "begging for forgiveness" instead of "asking for permission."*

She retreated as much as possible into her home office, spoke as little as possible with Gabe, and barely acknowledged even the kids until things settled down. Initially, this made matters worse. She was already inaccessible. The flip side was that whenever any of them came near the office, Julie was less than pleasant. *Maybe it wasn't so bad giving Julie/Mom space right now*, she hoped they thought. Julie hung a sign on the door to advise her family of the time she'd check back in with them, hoping that would lower stress and communicate her availability more clearly. *Working from home has its advantages, but, oh, boy! The disadvantages definitely are draining me. I can't give up though,* she prodded herself.

One thing became very evident: Gabe's disconnect increased, and Julie's patience waned.

"Your temper tantrums need to be kept away from our family, Gabe. You're even growling and snapping at the kids, who, by the way, are ready to move on. They get it! Why won't you?"

She says I'm having a temper tantrum, and I don't WANT to realize how spoiled I am. I liked things the way they were. Yes, I'd wanted Julie back at work for the money. Ever since I'd had to make the hard decision to terminate her position and salary within our company, money became a tough subject in our household. Thankfully, Julie loved to work. THAT wasn't the issue. Gabe often marveled at how she could juggle so many things in their lives. Then shortly thereafter, Gabe had to cut ALL salaries, including his own. The country was in recession, the event business was brutally affected, and money shriveled up—especially in Arizona.

The home issues were compounded by greater needs within the company. Gabe taunted Julie about taking a position within the company again, but she'd have to work for free until the company could afford to pay her.

"I'll find a way to make certain positions work within particular departments without ruffling too many feathers. Then," he reasoned, "we'll be keeping more of the money in the family, so to speak."

Julie wasn't having any part of that. "I *abhorred* doing the books. It was a sacrifice I was willing to make of myself at the *start* of our business. Now, it's way beyond my more elementary abilities. Furthermore, I've less than zero interest in it."

Gabe knew she was really serious when she'd continued, "In case you're doubting my words and feelings about this subject, let's just say I'd rather cook dinner every night than take on the books again."

Bad sign, Gabe knew, *because Julie truly loathes cooking.* She wasn't what one would call "domestically inclined." He still didn't listen when his wife accused him of forcing her into being someone she wasn't.

"I've made it very clear from the beginning: I'll cook as little as possible, dusting's a waste of time in general, and vacuuming will happen only when necessary. I don't want to mislead you, baby. If that's important to you, you can do it, or we'll have to hire a service."

Her lack of domestic ambitions has never bothered me—especially because she's always had OTHER domestic capabilities. He lasciviously licked his lower lip.

There was an underlying and unspoken concern that remained between the distressed couple: if their marriage was struggling now, what would happen once the youngest went to college?

CHAPTER 31

On A Roll

"**D**id you know that it's been said that all the world's gold that's been mined since the beginning of time could fit into just two Olympic-sized swimming pools?"

"Who told you such nonsense?"

Laughing at the seeming absurdity, she pouted coquettishly, "I loved that little fact! Especially because you're helping me fill another one!" Flattering a man usually was a sufficient diversion to change the subject. Her next trick was to create enough of an illusion that she cared for him more than her newest role—gold miner. While he was yummy handsome, dressed like a dream, and lusted faithfully after her, he was more valuable in securing the land, starting the soil/rock removal process, and keeping her calm when her enthusiasm was premature. Rolling off him, fully sated, and smug in having secured a temporary extension on the property lease, she laughed aloud.

"OK. I'll admit it. You've got me curious. What are you cackling about?" feigning hurt feelings.

"Oh, baby! I'm not laughing at *you*. I'm actually laughing at my new title!" Sidling back next to his muscular physique, she delivered her next line with as straight a face as she could muster. "Gold-digger."

* * *

Ever since Julie had returned from visiting with her sick dad, she'd been contemplative. She and her dad had had many deep conversations once his tubes had been removed and he could speak again. Even in pain, Julie's dad had so much advice to offer. She laughed, musing that *she'd* been there to help *him*!

In just that week, they'd actually been able to converse about more topics than they had in years. While Sam Harrow's fourth wife was off getting coffee in the hospital's coffee shop with one of her adult children, he seemed to breathe a sigh of relief.

"I know she's concerned; she's a good woman. I just needed a minute to exhale." Julie grinned at her dad's unashamed honesty. "She just overdoes it sometimes."

"Dad, in all fairness, you *did* almost die. She kinda has a *right* to fuss all over you. She seems genuinely thankful you're still around *to* fuss over."

"I know. You're right. But consider this: I've been out of it for awhile and may just need a little room to process this whole ugly experience."

"Understandable. Be gentle, though. She's trying, Dad. Hey, since you're lying there, I'm sure you've had all *sorts* of time to think. Has it ever crossed your mind that this whole ugly experience—you know, the pain, the weird back trauma, the surgery, this hospital—is for a reason? I know that sounds pretty kooky, but how else are you processing or coping with it all?" she asked him.

Sam took a long, slow, deep breath in and slowly started, "Honey, that *is*, in fact, one of the *wackiest* questions I think you've ever asked me," he chuckled, shook his head, and continued, "but it's probably one of the smartest." Julie froze.

Compliments were the exception with her father. She just sat staring at him, wide-eyed.

"You heard me," her dad answered, as if she'd made the statement aloud. "I mean, what the hell else do I have to do around here but watch the idiot box and think, right? So, I've been thinking and wondering what the hell I'd done to deserve such an ugly lesson, because that's what it is—an ugly lesson."

"You mean, my saying that everything happens for a reason echoed in your mind somewhere, and you've been trying to figure this out?" Julie was amazed.

"Pretty much." And so their conversations went. At one point, though, Julie voiced her own issues very generically and admitted to her father, "I know that I've been put on this earth for another big purpose other than having and raising kids, which, Dad, I know is a HUGE purpose and commitment. It's life affirming, and honestly, I've heard it all before. If that were my only purpose, then God would likely kill me off now and quit teasing me with other notions. Perhaps being the crappy Christian that I am, maybe I haven't suffered enough to know my value." They both laughed so hard that her dad had to call the nurse for help quieting his coughing fit.

When he was breathing normally, Julie continued, "But seriously, Dad, I know I'm supposed to make more of an impact. I'm pretty certain I'm supposed to be writing—and more than just high school sports recaps in my kids' schools' newsletters. I wasn't born this curious with strong abilities to ask questions, even interrogate others, and talk with just about anyone about anything for no reason, was I?"

"Julie, honey, even though your mother and I are divorced a long time, I know there is one thing we *always* did, and still *do,* agree on: when you put your mind to something, we just need to get out of your way. Hmmm, now that I'm mentioning your mother, she's likely the reason I'm in this quandary. I really screwed up with her… ."

Julie returned home shortly after that last private conversation, leaving her siblings to have time to visit with him. Though it took several more weeks of radical therapies and around-the-clock intensive nurse care, her dad left the hospital and returned home on the mend. The conversations they'd shared since he'd left the ICU weren't nearly as intense; still, his sage words rang loud and clear.

She'd been thinking about that last private conversation they'd had, what her dad had meant, and how she might actually apply it. She recognized that her external chaos was clouding her internal turmoil, and that what she needed to sort through her many thoughts, feelings, and directions was some serious quiet time—no distractions.

Running always offered her that indulgence. It was one of her favorite means of coping with daily challenges, a.k.a. "daily triage," explained her friend McKenna. "Running away," as Julie oft referred to it, evicted overwhelm and embraced peace during her early morning runs. Literally, she enjoyed the time and space to think that it brought her. It was like a luxurious therapy—just breathing in the cool, early morning air under the stars as the dawn considered breaking.

Today was another day of running, both literally and figuratively. Julie knew that she wouldn't solve the world's problems, but she *did* know she needed to get some clarity on managing her own issues: where was her marriage actually going? What did she want in five years? Ten years? Twenty? From herself? From her marriage? Where did she want to be living? Was Gabe even remotely interested in growing? Was *he* happy with whom he'd been and whom he'd become? Would romance become more or less important to them as a couple?

Gabe was barely romantic as it was, so what tiny crumb he flung Julie's way was pitifully savored. She knew that wasn't enough, though. She knew in her heart that their amorous stagnation wasn't sufficient to sustain her in marriage, yet, was it a deal breaker? Did she have an adequate amount of love and romance, or, as Gabe called it, "hearts and flowers and all that gooey stuff" for them both? Did she *want* to have enough for them both? She remembered how he definitely showed that he wanted to give her more when they were dating.

"Let me just get my own business going, and we'll have more time for that," he'd assured her.

Weeeelll, she thought, *he'd been very successful working for a large corporation —then for himself as a start-up—until the economy went south. Aren't we supposed to reap a little of what we sow once in awhile?* Gabe hated when Julie pulled the "you're the boss" card on him, scolding her that he wasn't *that* kind of boss. Having grown up as the boss's daughter, she was extremely aware of how seldom her parents exercised that option. She recalled, however, ownership being one of the numerous reasons why they'd started their own business. *All work and no play make us owners a drag!*

Again, she sighed and admonished herself. *I'm such a hopeless romantic. What I need to do is focus on what I DO have. After all, there ARE men out there who are FAR more romantic, but,* Julie reasoned, *they aren't nearly as level and responsible as Gabe. Besides, he can be surprisingly romantic. It's bringing that out in him that's the tricky part. Is there a tactic to help him understand that I need him in other ways?*

At that moment, Dane drifted into her thoughts.

CHAPTER 32

Legal Client

As soon as Tate realized that the international law firm he was considering hiring was where Dane Michaels was a partner, he made his businesses look irresistible to the firm. As he was about to sign a contract employing them, he insisted that Dane was to become his legal counsel as soon as the partners believed the new lawyer was ready to do so.

There was just one catch: the firm lawyer who initially represented him, and his company were not to divulge Tate's identity to anyone inside or outside of the firm, until Tate revealed himself to Dane personally—at the appropriate time—"kind of like an old classmate reunion." By then, Tate knew, the firm would be so invested in his company as a client that they wouldn't want to lose him.

When the time had, in fact, arrived, Dane had been aware of Victor having a U.S.-based Canadian client for several years that Victor attended to personally. Dane had always been too busy paying attention to his own workload to notice the workload of the partner in charge of him. Naturally, he was shocked that Victor seemed so willing to share this client with him to any extent. The first meeting to which Dane had been invited was expected to be a meet-and-greet—until Tate walked into the contemporary-appointed conference room. Dane was seated with his back to the door, so he hadn't seen his old high school classmate until he was the last to enter the room—with a discernibly smug strut.

A room that Dane had always associated with extreme professionalism changed in that instant. The crisp, white walls and shiny, white floor, an unusual décor for a legal firm, no longer lured his organized, methodical approach. His senses were in complete disarray, as if the room had become sterile, cold, and calculating, like some sort of psychiatric institution. Immediately, he performed a quick involuntary mental-systems' check for his sanity. *Am I seeing things, or did Tate Parker just enter the room as a client?*

The center attraction, a huge conference table, was a recycled airplane wing from a Boeing 747 jumbo jet. It had always represented his career taking off, but now made him feel literally "hung out to dry." He became aware of the sweat that beaded under his collar and armpits, a reaction less to Tate than to his mentor's frosty demeanor toward him. The quiet, smoothly rolling black chairs all of a sudden swallowed Dane—like sitting in the principal's office.

"There must be a mistake," Dane murmured to Victor to excuse himself.

"Stay put." Victor issued an unusual order without even looking up from his file at his young protégé.

The hair on the back of Dane's neck prickled with warning.

"Dane. Good to see you," Tate caustically greeted his former peer. Dane felt rocketed back to another place in time and imperceptibly nodded at the client. Victor heard the nasty tone and knew immediately something was horribly wrong with this arrangement. He looked at Dane wide-eyed and felt not only as if he had deceived Dane, but also that this client had deceived him all these years. Still, he knew not to change his tone or demeanor with Dane, especially in front of this cunning client. Any backing off in Victor's behavior would signal to both men that Victor had been duped, too, announcing weakness; he recognized both he and the firm would likely pay for such a shortcoming.

Again, Dane tried to remove himself from the unanticipated situation. "My apologies. I appear to be in the wrong meeting," Dane stiffly replied.

Tate sneered, "You're in the right place at the right time, Michaels. Isn't that right, Victor?" Tate's eyes never left Dane. Dane refused, at first, to look anywhere but at the file in front of his boss.

"Dane," Victor quietly insisted, "please sit down." The two men looked at each other. One apologized silently to the other.

"Did you know about this—ambush?"

"Yes and—no. I'll explain later," Victor squirmed.

"Oh, Victor, perhaps now is as good a time as any. I'm here and can make sure my old friend," Tate acidly clarified, "gets all of the facts. Do be sure to share with Dane how much my business is worth here, to this firm, as you explain."

"Still making less than tasteful choices, are we, Tate? I'm sure you want a more qualified attorney than me," Dane interjected as he began to regain his balance a little.

"Victor, are you going to do the honors, or shall I?"

Victor sighed resignedly, "Tate hired this firm years ago under the condition that you become the lead attorney when we deemed you ready. He made it seem like a good thing at the time."

"Really, Victor? Is that all you're going to share? Allow

me. Dane, ole buddy, ole pal, I've made it one of many goals in my life to win at anything and everything I do. Hiring you meant I won. Now you work *for* me. After all the years you acted superior, received the scholarships I was supposed to get, dated the girls I was supposed to date, won starting positions I was unmistakably to claim, it was just a matter of time before I got my head together and…beat you. Now, here's the giddiest part. If you walk out that door, so will I—taking my company's legal business elsewhere."

"Parker, you don't want me." Dane decided on another tactic. "I'm not the best. A guy like you who's pulled himself together and is clearly accomplished has so much to lose and needs the best. If I'm not the best, why would you want me?"

"How very self-deprecating of you, Michaels. Nice try. I already know all about your track record here. Even the word on the street is that you're more than a formidable legal opponent. It's my turn to not only have the best representation but to call your shots. You called mine in our high school years and caused me such turmoil through my formative college days. You're mine now—unless you feel *no* loyalty to the firm that's taken you under its wing all this time. I have to believe *that* word would spread as well, making you rather…unemployable."

Victor shifted very uncomfortably in his armchair and remained staring at the unique conference table. Dane knew he'd no choice—for now. "What are the rest of the terms of the previous agreement?"

"You abandon me as legal representation, then I leave the firm as a client. Really quite simple."

"Time period?"

"There isn't one," Tate flatly replied.

"We'll discuss this privately later, you and me. For now, what is it that you need from me?" Dane finally conceded, albeit temporarily from his perspective, and Victor breathed a small, almost imperceptible, sigh of relief. Dane would deal with him later.

Now that Dane finally understood why Victor had turned this client over to him, he would release his assistant, Isabella, from that search mission. He reasonably assumed that Tate was somehow behind the missing money issue. *If I know Tate, he'll start spewing all sorts of information in a bragging rage. That's just a matter of time and the right bait,* he considered. Dane knew he needed Isabella's research skill set elsewhere. *There's still more to this relationship than is clear. I know Tate's requiring me to represent him is ominous at best. No good will come from this alliance—for the firm certainly, but even more so, for him personally.*

CHAPTER 33

Direction Change

Julie knew it was important to write about practical issues, child rearing challenges, and high school sports. Those freelance pieces added immediate income to the family's budget. Nevertheless, what she really wanted to write were romance novels. She'd been talking herself out of writing them due to the constant glut in the marketplace. *So why keep thinking about it then?* she'd asked herself repeatedly. *Was it because there seemed to be so little bona fide romance in real life that reading and writing about it was better than not having it at all? Perhaps it was that deep, aching need every woman sought, at some level, to be worshipped without it being over-the-top or distasteful?* A deliberate touch, an appreciative ogling, a sweet compliment, a heartfelt peck, a watchful gaze for the sake of romance—not just for the sake of sex, but also for the sheer joy of sharing genuine passion right down at an atomic level. Julie's mind flashed to Dane and the night of the high school reunion.

She was, as were most honest women, drawn to descriptions of courting and dating, of bodies intertwined, consistent recall of magical moments, quiet poetry readings shared, and tender smiles only an adoring couple would treasure. Erotica held an imagination captive to a certain extent, yet readers often felt dirty or exposed if caught reading it.

She'd wanted to keep her rose-colored, daydreamer glasses on, but she was being drawn into a very different world unwittingly through her daughter's basketball experience. A teammate's parent, an old-car aficionado, had read Julie's basketball wrap-ups. He was also interested in fun summaries written for the car shows in the Valley. Julie had indulged her "fan," wrote a well-received recap, and now other car events in the Valley wanted her light-hearted rendition of their events' activities. Her rundowns tamed the wildly intimidating world of high-end car collecting. She empowered men and women alike to feel intrigued and undaunted by the crazy displays of money with practical knowledge, simple language, and a sense of humor.

As was her style, too, she amassed more knowledge of the industry to create more sophisticated and informed summaries. She invested time to gather, research, analyze, question, and even investigate events. As her reviews developed to be more informed and valuable, events occurred not just near or around her; they seemed to *enfold* her. She'd actually become a *part* of the story unintentionally. *Either my imagination is out of control, or I'm on to something.* Julie noted a huge benefit about her changed writing direction. *Feedback from readers has been intense. Overall, they seem to be pleased by what I have to say and how I say it.*

"At least someone cares about what I'm writing," Julie uttered to her dogs in her office one late morning as she finished another car event recap. "It may be about cars, but at least I'm finding my voice somewhere. I wonder who else might find my style entertaining or interesting? Must be another audience somewhere, right?"

For months, Julie didn't just feel unappreciated, she felt completely invisible to her family—until they needed something. She felt unheard, until she got angry. She felt unwanted, as if no one would even notice her absence. *So,* she considered, *why not use that apparent ability to be unseen in the world?* Her "ability" to disappear didn't translate into the real world, though. Out in the world, people wanted to speak with her, wanted to meet her, and wanted to listen to her. She decided that God was definitely trying to tell her something.

Evidently, the time had arrived for Julie to reach out to a couple of old friends who might be capable of helping move her in *her* direction—except one of them made her very nervous.

* * *

Julie's car-show synopses brought her more attention as a writer than she'd anticipated. Car collectors contacted her. They sought industry insight about not only the shows themselves, but about other collectors (often some purchases weren't in her wrap-ups), individual sub-contractors and remodeling companies (who did the high rollers hire), and how to get invited to private deals made "behind the scenes" (during non-show hours). She'd been sincerely flattered that they thought she might know.

Early on, Julie had decided that it was best to know at least enough to report on the events' results intelligently. Perhaps later on, she'd change her mind.

That later on had already arrived.

She'd gotten the kids situated for the evening and

decided it was time to wander across the street to connect with her car enthusiast neighbor. He was bound to be able to shed light on which direction she ought to pursue first in her quest for greater industry knowledge. She also suspected she ought to share a little about why it was time to get educated, though she preferred to keep her private life completely separate. Bob was entitled to a little information; perhaps he may be more generous with *his* knowledge then.

CHAPTER 34

Fallout

*C*losure. *Well that concept's good and screwed up! I knew flying home that there'd really been little closure. I'd shared my gratitude with Dane in who he was in high school, as well as how he'd made an impact on my choices later. What I hadn't anticipated was any re-opening of feelings—his or mine. He's got continued interest in me? How? Why? And what about that kiss ... on that last night? Was it real, or did I just imagine the passion there between us?* Julie sat frozen in front of her cell phone. *No, no, no. It was real all right. In fact, it was too real. It was too intense to be imagined. It was too intense given I'm MARRIED!* She scolded herself. *It had been completely inappropriate.*

Months later, staring at her phone uncertainly, she was still stunned at herself, especially since she wanted and needed to speak with him. *Had I been so deprived of intimacy or connection that I'd allowed a line to be crossed? I hadn't initiated anything; in fact, I'd discouraged him from walking me to my room that night,* she justified. *His room being on the same floor was either an ugly test or an angelic message. I'm still uncertain as to the answer.*

Though she'd really wanted to work out that morning before getting on the long flight home, she hadn't wanted to take any chances on seeing Dane in the hotel's fitness room.

She couldn't trust either herself or him to keep it simple, professional, or even at arms' length. She just wasn't willing to take any chances. She was, sadly, running away again. *Ok,* she voiced to herself mentally, *that's not exactly true. That was more…conflict management than running away. That's not the same thing, is it? Ok, let's rephrase it as being respectful of all parties potentially affected by questionable choices.*

What other options were there really? Her marriage was already strained. Though she and Gabe loved each other, their love had constantly been tested with strong wills. They knew that was both their relationship's strength and weakness. It used to be trickier, though. Thankfully, they sought counseling, worked through a number of issues, and began to communicate more fairly with each other.

Recently, new concerns had crept into their relationship—scary topics such as inappropriate co-worker behavior and business development, typical growing pains for an evolving company. Adding homeowner responsibilities, disciplining children, rising education costs, and sudden budget expenditures threw them back into a divisive world needing more conflict resolution skills than counseling. Because communication was their weakness, often out of balance and riddled with misunderstandings, Gabe frequently assumed Julie didn't believe in him; hence his constantly feeling questioned by her. He didn't know if this was normal marriage stuff or a wife doubting and disbelieving in her husband.

Julie knew asking questions was crucial to understanding, though. *Confusing times. Will we ever get it right? Does talking through concerns and problems always have to be so difficult?*

Now, she faced not only needing to pick up the phone,

but in doing so, the issues she'd stir from both the one questioned … as well as from her husband.

* * *

Though it had been just months since they'd last spoken, Julie and Aubrey hated going too long without touching base. Ever since the college roommates had graduated, they'd promised each other to remain "partners in crime." Ironically, the Feds had just promoted Aubrey Pulaski. Her new position in their international crime division required travel to Europe—an operational detail for which she couldn't resist volunteering.

"Seriously? Europe? Aubrey, that's amazing!!! Congratulations! When do I pack my bags? You'll need a non-federal chaperone periodically, right?"

"I know, right? Kinda crazy; who'da thunk, right?" Aubrey tried to sound humble.

"Screw that humble crap with me. You know better. If you can't brag a little with your college best friend, who can you?"

"Ya. Ok. Good point. In that case, I fuckin' BLEW the competition outta the water, Jules. I really left them with no choice *but* to promote me. Between my aptitude test scores, my recommendations, three levels of interviews, and my operations follow-through, my youthfulness, shall we say, never even came up. My more experienced competition was lazy in comparison. Simple as that."

"WOW!! That's something you've *never* been—lazy! How's your hubby? He must be so proud of you!"

"Well, he says he is, but honestly, I'm not too sure he's as thrilled as he's claiming."

"Sounds like he's hit your very own personal suspect list.

Sheez, Aubrey, are you sure this career isn't getting to you on another level?"

"Jules, I asked myself the same question, and I'm not liking the answer. I even thought about not going for this advancement."

"That's not good."

"Exactly, so we'll see. OK, your turn. What's up with you?"

"I need your advice."

"Hopefully, not about marriage, since you've been happily married longer than me." The two women laughed. "Is it?"

"Well, not now, though we're struggling, too."

"Oh. I'm sorry," Aubrey mumbled.

"Yeah, well, must be in the atmosphere! Maybe that'll make you feel better, knowing that you two aren't the only ones struggling right now. Anyway, I'm actually shifting my focus in my writings. I'm moving away from high school sports recaps and have been concentrating on car shows."

Aubrey sputtered, nearly choking on her midday coffee.

"Sheez. Does that sound funny for a reason?" Julie tried not to sound as irked as she felt.

"Sorry. I don't mean to upset you—and you're not gonna like how this sounds—but I've never lied to you before, right?"

"Riiiight… ."

"You've never liked or given a rat's ass about cars before, except that they better work when you turned the key. So, why now? And how can you? You don't know anything about them."

"OK, fair enough; good points. Well, it turns out that

my crazy inner research junkie can write about anything—as long as I don't have to be too serious, can research and ask all the questions I want, and then regurgitate info accurately. Pay's better, too."

"Sweet! OK, now *that* all makes total sense! Sorry, honey, I didn't mean to upset you, but you understand where I was coming from, right?"

"Yep, but I think that's been part of my problem—not you, but in general. I've been limiting myself to write about only what I know. While that's all useful, and I've paid a few bills here and there with my *huge* earnings, this car show stuff is far more intriguing than I'd expected."

"So what advice do you need from me then?" Aubrey looked at her watch, knowing that she needed to scramble to make the department's weekly briefing.

"Asking how you're making marriage and career work *was* actually one of my questions, but we'll strike that one from the record for now," she chuckled. "My other concern is actually about this industry. Car renovating is huge money."

Unknowingly, Julie now had the federal agent's complete attention. "That's an understatement."

"You're familiar with it?"

"Every day we deal with some crime or criminal in that world."

"Aubrey, I don't mean theft, I… ."

"Sorry to cut you off. I've only got a few minutes to make a meeting I'm definitely late for already. I know you don't mean theft. But let me warn you—those car shows, like the Barrett-Jackson in your area? They sell legitimate, renovated, antiques, registered, etc. That's not the warning. Here's the warning: not everyone or every car is legitimate. Does this make sense?"

"No. Clarify, please." Julie went into her pro mode, too.

"What you see isn't always what you're getting. Be careful. Do your research."

"I'm really just reporting results, quirky events, etc. Kind of like a social recap, really."

"Knowing you, my friend, you'll get bored with that, or upset someone who will say something, and then you'll expose—unintentionally or intentionally—something, that maybe you needed to refrain from exposing and, well, then we're off!!"

"Um. OK," Julie mumbled, more confused than before.

"Listen, girlfriend, I've gotta run. Call me if you have any questions or really need to run something past me. Hugs to all!"

"You, too—and thanks." The line disconnected. "Well, what the hell was that all about?" Julie wondered.

* * *

"She constantly blames me for all of our communication issues. Apparently, she's so perfect, and I'm so wrong about everything," Gabe lamented. "How can one person be so wrong all the time?"

"I'm not always right. I'm just not going to be bullied and roll over," Julie grasped at evenhandedness.

Julie felt like she was having an out-of-body experience. It was almost as if her soul was somewhere else, and she was simply evaluating her place in time. *This counseling session hadn't been called due to crisis or emergency. There hadn't been any major conflict, just a series of smaller ones—or so I thought.*

There was, however, definitely a building up of issues. In her heart, she trusted that time together would probably solve most of them, if not all. *What we need desperately is the fun and joy of being together, like when we first met, as well as the quiet and peace we've often shared. Our lives just keep spinning faster and faster, teetering on the edge of brilliance and disaster. I thought that was really why we'd agreed to attend the latest session. Now I don't know what to think.*

"Thankfully, we're smart enough to know that we either lacked the skills or the know-how to solve our challenges," Julie lectured herself aloud, despondent and more frustrated than when she'd arrived. "I'm just not seeing that we're evolving, especially after that session."

Exasperating as it was, they both easily blamed the other. Taking responsibility seemed to constantly fall more on Julie as the more "evolved soul," according to their therapist. Though Gabe accepted whatever the counselor advised him was his part, she reasoned that the "workaholic can only handle so much."

Well, what the hell is that supposed to mean? He's excused from trying here? Being a workaholic is acceptable and healthy? I'm solely in charge of any and all emotional development in our marriage? Is that what marriage is actually about? Well, nobody told me that. That was NOT part of any vow I took.

Julie grew tired of these sessions. Not because she didn't love Gabe; she did. Not because she felt they were a waste of time; learning something new was never a waste. Not because she wanted things to fall apart; she eagerly wanted her marriage to flourish. Alarmingly, she'd begun believing difficulties between them weren't ever going to resolve—that Gabe either didn't want them to, or he was afraid that the transformation would be emasculating; he was "safer" without them. Julie couldn't convince Gabe that she wanted them to mature and improve together, not with one dictating to the other.

According to their counselor, for a while, sometimes men are only about their businesses developing. "Remember, it's a very primitive instinct, like hunting, killing, and providing for their families. This is the modern world rendition. That means for a while, the wife picks up the emotional slack. Doesn't seem fair, but that's kind of reality. Sometimes the roles even reverse, and sometimes men catch up—sometimes."

"The funny thing about beliefs and thoughts," according to an artist from the late 1890's whom their counselor had quoted, "was that they return, sooner or later, with astounding accuracy," and that "life was a game of boomerangs." Knowing that, Julie freaked out about the thoughts she had been having.

I don't want to bring negative energy to our marriage, but life definitely would be easier for both of us without this challenge. Am I holding back making a sweeping change due to fear, or am I staying in this marriage out of guilt or love? What about Gabe? Why is he staying? Or, is he just waiting for me to make a big move so he doesn't have to? Are we capable of growing and moving forward as a couple through these challenges? What's plaguing me about this session? She knew these thoughts were warnings of some sort.

And *why* had that woman's face from the airplane flashed in her mind in the midst of this strife? Who was she? Julie's inquisitive instincts screamed at her. Maddeningly, they were all screaming at the same time, so she couldn't understand even a single one of them.

CHAPTER 35

"Biz" Trip

A few years after Dane had started his new position within the firm, his new boss had invited him to check out his hobby: rebuilding old English sports cars. Victor and Dane came to appreciate their mutual interest in old cars. Victor liked to invest in fixing them up, then selling them. Dane liked to test drive them once finished to ensure they functioned correctly, then to sell them. Soon thereafter, Dane bought the cars in need of renovation; Victor spent the time needed to restore them. They'd split all expenses on parts and then all profits on sales. They'd both get the enjoyment they were seeking. Dane appreciated the diversion. Since his divorce, he'd been without one—other than his kids.

Victor had little spare time for his very expensive passion, but he truly enjoyed tinkering with the mechanics, finding parts, and restoring a classic to its original glory. Dane shared a great admiration for the final product and the return on their investment, though he relished the brief opportunity to drive and enjoy each one. While Victor occasionally relived the car's glory with his wife of 42 years in roadster groups, Dane preferred the quiet drives through the beautiful countryside and maybe a night or two at various bed and breakfast inns. He usually spent the time reading, sleeping, and enjoying the quiet space he rarely experienced in his regular life filled with kids, work, functions, meetings, case studying, etc. His brief jaunts out in the roadsters allowed him an escape. He just wished he'd had someone with whom to share such tranquility and appreciation.

On a low-key Sunday when Dane was making his way back to the city in one of their recent rebuilds, Victor called him excited to share that he'd found a buyer for their investment, who also had been a client of the firm over the years.

"Actually, the buyer found us. Bob Couvey is here looking for some very specific parts for another virtually completed car he's been working on for awhile. We were talking about our latest project, and Bob may have a party interested in acquiring it. I know better than to bother you with the specifics, Dane. Let's just say Bob was led to me years ago from the States. Then he became a client, as he needed legal representation for auto transactions to and from all over Europe. Anyway, we've agreed upon what he needs, and he has a deal for us. How soon are you back this afternoon?"

When Dane got to Victor's home workshop, Bob Couvey was still there. Brief introductions were made, and the deal was simple: exchange the part for free entry and representation of their classic in the famous Barrett-Jackson Car Auction and Show in the U.S. in late January.

"You both are more than welcome to stay at our home as well. We've a separate guest casita that's actually part of the car showroom next to the house."

"Victor, you go. I have those two big launches happening at about the same time," Dane reminded him.

"Dane, really? Frankly, our assistants are more than

capable of handling those transactions IF they even happen. It's the perfect opportunity for them to give it a go on their own. Promise. Even if they screwed it up, the consequences are minimal, if any, and not at all dramatic. A little extra attention from us, and the issue would be over. I'd tell you otherwise, because we'd both be on the line."

"Besides," Bob continued, "it's a perfect time of year to be in Arizona." Little did either Bob or Victor realize, but they had Dane's attention now.

"The car show's in Arizona?"

Bob smiled. "Craig Jackson wouldn't live anywhere else. He's threatened to move the show to Las Vegas, but he doesn't actually want to go there himself. You know anything about Arizona?"

Victor interjected, "Dane had a stop-over there during the summer…"

"Ouch! Tough time to come through our desert. Summer means monsoons, crazy heat, and bizarre weather patterns. Whoever booked your travel plans ought to be fired or demoted severely," Bob teased.

"The connecting flight I was taking out of L.A. had mechanical failures that forced us to land in Phoenix." Dane was suddenly thoughtful. Neither man had noticed. Dane was stuck in a brief reverie marveling at the circumstances beyond his control; but, just as Julie had pointed out at the time, *obviously very meant to be. I was supposed to see her. Now, suddenly I'm aware of the universe conspiring to bring us together again. But why? We've lived worlds apart, led very different lives, and neither of us is able to change what we're doing.*

"You know, on second thought, Victor, I *will* go. I've only stopped through when it was 118 degrees, so why not show up when the weather's at its best? Since I started this hobby, I've wanted to attend several car shows. Unfortunately, the timing's just always been off. I can also take care of some of those Southwest clients who usually just get video conferencing with me. Maybe I'll even use a few of my many vacation days." He paused, took a deep breath. "I'm in," Dane decided.

WHAT am I doing?! he screamed at himself in his head. As he'd done many nights since returning from the reunion, he dreamt of making love to her again that night.

* * *

Days after that meeting with Bob and his decision to go to Arizona, Dane walked into Victor's office as his boss hung up the phone. The senior partner seemed perturbed.

"You needed me in person?"

"Yes…for a few reasons," Victor answered distractedly. Dane sat in the large, soft, brown leather wingback chair patiently waiting for Victor to continue. It was rare when the man actually called him to his office instead of just stopping by Dane's.

"It's a really good thing you're going to Arizona soon."

Dane tried to remain calm, but hearing Arizona mentioned in any conversation didn't just immediately get his attention. His pulse quickened, its tempo awakened as if he'd just returned from a brief jog. *I'm ridiculous,* he thought. *We've not even communicated since the reunion, so why I'm planning to see her is ludicrous. Thank God I've had the intelligence to keep my mouth shut about that whole event with anyone.*

"That was Bob. He said he's anxious about confirming

our plans to attend the car show there in January. His wife was trying to reserve their guest casita for some other friends who are likely to attend as well. However, Bob's business people always come first—unless she secures the space first. So, you're in, right? I can book our tickets?"

"Yes." Dane thought the less he said the better. He didn't want to give anything away.

"Good. I'll call him back as soon as we're finished here. I'd have kept him on the line, since you were walking in at that moment, but his lovely, young neighbor had stopped over to ask a car question. Since this, um, Julie, I think he said her name was, rarely, if ever, bothers him, he knew it must be pretty important. He'd never let his wife communicate with her if possible—long story, but essentially his wife is not the nicest person, in general."

Dane was on alert. Arizona. His car hobby. Neighbor named Julie. Couldn't be. There were tons of women named Julie.

"Oh, boy. Hang on. That's him again, and he always waits for my call. Something else must be up."

"Hey, Bob. I have Dane sitting right here. I was just confirming plans with him. What's up?"

Victor shifted in his desk chair, clearly intent on listening to the voice on the end of the receiver. "Well, that's too bad. Anyway, Dane and I are a definite for the car show week. If the invitation is still open, we'd love to stay at the casita as well. Very good; I'll get you our travel plans later this week. Thanks again."

Dane grew anxious.

"The second reason I've called you in here—Tate."

Dane looked impassively at Victor and took note of

his blood pressure rising at the mere mention of his former classmate's name.

"He said he's tried to reach you twice this morning?"

Dane stonily replied, "His timing's a bit off. I'm in the middle of preparing for those launches while I'm away, and he's asking about something for months from now."

"When he calls, Dane, take his calls." Victor looked up from his desk at Dane with a coolness he'd only experienced that one time in the conference room with the older man. Dane again felt uneasy with Victor's turning over Tate's account to him.

I know Victor hadn't had a choice, but I just can't understand what hook Tate has in Victor, or the firm, for that matter. There's certainly something there, but Victor protects that information somehow—for some disturbing reason. He insisted there was nothing but the firm's reputation and bottom line at risk. What is he keeping from me and why? That's the question.

Dane had asked Isabella to keep her ears open about why the change in who handled this client. She'd been trickling information to Dane as she'd heard it. He'd cautioned her to trust no one and ask few questions when with her colleagues, and she'd been masterful to date. What she'd turned up, though, left Dane increasingly concerned for his long-time assistant, as well as for the firm.

There were whispers about stolen firm money, but no one seemed to know any particulars. Victor's tone regarding Tate was unsettling. He waited for more information before starting any private digging. *I believe, with certainty now, that Tate has something to do with it. If Tate's involved, then so is Victor. Were they the only two?*

"I'll call him back when I leave here. Will that be soon

enough?" Dane had an edge in his voice he struggled to conceal.

Victor was distracted (or professional) enough to have appeared to have missed it. "Yes. Fine."

"What's up with Bob's neighbor, Julie, I think you mentioned?" Dane tried to sound casual.

"She and her husband are just having trouble. They're successful business owners in town, so she was reaching out to ask for a little help, I guess. Apparently, that's a first. Anyway, he isn't normally nosy, but I had asked him to keep an eye on her—just because of who we are, what we do, as well as because of Tate's latest demands on you and the firm. None of us need an issue. But Bob's assured me that they're not that kind of people. They keep to themselves, are really into their kids, and her husband works crazy, long hours. She's very sociable, but not open. She's *very* private. He knows virtually nothing else about them, though they've lived next door for years," Victor finished.

"What do you mean, 'given what we do?' What do we do besides play lawyer?"

"That's what I mean, Dane. Tate's a challenging soul to deal with, as you already know, and privacy is almost a safety issue for him."

"So, then, the neighbor's really a non-issue, since she's very private as well. Who's this neighbor again? Julie you said? Last name? I may need to do a little research myself if I'm to help both Bob and Tate." *Good thinking, Dane,* he applauded himself.

"Here," Victor flipped through the file sitting on the left-hand side of his desk, then handed it over to Dane. Dane scanned the part about Julie and her husband.

"Archer is their last name. I asked him to become a little chattier with Julie when he saw her. He told me that might be difficult, since his wife had had less than pleasant words with Julie a few years back. Given the wall of privacy between these neighbors, I had to ask why. Bob said it was over some construction issue that his wife had been a bitch about. He thought Julie handled it in a very neighborly way. She and her husband have done pretty well in respecting Bob's 'charming' wife's concerns. Bob said that he has neighborly chats periodically when his wife isn't within ear range." Victor chuckled, knowing Bob's wife. In spite of her tough, caustic demeanor, she was very generous when it suited her—but there had to be something in it for her.

"She's separated?! Who told you this, Victor?" Dane demanded. Oh, *shit, I just gave myself away,* Dane realized as he met Victor's blank but fixated stare and raised eyebrows. The older man processed this instantly.

"Dane, who is this Julie to you? Why do you care so much?"

Dane pushed, "So, what did Bob say? About Julie's separation?" Dane knew he had to be forthcoming with his information, or Victor would be very unforgiving later—in spite of his boss's less accommodating spirit even now. "We went to high school together," Dane shared dismissively in an attempt to downplay the impact of this revelation.

"Oh, my. She was the reason you went to that reunion, wasn't she?" Victor was too perceptive.

Dane slowly let his breath out. He hadn't realized he was holding it.

"No wonder you changed your mind about going to

Arizona with me," Victor teased, seemingly more like himself again.

Dane knew it was best to keep his mouth shut unless asked a question. *You've blown it. Now it's going to get to Tate, if he doesn't already know—which he may.*

"He said that Julie hadn't offered any information about Gabe, so Bob asked in a roundabout kind of way—you know, how's business? How's your husband? How are the kids? Neighborly stuff. Julie said nothing about it to him, again, very aware of her boundaries. Bob was talking out of the blue with another neighbor who *does* speak with Julie often, and that was when he found out she and her husband have been separated for the last two months." Victor silently observed his protégé's expressions as Dane did the math quickly.

"Victor, granted I last saw Julie months ago, but she said nothing to me about any issues." Dane had no idea what to make of his thoughts, the situation. He was acutely aware that his heartbeat had gotten faster again. *Why hadn't Julie said a word? I understand the kiss a little better now,* he thought, *but even that's not very clear. What's going on? Why hadn't she at least updated him? Didn't she consider that Dane might have an interest in such a development?*

Victor stood staring at Dane. "What are you thinking?"

"I honestly don't have a clue—yet. I don't know what *to* think. She clearly did *not* want to influence any decision; she's also obviously not looking for a rebound relationship. She must be horribly confused herself … ." His voice trailed off, realizing he'd said too much. "Excuse me, Victor."

Dane ran for his phone, immediately dialed Julie's number, and hung up. *What was I going to say to her? 'Hey, heard you were separated. Wanna fly over?' WHAT was I even THINKING? Maybe she's trying to figure it all out. Maybe they're in counseling and trying to work things out. Why wasn't hubby doing this living at home? Was there someone else for him?*

"No way," Dane reasoned aloud to himself, as the normally cool attorney paced in front of his office window. "Gabe knows what he has in Julie, I'm sure." *He'd definitely married up. She's an incredibly special person. He wasn't cheating on her—was he? Why would he? His own insecurities maybe? Hmmm. Insecurities—sounds like another guy I know all too well,* Dane upbraided himself.

Dane decided to ask for some advice. It was rare that he ever needed advice, since that was usually what *he* dispensed. He left work early to see his parents. *They'll talk me out of my crazy notions. They'll help me see through the emotions to the logic. What's logical right now? All I've wanted to do for months was call her, or get on a plane and surprise her or … no. Wait. I won't surprise her. What if that very same day I showed up, Julie and Gabe had reconciled? That would just about kill me.*

I'll talk with my parents and think. In fact, Dane decided, *it might be the perfect time to start really praying. Yes, that's what I'll do—pray for divine intervention.* A smile crossed Dane's face on his way to his parents' home.

CHAPTER 36

Turmoil

The turmoil in her gut was clear in its message: she was denying too much of who she was and what impassioned her. Julie was negating herself to be honorable, right, and fair to the marital commitment she'd made, all the while pushing herself aside and agonizingly losing sight of her future and *her* dreams. How does one brave a transition when the pattern's been set for so long? The ripple effect potential was considerable. Writing, researching, investigating, and hours spent alone in doing so were seen as threatening and scary.

She loved her family, her husband, and her life in so many ways, yet she knew she was missing a deeply significant piece of her essence: the piece that called to her soul and her spirit. She was a spiritual being with a deeply romantic side. Her husband often shunned it as nonsense and told her she was being silly. Her now rare advances (especially in public) embarrassed instead of flattered him even though they were married! She knew that what had attracted him to her in the beginning seemed to be less attractive now. Was he changing or was she?

As life took its turns, she was expected to rise to certain occasions and be someone she wasn't—to do what was right, to be who and/or what he needed her to be at that time. Dutifully and out of love, Julie pushed through the increased and confusing demands for Gabe—even when it failed to make her happy. Did he do the same and she was unaware of his part? Was that what happened in marriage? Was that what compromise was about?? Did every woman feel this at some point? Or, was that what happened when it was time to move on? When change was imminent?

Immediately, Julie's thoughts turned to guilt. How could she even think this way? What had Gabe actually done to deserve being left? Or, was he as unhappy and that was the vibe she'd picked up on? Their last counseling session left an uncertain and indelible mark on her soul.

Julie decided she needed to take control of her own life. *That's all I really can control. It's time to cease allowing fear to rule my actions. Yep. It's time. Another birthday's just passed, and life's pace is picking up speed. I've got to focus on all that I can control: MY emotions, MY thoughts, MY choices, MY writing.*

* * *

She still couldn't believe it weeks later. *This cannot be happening*, Julie thought, stunned. *Did my husband really say what I think he said? Was he really so unhappy, so jealous of my new career path that he'd be willing to walk away from our marriage? Or, was something outside of our marriage triggering him? He wanted me to return to work. Evidently, work HE deemed acceptable or necessary—not what would make me happy. Our marriage lasting had never even been on the list of discussion topics before. We've definitely had our share of disagreements, of anguish, anger, and gloom, but divorce?*

She'd been launched into a state beyond mere concern; it was more like fear with the shivers to show for it. *I know I'm not perfect. Who is? That's what happens in marriage, right?*

Couples actually grasp their humanness, imperfections and all?
There was usually just one reason for a spouse's growing
unhappiness: 1.) one spouse was not growing enough (or the
other was outgrowing them), or 2.) someone else—a third
party—had entered the picture.

Julie toiled with this thought. *Gabe has always been the
most loyal person I've ever known. His college buddies used
to tease him about how he wouldn't even date because of his
commitment to his high school sweetheart. Loyal to a fault, they'd
tell me. Shortly after college, Gabe broke up with her, only because
she'd cheated on him—twice.* Months later, he met Julie.

*So, was all that loyalty getting to him? Did he need to lash
out and just do something different? Be someone else for a change
while he was still young maybe? Mid-life crisis?* Her head
was racing with so many possibilities, each option more
nauseating than the last. She reprocessed that contentious
conversation …

Hoping to make a positive impact on Gabe before he
said anything permanently damaging to their relationship,
Julie opened their discussion. "Let me preface my
concerns with this clear gratitude: our differences
aside, I'm married to a very kind, generous, lovable,
handsome, responsible, and faithful man. You can be
adoring, sensitive, fun, connected, and loving. With that
said, our differences can be staggering."

Julie quieted her breathing with a slow, deep intake
and expelling of air. She knew having this meeting in a
public place was crucial to both of them remaining calm
and respectful toward the other. The tension that existed
between them—even in the large restaurant space—felt

suffocating, as if each was just waiting for the other to make a drastic move.

When Gabe sat her down to explain his feelings, he was prepared for an explosion of nastiness and blame. He was shaken and immediately felt off-balance when Julie began first. He knew it was easy to walk away from someone when you were angry with him or her. Julie screwed up his whole exit plan.

"Julie, I know things have been strained between us for quite awhile. We've been smoothing rough areas, talking through some issues, and generally struggling to find common ground. Ever since you started that new writing focus and then shifted your existing writing commitments to this very consuming project, we've been more challenged than normal. I know I've definitely contributed to probably most of those challenges, and that I've disappointed you in how I've dropped the ball of active support."

"Gabe…"

"Wait. Please let me finish. OK?"

Julie somberly nodded her agreement.

"I also know that ever since you came back from that class reunion, you've been different. I guess almost restless. It's as if a piece of you didn't come back. I can't really explain it. It's pretty weird that I'M talking like this, right? I usually don't pay attention to details, like when you get your hair cut or how nice you look. 'Course, you always look nice, so why say anything? I'd bore you with how often I told you!" Gabe chuckled.

As he looked at Julie, fully waiting for her to debate him or accuse him or interject something, she just waited quietly for him to continue, staring at him both apprehensively and thoughtfully. He suddenly became aware of his stomach clench.

"What I keep running into, though, is how I know that I can't be what you really need, or who you really need me to be. I've also finally started to realize that you've been the most amazing woman in my life and are the most amazing mom, but… ."

Julie's stomach knotted itself. *When "but" enters a conversation, it cancels out all words prior, and here it is. I can't even believe I'm sitting here…listening to this. It's so surreal.*

"… because I refuse to cheat on you—and we swore to each other that we wouldn't embarrass each other by doing that—I know that we need to make some changes."

The silence was deafening. *Holy shit! There's another woman!! What haven't I been to him that he needs someone else? I know that someone else really has nothing to do with me and everything to do with him. It's still making me fucking ill. Is stability a sham?? Is growing old together truly unrealistic, as educated and smart as he is? Maybe I'm being forced to let go, so he's forced to grow. Then, God willing, we'll find our way back to each other. Was this really how it's supposed to go down?* She processed all of these thoughts in fractions of seconds. At that moment, Julie realized she'd been contemplating these same thoughts for longer than she cared to admit. She gently closed her eyes as she released the breath she'd been involuntarily holding.

Gabe was shocked that all he got were Julie's closed eyes. *I was completely ready for her defensiveness, welcomed it even (something I'd have felt) and am getting none of it. She's been getting better at just listening; yet, right now, I'm beginning to feel guilty about her ability to do so. Has she been growing, and I'm actually far behind after all? She's actually calm, eerily quiet. What's really weird, though, is that she seems okay. Am I imagining this? Has there been something to that reunion that she's not shared after all?*

"Please say something," he firmly urged, as he looked around at the diners who'd been seated near their table, distracted long enough to note how busy this California Pizza Kitchen location seemed to be even at 11:30 in the morning.

"What…do…you…want…me…to say?" she very deliberately articulated, slowly opening her eyes. She noticed, sadly, that even in this heartbreaking moment, Gabe was distracted. "I don't know what you mean by 'make some changes.' Basically, you just made it clear that you don't want me any more. You're even seemingly over the concept of 'us' so fast that you're paying attention to our environment." She was almost inaudible.

Julie knew in her heart that staying married for the kids was wrong. *I've constantly believed that our passion for one another would always triumph over our anger, disagreements, and differences.*

She suspected, deep down in her heart, that Gabe might not have ever been her soul mate, her true life's companion. *Scorpio and Gemini were never the ultimate combination. We'd just believed that we'd get through anything with our pledge to each other. We'd made a life's commitment. What question was*

*there in that? I get perhaps a separation to re-evaluate, maybe;
but ... divorce???*

Gabe packed a suitcase and moved out that night.

Julie still couldn't believe that was just shortly after she'd
returned from the reunion.

CHAPTER 37

Exes Meet

Dane was long over his marriage. It had been over fifteen years, after all. Looking back over their six-year relationship—two years of dating and four married—he knew it shouldn't ever have happened to begin with. He thought because Rachel was striking, smart, educated, and impeccably mannered that she'd be a great companion and that he'd grow to love her. He was right—*and* very wrong.

She was an acceptable companion for Dane, but only for short periods of time. Their initial attraction evaporated swiftly. He often thought the problems in their marriage were all her responsibility until their children were born. It became very clear to him then that *he* was the problem. He'd never loved Rachel; he'd been attracted to the *idea* of her. He'd never heard her thoughts or concerns in life, nor had he even asked. He'd only assumed they weren't a challenge to his own, which he hadn't shared, either. He'd been an absolute chauvinist jerk, completely unfair. He knew that he hadn't been raised that way, either.

He was rarely intimate with her, though he fulfilled his marital obligations to her, as did she, giving her two children; then he blamed his career for his fatigue and disinterest in sex. He'd never really felt connected to her, so it was easy to keep his distance from her. The children kept them connected more than they would've been otherwise.

He caught himself wondering, *At what point had I made a lifetime commitment to a woman whom I'd held no genuine interest in, who barely really knew me, and who seemed to not care one way or the other anyway!* Though he'd not given her much of a chance to know him, she never seemed all that intent on doing so anyhow. *WHAT was I thinking?* It was at that point that he knew he needed to stop misleading her; he needed out of the relationship. She thought at first that he'd been having an affair. After all, what man makes the effort to leave a marriage that's convenient? Why else would any man break up his family and cause such heartache?

The rumors flew. Rachel had a private investigator tail him for months. *What a waste of both time and money. Not only wasn't I cheating on my wife, but I also knew about the P.I. the entire time!* He scowled as he shook his head slowly. Rachel had even gone so far as to accuse his assistant of being the "other woman," since Isabella spent more time with Dane than anyone else at that point. It was quite a surprise to find out that Isabella was actually a lesbian.

The legal proceedings were ridiculously dull, too. Dane cooperated with whatever time she'd wanted regarding the kids, but made it clear that he wanted very much to be a significant part of their lives. In his despondency, he gave her pretty much everything else, despite his legal counsel's recommendations. Rachel hadn't acknowledged any level of Dane's generosity. Her attorney couldn't convince her otherwise. She'd been so hurt that she'd failed to see his misery—even in the end. He'd caused it, right? Yet, she, too, came to understand that they should never have married.

It's been years since the final divorce papers had gone through, the dust has settled, and I'm just about to leave for the U.S. again. Why, then, has Rachel called me for a meeting telling me it's to call a truce? I thought we've had one for years. Can't remember the last time we disagreed or even had tension between us. Dane knew to be on high alert with the Rachel from the past. *But something about her calling for this meeting makes me exceedingly uneasy.*

"I cannot believe how miserable you looked after the papers went through and how much better you look now," she stated flatly as he approached her café table outside.

He tilted his head and gave her a questioning look. He looked down at himself mockingly and shrugged his shoulders.

"So, what's this about? You didn't call a face-to-face meeting to tell me how I looked years ago, did you?"

"No. I didn't. I was simply making an observation that perhaps you might not have been aware of yourself. You often do *not* really *look* at yourself. You don't look glum any more, but I'm not sure what adjective I *would* apply," Rachel reminded him.

A brief silence followed as she collected her thoughts, and he settled into his chair. She definitely made a much better friend than spouse. Her honesty had always been one of her finer qualities. Still, he speculated when she was going to be forthcoming with the purpose of this meeting.

"I've a few things to share with you in their entirety, and it will be very important that you let me get it all out before I lose the courage to say it all. Agreed?"

"OK."

Rachel reached out to Dane, laid her hand on his shirtsleeve, bowed her head, and firmly apologized. "I…

am…sorry," she spoke each word quietly, haltingly. "I'd been hurt and angry, mystified and embarrassed. All of those feelings were, and still are, mine to own, however, and not your fault. After counseling, soul searching, and a few too many bottles of wine, I've come to the same grand conclusion as you—that we never should have married."

"Rachel, we've been through this confession before. What's … ."

She sniffed and pouted, "Now, you just agreed to not interrupt me."

Dane raised his eyebrows in agreement, took a deep breath, and nodded his assent.

"Thank you. You were just too many steps ahead of me, as usual. I was too proud to be realistic, though deep down, I'd known this for years as well." Rachel ordered a glass of red wine from the waiter who'd just approached their table, then took a sip of water before she continued.

Dane quietly observed her and waited for what brought about her requesting this meeting. He knew money couldn't be the issue, and they'd recently agreed that the kids had adjusted well to the unfortunate changes.

"I was so cocky and arrogant about whom I'd married, I virtually forgot that you were a human being with thoughts and feelings. I saw us as a dynamic power couple—good-looking, smart, successful, and with two perfect children…"

"Rachel, we—have—been—through—this," he patiently, but tersely, stated in spite of getting impatient. "*What* is going on?"

She continued as if he'd not said a word. "I was so caught up in the superficial 'who' we were that I was practically disconnected as a parent and person from reality.

"Then you came home that night and told me that you'd been unfair to me, to us, and to yourself, and I lost it. I lost myself in my anger, though I knew what you'd said was spot on. I lost my confidence as a mom, as you know, all but abandoning our children and leaving them with you. Now, don't get offended. I know you're a great dad, but the mom is supposed to be the main caretaker. I ran away. When I got my head back on straight, you were again a gift: fair, kind, very generous, and worked out whatever I asked of you.

"I lost my confidence as a woman until I went through a significant amount of counseling." Rachel smiled at herself, shook her head, and went on. "I'd recovered my balance, started dating again, and met David. He's kind and thoughtful. He dotes on the children and me. He doesn't overstep his bounds as a stepparent, either. You agree with that?"

Dane nodded his head, having grown more than wary of the conversation. Some alarm had sounded off in his mind. This was the "Old" Rachel resurrected.

"Great. So, I'm here to ask you for your forgiveness—again. I'm here to thank you, again, for forcing me to grow. I'm here to call for an extension to our truce, to continue to be the friends that we were really meant to be, and to start again, except we have children." She laughed a small forced laugh that didn't reach her eyes.

"Truce." Dane sat back, removed his arm from under her touch, raised his eyebrows, stuck out his right hand to shake Rachel's, and then released it. "Now, tell me, Rachel."

She looked at him quizzically.

"Why did you really call this meeting between us?"

"I don't understand your question. I've already told you why: to call a truce," she tried smoothly.

"Rachel, we've been fine for a long time, at least I thought we were. In fact, I thought we'd even become more pleasant. Now you suddenly need to formally announce a truce between us? Again? What's going on? Does David know you're here?" Dane probed evenly while his lawyer suspiciousness kicked in. Something was up.

"David's a good man, Dane."

"Rachel, cut the bullshit," he calmly shot back.

She looked at her hands. "Fine," she snidely snapped. "I heard you were going back stateside and just wanted to touch base before you left. I'm just making sure all papers are in line in case of…well, of anything."

"That was why we needed to speak in person? I know you better than that."

Dane stared at his ex-wife, knowing she had an ulterior motive. *I recognize she's up to something and not ready to share what it is yet. Who's told her I'm going back to the States? My assistant? Not likely. Isabella holds no love for this woman. After all, Rachel had threatened Isabella's position with me wrongfully. Victor? Why would he? He knew what hell I'd gone through. Then again, Victor has seemed off ever since he handed over Tate's account, so who knows why he might have offered the ex anything.*

"I'll stop by later to let the kids know what's going on." He quickly reached into his inside-suit jacket pocket for his billfold, snagged a few bucks out of it, and left the money on the table for her drink. He just looked plainly at Rachel, pushed back his chair, and left the café. He saw her eyes gaze downward without a word—another sign that they just weren't made for each other.

CHAPTER 38

Paint And Upholstery

Once the exterior shells had dried from having been painted and the interior upholstery install had been finished, the small sports cars were rolled into a large, elegant, private showroom. The doors of the showroom were pulled closed by the next level of security guards, and then locked. An automated curtain closed once the doors sent a signal that they were sealed.

CHAPTER 39

Admonish ... Again

"I don't understand." Gabe clashed with Julie. "You first were writing brief summaries about car shows, and now you're starting your own investigation? How did you make that leap?" He strongly challenged her on the phone while he was still at work.

"I don't know how to explain exactly, other than to say that there's some sort of bickering and battling with all the posturing at the recent smaller shows. According to the rumors and innuendos, there's more than just selling cars at stake here. I've asked Bob, our neighbor, a few questions, but he said he stays out of as much of it as he can." Julie didn't share with Gabe that Bob had suggested she do the same. She knew what her husband was about to say, though.

Gabe didn't have any problem picking up on that missing comment, however. "I'm sure our wise, older neighbor suggested you do the same?"

"He did."

"But you're not going to listen?"

"Depends on what my 'innocent' questions turn up."

"So, does that mean you won't be taking Maddie to her retreat up north this weekend?"

"No. Should it? I can read, research, write, etc. up there, too. This cool new invention called the Internet extends up there as well, I hear." *I shouldn't be such a smart ass,* she thought to herself. *That attitude rarely helps any couple's communication.* Julie's crinkled brow and turned-up lip hinted at her annoyance with her husband. Thankfully, he couldn't see her expression. "Why? Were you worried I might ask you to go in my place?" *Since we've separated, there always seems to be another agenda in his questions—like he's got plans that I may interrupt. Ugh! I hate this discord between us,* she thought sadly.

Shit, I hate when she's sarcastic like that. I'm working hard to cut back sounding like that. She's been right all this time that it's pretty hurtful. "Not at all. I just don't understand what your next move is with this research. Frankly, I'm a little concerned with you thinking you're now an investigator; plus, given our current marital challenges, I guess I'm just confused in general about your direction in life."

"I'm still taking Maddie up north. I'm still working on, shall we call it, a 'clarification' instead of an investigation. I'm also doing research so that I have accurate information for the new book project—though it's fiction. Yes, I have 'several irons in the fire.' Yes, it'll require more juggling and priority tweaking. That's typical for us, isn't it? The ole ten-pounds-of-shit-in-the-five-pound-sack trick? Our issues suck. But, we're either going to figure them out, or we're going to continue this separation to sincerely think through what we want personally, unless you've already figured that out and are considering your exit strategy. So, I understand the whole being confused thing.

"One other thing—I'm going back to New York soon. Remember the agent I've hired and have been communicating with via phone calls, texting, and emails?

Well, she recommended that I get back to New York for further research for this book, and also to meet with her in person. She loves what I've stumbled onto. Apparently, she has a few places in mind for me to observe to add a real touch to two characters, as well as certain parts of my storyline. She also wants to introduce me to several potential publishers. So, I'm guessing you'll want to likely stay here while I'm gone. I'll keep you posted, though, as I know. If I'm assuming incorrectly, please let me know, and I'll find coverage for the kids."

Gabe didn't like the sound of her traveling. He knew he couldn't argue, though.

"I guess I don't have much say on these issues, do I?" he commented resignedly, knowing he was opening the door to confrontation with his tone. *What the hell did I ask that for? I know better. She has a right to pursue this career path, just as she's supported our company and me. What is my fucking problem?*

Quite surprisingly, as sweetly as possible, Julie didn't take Gabe's bait and unexpectedly responded, "Nope. Makes life a little easier knowing that, doesn't it?" She made an excuse to get off the phone quickly.

Gabe sat at his desk shaking his head. "What am I going to do?" *I'm losing what little connection Julie and I have. Pretty much anything I say to her at this point about this book, or her writing in general, would sound unsupportive.* He wavered between wishing she'd stayed completely focused on him and the kids and wishing she'd taken a conventional position somewhere locally. *This writing is very inconsistent from several approaches. Monetarily, payment depended on deadlines and publishing dates, which, of course, depended on how often the car shows happened. Scheduling is always challenging between my calendar, hers, and the kids'. I also often don't know where she is or when—a fairly recent issue between us.*

His intercom buzzed. "Gabe, line one."

"Who is it, Beth?"

"She said her name is Jennifer Fioroni with Premier Resource Mining."

Gabe swallowed hard. "Thanks, Beth. I'll take it." He looked at the blinking phone button, took a lung full of air, and breathed out slowly. *I really need to simplify my life. This is definitely a complication I don't need right now*, he scolded himself.

"Hello?"

CHAPTER 40

Everyone Loves A Parade

Julie sat minding her own business, reading quietly in a beautiful park in front of the courthouse. The weather was a perfect 82 degrees with blue skies—a rarity in Arizona. After dropping off her daughter for a school retreat, Julie knew she had the afternoon to herself. Gabe was with their eldest daughter and youngest son, and their first son was with his football team. She sighed at the luxury of being able to read and journal quietly in broad daylight, and especially without knowing a soul— an unusual and peaceful treat.

She set herself up at a picnic table, when a sudden pounding on it startled her. A small shriek escaped from her involuntarily, sending giggles through the teenage boy who'd used her table as a skateboard ramp. She turned around to follow where he'd scrambled off to and laughed at herself, stating to those staring, "That caught me a little off guard, huh?" She chuckled and knew it would happen again at least twice, since she'd reacted the first time. She smiled at herself not realizing how entranced in her own little world she'd been in the short time she'd been sitting there.

When the boy looked to startle her again, she was ready this time and didn't even flinch as he scurried over the picnic table. She said nothing, in fact, until he came around a predictable third time. Then, in her best firm I've-had-it-Mom voice, intoned, "OK dude. That's enough now."

The teasing ceased.

Returning to her reading and her own little world felt healing somehow. At home, she stole moments to read and even used the kids' required reading time often as her own. She knew this break was completely overdue. It wasn't long after that, however, that the universe kept testing her powers of focus and self-preservation.

Since the date was September 11th, the town honored it with a parade. Actually, it was more of a showing of unity and celebrating lives. She marveled at first but became keenly aware, quietly observant and properly reverent as the emergency vehicles, military equipment, and scores of motorcyclists revved their engines through town. She tried again to restore her focus and mentally withdrew from the festivities to return to her journaling.

Give it another shot, she silently redirected herself, *before you call it a day and retreat to the hotel*. But as she looked away from the procession, Julie froze in her seat. She recognized a woman from a distance. *I don't know why, but the face is familiar. My reference point's evidently unfocused. Somehow, I know to just sit tight, observe her, and not approach her. Why, though?* An unsettled feeling gnawed at Julie as she scrambled through her mental Rolodex.

Two older ladies interrupted Julie's thoughts this time.

"Mind if we join you? We need a table to play a quiet game of cards."

"No. Not at all."

"Thank you. We won't disturb you. You have such a lovely shaded spot here."

"No, thank *you*! You're both actually offering me protection from further invasions." Julie briefly explained about the skateboarder when she noticed their confused expressions. The older women smiled sweetly and nodded their understanding. Then, as initially established, they busied themselves with their quiet game—two old friends making time for each other.

Guessing her guardian angel *had* to have sent them, Julie silently thanked the invisible energy for the help. *Gotta love the way life works.* Within less than thirty minutes, a man approached the table with credentials in hand. *Call me crazy, but I'm going out on a mental limb here and saying I'm really not meant to get much done right now.* She chuckled at her futile attempts. *Just sayin'.*

"Hi. I'm Dave Krane with the *Prescott Daily Update*. Would you mind if I asked you a few questions about this September 11th celebration and how we, as a country, are progressing in our…"

As Dave prattled on, Julie was terribly aware of two things: first, she wasn't going to finish her journaling here in the park; and second, there was some other force at work here that she just needed to go with.

Smiling, she agreed and asked him to be very conscientious about his quoting her.

"You married, Dave?"

"I am, actually."

"Good. So when I state that I don't even like being misquoted at home, my concerns are clear?"

Dave grinned back at her and said he wasn't one for misquoting for the same reason. After he showed her his tape recorder, he reassured her that he was also taking notes. Julie relaxed—a little.

Turned out she was the third of five people he interviewed for the article. She was also the one he predominantly quoted in the paper the next day. She was pleased with both his accuracy and fairness in how he'd shared her opinion.

She finished reading the article sitting alone at breakfast the next morning and realized she was still hungry. Getting up from her tiny café table-for-two, she did the classic double take. Something in the article's photo caught her eye. Actually, *someone* had caught her eye. It was the same familiar-looking woman she'd seen near the parade. *How can this be? Uh, oh—goose bumps— that clearly signals to me that something isn't right. Again, though, she's unclear, just out of focus.*

Needing to reorder her thoughts, Julie pivoted in the small dining area to the self-serve kitchenette. Having tussled with the waffle maker long enough, Julie opted for another hard-boiled egg and English muffin instead.

"I wrestled with that thing my first morning here. You still hungry for a waffle?" the attractive stranger asked Julie. She nodded and smiled. He had kind eyes, rugged skin, and spoke with an accent, revealing a nationality other than American. *His work takes him outside more often than not,* Julie decided.

"I am, so would you be willing to share your learned waffle iron secrets with me?"

"Happy to," the stranger chuckled and paused. "How long are you here for?"

"I leave later this morning. You?"

"Too bad. I'm likely here another three days."

Curious about his remark, Julie prompted, "Why too bad?"

"Outside of the owners of this fine establishment, you're the first person I've spoken with since being here."

"Which has been how long?"

"Eleven days."

"Ah. Lonely. Check." *Oops. THAT was blunt.*

"I like a woman who's got no problem callin' it as she sees it. Refreshing, actually."

Julie laughed and couldn't help the additional words that stumbled out of her mouth, "That's what you say now! Tough to manage long-term in a partner."

"I totally disagree. That's actually why I'm divorced. She had a brutal time with the truth, sadly."

"Well, there's that." She paused. "Sorry," checking back in with her compassion.

"No problem. It's been several years, so I'm over that pain. You married?"

"Ah. You're direct as well. Refreshing. I am, indeed, married."

"Where is he now? About to come in here and beat me up for talking with his wife?"

Laughing at that visual, but keeping her status private, Julie shook her head. "I'm here alone because our daughter participated in a retreat, and I'm the local parent chaperone. You've flattered me. Thank you for that."

"You've been a kind listener. Thank *you* for that. Here's my card." He scribbled on the back of the business card. "Call me anytime *you* need a sounding board—if you need anything."

"Thank you." Julie smiled politely, put the business card in her purse, and shook his warm, firm grip for a moment longer than customary.

It'd be months before she pulled his business card out again and realized it had only an emergency phone number on the front of it, but a handwritten "Waffles" on the back.

CHAPTER 41

Upside Down

"**S**on of a bitch," Dane cursed under his breath as Isabella delivered the latest office gossip. "Where does this information come from? How does it get started?" Dane's ex-wife was apparently leaving her husband of two years. *She hadn't said a word to me when we'd met earlier. No wonder she was behaving so oddly.*

"Rumor has it that she still wants to work things out with you, Boss, and that she was hoping when you saw her with your children and another man, well, that you'd become jealous." Isabella knew to just stand there very quietly until her boss was ready to absorb anything further.

"Really."

"Really."

"Who started this crap this time? And you know what I'm asking, so don't tell me 'I can't tell you,' ok?"

"It came from one of the partners' offices. That's ALL I'm sharing."

Dane approached Isabella, but she knew to block his doorway. "There's more. You better sit down."

With his hands up in an obvious surrender, Dane backed up to and slumped down in one of his own wingback chairs.

"I know we don't speak of personal issues, you and me, in general. We've pretty much always been about business.

I'm thankful for that. It's kept my worlds simpler. So, believe me when I tell you that I'm not thrilled about sharing this." Isabella looked straight at Dane.

"When I tell you the rest, you *have* to promise you will NOT run out of here and go for anybody. Promise me, Boss, or I can't tell you anything."

"Oh, boy. This isn't good. I can tell."

"Promise me," she politely, but firmly, demanded.

"Fine. I promise I'll stay right here until we discuss the game plan."

"If you sincerely care about my safety—not to mention your own and your children's—you'll follow the prescription you just dispensed for us both." Isabella took a deep breath and lowered her voice even more. "Dane, you're going to know exactly who has been starting the rumors when I tell you the next parts."

Dane wasn't sure he wanted to know now. He wore an unemotional expression, but his heart was pounding.

"You asked me if I'd shared your travel information with Rachel. You knew the answer before I'd even spoken. Of course not. You'd hung up so fast that I hadn't told you with whom I *had* shared the information." She paused, knowing she took a huge risk in what she was about to say. "Victor." Again, Isabella waited.

"*Victor* told Rachel I was returning to the U.S.? Why would he do that?"

"There's more. She apparently thinks you're returning to the U.S. for more than just business. Rumor has it that you're going back because of a woman."

"Go on," Dane intoned.

"The other rumor going around is that someone is

stealing money from the firm. They can't figure out who's doing it or how. But, Boss, your name is swirling around with the rumor and why you're going away." With that, Dane leapt from the chair.

Isabella stood in front of the office door with her hands on her hips. "No! No! No! You promised to stay put until we had a game plan!" For as petite as she was, Isabella seemed to fill the space with her presence.

Dane stormed around behind his desk, ran his hands through his hair, and stopped in front of his big window. "MY name is being dragged through the mud in a rumor that *I'm* stealing money from the firm and running off with it to the States? THIS firm? Here? Where we work?? And you want me to *not* storm out of here and punch or strangle someone? You think I'm super human, Isabella? I have one thing I can go to my grave with, just one: my honor. Now, let me out of here, please."

"So you can give them what they want—a show? A reason to believe you're the bad guy? MY honor counts here, too, ya know, but if nothing matters at all to you, then be my fucking guest. Take us both down." Now he *knew* his assistant must be pissed. He'd heard her swear just one other time: when Rachel had accused her of having an affair with him.

"OK. Fine," he backed off. "Sorry. You DO understand I've every right, correct? You *know* what we do here. You *know* how *hard* we work." Another pause. "Holy shit. I know this has something to do with the Tate Parker account. Everything has gotten confusing and overwhelming since being ordered to take it over. But why?" Dane muttered and paced back and forth in front of his window. He turned and stared open-mouthed at Isabella.

"What do you think we need to do? Who exactly has told you what? Who else may be in trouble?"

"Dane, there's only one person who can spread Victor's rumors—which means she's in grave danger, too. There's apparently a lot of money at stake. A LOT."

"What does Rachel have to do with …?"

"Dane, Rachel is …" Dane's office door burst open dramatically as Victor stormed in.

"I need a word with your boss alone." There was nothing but cold venom in Victor's tone and glare.

"Yes, sir." Isabella looked at Dane, who nodded once at her; then she turned and left his office.

* * *

"What do you think you're doing?" Victor snarled at Dane.

"What are you talking about?" Dane drew a long, deep, steadying breath. *Be calm,* he thought to himself, *and try to look bored. Give away none of what Isabella just disclosed.*

"I'm sending you out of the country on business—law firm business as well as our hobby business—and I just got a call from your ex-wife asking where you're going and why. She sounded very accusatory. Are you having communication issues with her? If so, please keep them out of this office. To date, you've been successful. That call was absurd."

Ok. Ok. It's not what I thought he came in about. Relief. Dane calmed his heart rate further. "Interesting."

"What?!" snapped Victor.

"Rachel gave me the impression that *you* had called *her*, offering my travel information, which now makes sense about why she'd called for a face-to-face meeting earlier. She wanted to confirm that my Will was in order prior to travel." Dane tried a little diversion with his boss.

"I've less than zero reason, time, or inclination to initiate a call to her—not that I need to tell you that," Victor eyed his protégé. "But I'm sure your young assistant has already informed you that I gave your ex information."

"Actually, Isabella had just come in to brief me on a number of cases. As you *must* remember, I do *not* speak with anyone here about my personal affairs—except for you," Dane calmly postured, raising his eyebrows just enough to cause Victor to uncomfortably shift his stance. "Why would I be asking Isabella for such information? Anything I need to know? That line of questioning would be highly unusual coming from me, as you know my policy about personal issues in the office, but I'm sure she'd accommodate me regarding most any request."

"No, I … ." Victor stammered.

"So," Dane remained behind his desk standing, "to make sure I have the story straight: Rachel called you for some out-of-the-blue reason; asked about my travel plans; you gave them to her; she then called for a face-to-face with me. Do I have that straight?" Victor knew Dane was using his courtroom interrogation skills on him.

"Actually, you've missed a step. My error, though. Rachel called me leaving a message with my secretary. She left several calls, actually. I returned the calls out of respect for you. Turned out she wanted to know how you'd been at work since returning from that reunion you attended. She felt like there had been some sort of shift, or change, I guess is the better word, in you. You'd been really sideways for quite awhile, as you know, and hadn't snapped out of it—until returning from that stateside trip. Now you seem actually, um …" Victor looked at Dane, "… well, happy."

"And you told her what, exactly?" Dane now felt a little off balance. *Uh-oh.*

"I told her I agreed. I told her I was thankful, because you were even more productive than you had been in the last few years."

"Her follow-up question was?" Dane knew Rachel. *There would definitely have been a follow-up question.*

"She asked why." Victor's poker face betrayed him.

"You've never been good at telling stories, Victor."

Victor knew that he'd screwed Dane for a second time. Dane knew this, too, but he didn't understand why. Victor wouldn't ever admit it, either. Dane determined that he'd figure it out eventually, especially because he thought he could trust Victor. The senior law partner knew how few people Dane *had* ever trusted. *Thank God I never told Victor he was in my extremely small circle of trust, because I clearly need to remove him as well.*

"I told her I didn't know, but that I had definitely suspected it had to do with getting away from work for a few days, and that you hadn't taken almost any time off in months until then. I tried to shrug it off with her and then made my mistake." Victor looked down at his hands. "I confess, Counselor. I told her I had high hopes that you'd be in a much better mood after this next trip, and that she ought to notice, too. I thought your being in a better mood would have been a good thing, but apparently I was very wrong with regard to your ex."

"Oh, crap." Dane rubbed his lips back and forth slowly in thought. *Now what the hell is she up to?* As he processed

Victor's words, he turned toward downtown and stopped at the corner of his window behind his desk.

"Listen, Dane, I'm sorry. I guess I shouldn't have come in here all fired up when you're the one who has to deal with her fallout. I'm sorry. I know we talked about never taking her calls, but she'd sounded sincerely concerned."

"Victor, I've told you: that's her act. She's concerned, all right; it's not *for* me, however. It's for her *wallet*. Do *not* take any of her calls. Period. Have your secretary forward them here. If she insists, then let me know. I'll deal with her."

"I've got a meeting right now. I'm sorry. I'll see you this afternoon to finalize any papers and procedures regarding your trip." Victor looked at Dane's back, waited for him to turn, but left without another word spoken between the two men.

Isabella saw Victor leave. He said nothing to her on his way out of the office suite. There'd been no need to—she'd heard everything. She knew not to rush into her boss's office after any type of trying conversations; better to wait until Dane called for her. It worked best that way. She grew concerned when he hadn't buzzed for her after forty-five minutes, so she peeked in to his open office. He was glued to a file on his desk but sensed her presence.

Chillingly calm, Dane forced a polite face, "Come on in. I believe your last words prior to Victor's barging in were, 'Rachel is'? Bring your pen and notepad. In case we're bombarded again, they'll serve as props. Close the door, and let's finish our earlier conversation. We haven't game planned, and you must have heard my conversation with Victor."

"Yes, I did, and thank you. Be right back." Isabella did

as she was asked, also grabbing the office's portable handset in case it rang.

"Continue, please," Dane coolly ordered.

As a new assistant, Isabella had once cringed with such a tone. After a few months and several conversations with her new boss, Isabella recognized that when he fumed, he chose to censor as much emotion as possible. His theory, he explained to her then, was that *his* feelings were *his* problem. Venting them on her was inappropriate and unproductive.

Still whispering, just in case ears were close by unexpectedly, "Rachel isn't who you think she is— apparently." She had his attention. "The scary part of those two rumors is the link. It's being said that you're the link."

"You lost me."

"Apparently, you divorced her because you two didn't want it to look like she was involved in your illegal activities. She remarried her second husband as a cover, but he didn't actually know that. The story continues that Rachel was ok with that until you went back to your high school reunion and returned happier than anyone has ever seen you. Now your ex assumes this newfound positive state is because of someone from your past, which has always been her biggest issue with you. In a nutshell, she's jealous because she's still in love with you. The chatter says she's also angry at your abruptly ending this lucrative 'arrangement.'"

"I've been up to all that?" Dane had to chuckle. The rumors and innuendos in the office were as bad as or worse than any tabloid in the newsstands.

"Boss, seriously? You know this is actually menacing stuff."

"OK, sorry. So, according to your hearsay, why do *you* know all this? After all, you work with me."

"OK, for a smart guy, you're just not thinking. They tell me stuff because they think I'm overworked and feel sorry for me. They don't believe that you and I work as a team because you're beyond narcissistic—*their words*. They believe that given how lazy the other lawyers are here, you must be cracking the whip over me, but not sharing any of the credit or profits. They're actually trying to help me find another position within the firm. They don't want to see me get tied to the accusations against you—when they happen. They don't know how much work you and I produce together.

"Well, you and I know we're a team. We thought Victor knew we were a team, right?" Isabella waited for Dane to catch up to her world of gossip, innuendo, and slander.

Bingo. Dane's wide-eyed look signaled that he was there.

"I'm missing some connecting piece of information, but you're on to something regarding that Tate file. Victor has a deeper connection to that account than he's let on. So does Rachel. Rumor mill doesn't know what that is yet. This much IS clear: the other lawyers aren't nearly as industrious as their assistants. They dump on them. It's assumed that you work more as a diversion, so you bring less attention to us—like we're doing just what we need to be doing. You're making the others look really bad, so they automatically figure you must have your hand in the proverbial cookie jar."

Dane was confused, silenced. *I thought all I had to do in life was work hard, invest well, and make partner. Tate's behind this. I can almost deduce several scenarios about Victor's position, but Rachel? She's a different twist. What did she have to do with this? With Tate? With Victor? It's not all about the money; control or power makes more sense. Why? How?*

"What have you told your grapevine, so I can either back-up your story or just remain silent?"

Isabella smiled, almost conspiratorially, "It's not what I *told* them; it's what I *didn't* tell them." She paused. "Understand?"

"In other words, you'd complain about a workload, seem unavailable to talk and be aggravated, then keep quiet as they talked around you about how crazy it's become for you? You didn't correct them. You let them just … 'run' with it. Do I have that right?"

"Bingo."

"OK, let's confirm what we know, and what we don't know, to guide us from this point," Dane established as he finally sat down behind his desk. On the blank legal pad, he jotted notes. Isabella took some as well. "We have a firm partner, Victor, we believe, who's stolen money somehow from the firm. He's already figured out how to frame me for it, though we're unclear about those details. He'll likely disclose them sooner if I turn him in, or continue piece by piece, as he is now, to make me anxious—I suspect not by his own doing, but by someone else's. You with me so far?"

Isabella nodded her agreement.

"We know that Rachel is involved, but we don't know how yet; she's purportedly divorcing her second husband and is up to something to try to figure out who I'm allegedly flying to the States to see."

"Are you?" Isabella interrupted.

"Am I what?"

"Well, since we've officially crossed all sorts of personal/business lines, I probably ought to be clear on a few of them."

"Don't you think the 'don't ask/don't tell' policy, or the legal phrase 'plausible deniability,' might come in handy now, or possibly in the near future?" Dane reasoned.

"So, that's a yes without a yes."

"No, that's the 'let her think what she wants' just like what you did with the 'mill'."

Isabella considered pushing Dane to reply when he shockingly offered, "I went to my high school reunion to tie up some loose ends, shall we say, and was successful in doing so. That sort of closure is extremely relieving and affirming. I've seemed happier because I am. I'm no longer carrying around emotional baggage from then or my recent past. It's quite liberating, really. Make sense?"

"I'm impressed, Boss. I didn't think you were capable of that much deep thinking outside of your legal world."

Dane smirked, "Me neither." They both laughed and then completed the list of what they knew and didn't know, since ugly accusations were likely imminent.

Dane, who wasn't one to disclose such private thoughts, trusted that Isabella wouldn't cross that line easily in the future. He shared that he'd discovered, or at least discerned, some sort of fiscal impropriety, if not a theft, had happened awhile ago. He suspected that Tate Parker was involved, but, again, he didn't know how.

"Other than the 'scorned woman' issue, what is Rachel's connection? It couldn't be money; I've been generous with her since our divorce. I'm additionally confused as to how I've been set up to take the fall, by whom, and why." *How will I need to come forward without hurting those innocently involved?*

CHAPTER 42

Revenge

With Dane unwittingly orchestrating his own demise, Tate just needed to be in the right place at the right time. *Patience. You've waited this long. What's another few weeks?* he reasoned with himself. *This is getting better than either the boss or I could've possibly imagined.*

"That tail following Bob's neighbor keeps turning up connections previously unknown, a delicious revelation on several levels. Of course, I'm not going to share *exactly* that adjective with my brilliant, but emotionally insecure, and jealous boss. Somehow, I need to *reacquaint* myself with this special neighbor without distressing Bob. Then I need to redirect her writing interests from car show summaries to something more, yes, more involved; something that might divert her attention for a short while—perhaps just until I get Dane out of the picture." Tate talked himself through his impending plans.

Bob just needs to accelerate those finishing touches, so I can sell that car and get the next car body in here. This patience crap is getting on my nerves, but greed has ruined me before.

CHAPTER 43

Home Visit

They'd swapped cell phone numbers during a quiet, thoughtful moment at the reunion, both only hoping to see the other again. After Dane had kissed Julie in their hotel's hallway, neither knew what to do. They understood Julie wasn't going to break up her marriage and family or abandon her children and live overseas. Similarly, Dane wasn't going to leave *his* children, and his work was far from over in Europe. Moving right now wasn't an option for either of them. Truly, their lives couldn't have seemed any farther apart. They'd believed it was for the best, grateful for the time they'd had to reconnect. During brief but more surface discussions, they'd put various issues to rest and planned to move on with their lives as they'd been. Little did either know how much that kiss had thrown them both completely off balance.

When Dane had decided to attend the Arizona car auction with his boss, his sole thought was of seeing Julie. Of course, for all concerned, he was quite clear on what expectations had been placed on him as a professional. *A new auto body Victor and I are still considering needs evaluation, several legal clients requesting counsel require face-to-face assurances, and smaller matters ought to keep a necessary façade intact for me. Hopefully, I'll escape Victor's scrutiny long enough to connect privately with*

Julie. Besides, mid-January is evidently a great time of year to be in the Arizona desert. The temperatures cool significantly in the evenings and are far more tolerable during the days. I wonder if she'll make the time to see me—or excuses to avoid me.

* * *

Julie was stunned when she realized it was Dane's voice on the other end of the phone. She hadn't recognized the number on her caller ID, and debated about picking it up while in the middle of her limited writing time. Bob had shared some helpful information that she was pouring through for an article due at week's end. On the last ring, she opted to pick up the handset.

"Hello," she stated distractedly.

"You don't have caller ID?" the voice chuckled.

Too stunned to respond, she heard Dane try again. "Either you haven't actually picked up the phone, and I'm talking with your message machine, or you're debating about speaking with me. Which is it?"

"I'm...um...speechless. Dane?" She pushed her chair back from her desk and started to wander out of her office through her home.

"Were you expecting another distant admirer?"

"No! Of course not! I'm just incredibly, um, surprised—stunned—to hear your voice! Wow! It's been, m-m-months since the reunion." Julie stammered and felt her face flush at the memory. "Wow. Hi! Uh, long time no chat? Let's try, to what do I owe the pleasure of this call from out of the clear blue sky? And let me assure you, the skies are, indeed, clear and blue today here in Arizona," she giggled in an attempt to regain her composure. *This is ridiculous how I feel right now,* she thought to herself. *It's a very good thing no one's home to see me like this.*

"I know," he replied casually.

"Sorry?"

"I know the sky in Arizona is sunny and blue today."

She knew she was being taunted, so she only nibbled at the bait. "Watching the weather channel, are we?" she gently teased.

"You might say that I'm watching the, hmmm, live version, actually." She could hear him smile. Then he heard her footsteps and waited quietly; his heart raced.

My stomach's always a warning. Is it actually possible that ... She walked to her large, wood front door and stole a glimpse through the peephole. Though her jaw dropped open, her breath instantly vanished and her pupils dilated; she opened it with attempted poise. She kept the phone to her ear, though she knew she wouldn't need it any longer for the rest of this conversation.

"Oh...wow," she barely voiced, not trusting that he actually stood in front of her. "How did you know I was home? Do you usually just stop by unannounced?" She quickly regained her composure. *I'm a tangle of emotions: thrilled plus anxious, peppered with a mix of concern and curiosity.* A tango of emotions began their slow, internal dance. Julie quickly prayed: *Dear Lord, please don't allow this dance to actualize physically, though I'm deeply aware of my inability to control all the moves, since I'm just half of the equation.* While Julie never appreciated people dropping in unannounced, she considered this the rare exception.

"May I come in, or are we going to create a stir with your neighbors?"

"That depends."

"On what?"

"On if you can keep a certain distance from me. Nothing good can come of your being here. We both know this already." She was instantly reminded of how magnetic their attraction was for each other.

"I disagree. I think plenty can come of this," he smirked.

"OK, you need to go. I'm sorry you wasted your time coming here." Completely on a heightened emotional and physical alert, she started to close the door.

"I've told you already," he put his foot in the door, "I believe plenty can come of this, and I haven't come to waste time. I promise to keep a distance between us. *Now* can I come in? It's pretty cool out here."

She closed her disbelieving eyes, took a deep breath of his subtle scent, bowed her head, and let it out slowly. She opened her downward-cast eyes and slowly dragged them up to meet Dane's. Though she hardly even trusted herself, let alone Dane, Julie let him in, and then secured the deadbolt on the front door. Again very slowly, she took every extra moment to regain her footing—in her own home. Dane stood still in the foyer waiting for Julie's cue, taking in these new surroundings.

Julie's home was as warm and inviting as Dane had imagined. Creams, browns, and burgundies with pops of teal and tangerine on large, overstuffed couches welcomed adults and kids alike. Unlike his cool, almost sterile apartment, Dane felt at home immediately.

"Would you care for water? Coffee?"

"Nothing yet. Thank you."

"Come—sit down," she gestured to the chairs in the living room as she led the way.

"I highly suggest you stop using that word," he grumbled. "You have a lovely home."

"No playmates in all of Europe? Really? You poor man," she taunted back. "Ok, what really brings you across the globe to my humble home—and thank you." She remembered her well-bred manners.

"You."

Stopping immediately in her tracks just short of the seating area, she turned to Dane with an almost unreadable expression but a very clear tone, "Stop. Seriously." She grew irritated with his new game playing. *This isn't like him at all. It's leaving me feeling oddly vulnerable, almost foolish, and completely turned on. Uh-oh.*

Now aggravated himself with this new experience of not being taken at his word, Dane's tone became indignant. "Seriously? I'm telling you the unfiltered truth. You. To put it mildly, I was incredibly unfocused when we started the good-bye and stay in touch crap on the elevator. OK, and that kiss—well, I've been restless, irritable, and downright cranky! I was picking up my kids when my ex noticed, too. I told her that I thought jet lag was starting to bother me. Then the kids noticed I wasn't getting any better when *we* were hanging out. So, I decided to take a few days off, thinking I must be coming down with something. I even went so far as to call my mother, as absurd as that sounds. She suggested I get checked out by our family doctor, who, of course, found I was perfectly fine—physically." He clammed up, just drank in her presence, and waited.

It's taken me months to get his passionate look and enticing scent off my mind 24/7. I'm finally down to only a few times a day, as I've tried to console myself. Now, here he is, sitting in my living room, back with that insane intensity focused on me. She knew everything he touched would be marked. Such consciousness was gut-cloying now. Stunningly aware of how off-balance she felt, her insides pitched. Absurdly, she considered her disheveled presence and laughed, an awkward attempt to lighten the highly-charged atmosphere between them. Dane looked puzzled.

"Sorry, you're getting me as you found me. I obviously wouldn't have looked quite so—unkempt. I mean, I would've definitely been a little more put together had I known you were coming—visiting, I mean. But today I'm working from home, so casual and comfortable is the uniform of the day. Just be thankful you didn't visit yesterday when my hair was up and going in more directions than I can count." She chuckled at her self-control for not mentioning how scantily clad she'd been as well. *No sense in encouraging him with visuals, too.*

Dane had just been studying her. He was completely awed by her natural, unaffected state and pulled toward her enticing, sincere energy. With a gleam in his eyes, yet a very calm and kind demeanor, Dane reassured Julie, "You look perfect to me. You could be dressed to the nines, or, I'd bet, with nothing on at all and look amazing. Don't apologize on my account. As you said, I gave you no warning."

"I know you didn't come all the way across the country and halfway around the planet to seduce me. All teasing aside now, I mean, what are you really here for? And didn't we already talk about a little distance? That meant more than just physically. Please, Dane, I'm feeling so vulnerable right now."

He resisted asking her about that vulnerability. Her

feeling that way with him was like a glimpse of the sun after weeks of seemingly terminal rain: warming, reassuring, life-giving. *EASY. Don't scare her away. She has good reason not to believe you.* "I'm on the other side of the room from you. What proximity are you referring to? Yes, I came all the way across the world for you. Of course, I needed a reason with my firm. So, I'm officially here because of some legal clients, as well as the car renovator who lives—conveniently—next door to you." He smiled sideways.

"What is *with* you? You're beyond suggestive and over-the-top, especially for you! You're kind of acting like the Cheshire cat having swallowed a large canary. What's going on?"

"I knew I was taking a chance coming—um, traveling, I mean…to see you; you know what I mean," exasperated at needing to substitute the vexing word. "When the opportunity arose," he looked proud of himself for having navigated better verbiage, "to view and bargain for a car with the restorer for both me as well as my boss/partner, I jumped at the opportunity. My boss, who was supposed to travel with me, had to cancel at the last minute. Anyway, I've known for many years that Bob lives in Arizona. I didn't even know that you lived in Arizona until I ran into you at the airport, let alone were neighbors of Bob's until recently. That's when I was given this legal client to take care of here. Just more indicators that we were meant to see each other again, right?"

Dane left out any mention of Tate Parker, hoping there'd never be any reason that Julie would run into him. "I looked up your address, decided to MapQuest how far Bob was from you, and stared at my computer in astonishment. All this time I've wasted, and you were right here." He sadly and slowly shook his head, though he never took his eyes off her. His realization displayed deep-rooted pain; the torment clearly entrenched.

"I'd never even known where you'd been living until our reunion, so I understand your doubt. However, there's no reason for *you* to feel vulnerable. I'm the one pouring my heart out, potentially making a fool of myself. OK, not potentially. Clearly, I'm doing a fine job of it. I mean, what would the chances have been that I would've been on Bob's property, speaking with him, and actually see you?"

Thickly, she responded, "Lately? Rather good, actually. It *is* too bad you didn't visit Arizona sooner."

"So how are you?" Julie thought it safest to start with small talk. Spellbound, their eyes locked on each other, unable to veer away.

"Well, I've shared too much already. Other than acting like a pathetic jerk to everyone around me, I'm great. You?"

"About the same. You and I—we haven't done anything, but the question still begs asking: *what HAVE* we done? Look at how different we are; how different our lifestyles are. Your world is formal, proper, and seemingly perfect. You go to work dressed to kill in a beautiful office complex. My world is highly casual in comparison. I work out of my home/office in my jeans and flip flops, barely even dressing, let alone professionally, when I leave the house, or when I have to be on Skype, depending on my audience. Then? I'm dressed from the waist up." She laughed at herself self-deprecatingly and shrugged.

"You have assistants, many of whom are also lawyers, or, at the very least, are legal aids. I've a girlfriend whom I pay to come over periodically to help me with paperwork, house stuff, and dinner so I can keep up with my family. You have an established and flourishing career you've been building for years; my career is re-inventing itself—again, if you will—from scratch, after dusting it off from years in storage. You travel the world 'slaying dragons.' I travel in-state, typically either playing chauffeur to my kids, or following show cars owned by vain, pompous windbags who have few to no manners."

"I place no less value on what I do. In fact, I believe I've a better lifestyle than yours that will ultimately pay off longer term. Currently, you've a very different life from mine. You know I come from proper and formal. It was who my parents were. It was who my family was. It was where we lived, how and when we grew up. It was how we were raised. Most of the time, my life is not like that any more."

"You have to admit, once you've lost your tie and jacket for a while on vacation, it's hard to put it back on until you force yourself to get back into the swing of things. Imagine if you hadn't had to wear formal suits for years in general, and then, only rarely after that. That's me. Your firm would eat you alive in your world if you showed up to work informally. As great an arm piece as I might be for a week or two, I'd be detrimental after that. I'm out of that habit of looking so professional all the time. These days, that's only who I am when I go to certain events and functions. I can put it on and turn it on, if and when I have to. I sing my parents' praises that it was so ingrained. The rest of the time, I prefer the more *casual*, elegant style." Julie laughed at herself again. "Highly unprofessional, really."

"You make it sound as if we've no connection whatsoever, and you've given yourself no credit. You're such a positive person; so, I gather this is the big blow off, all this negative talk from you."

"Wait, I hadn't finished."

Dane groaned. "There's more?"

"I'm a huge believer in deliver the bad and/or realistic news first, and ALWAYS end on a positive note. OK?"

Dane nodded, his clouded look brightening just a little.

"Both of us have obligations and global responsibilities which are *very* different, but tremendous, nonetheless. I know we both see the value in what the other does. We help, we solve, we organize, we inform, and we energize. We're intelligent, tenacious, and connected in spirit. In some ways, we haven't changed at all; we're just better versions. Yet, look at how much we *have* changed over the years."

Dane needed to explain, "I'm sorry to interrupt, but I have to. As you said, in some ways, we haven't changed at all and are still connected. We're still the same core people, *real* people who care about real things. When I went back to Europe after the reunion, I felt empty, disconnected, fake even. I've known that the lifestyle I've been leading has been a mere existence until now. Now, I GET it and know there really *is* more out there. I know that I've felt empty and detached for good reasons; I just hadn't figured out why. I've also never believed it would or could change.

"I've kept myself so insulated—almost dead to actually living—until we reconnected. I knew standing at the Phoenix airport that *something* was happening to me; I just didn't know what. Next thing I knew, I bent down to help a lady. Crazy sounding, but I could hardly wait until we got off that plane! I don't normally think that way—excited or happily anticipating anything. Disturbing as it may sound,

I can't remember the last time I did, other than for my children. I've so many things on my mind: cases, details, etc. I'm usually only barely aware of breathing, existing. Downside of that way of living? Tunnel vision. Upside? Ability to focus like a laser. But I forget to *live*. I forget to appreciate why I do what I do. I didn't understand at that moment in the airport what I was feeling. I mean, I knew it was different, but I didn't *know* what that meant.

"I know I'm rambling. I don't do that, as I'm sure you remember." Clearly summoning courage with a deep breath, Dane pressed himself to expose a truth he suspected might make Julie throw him out of her house, and life, permanently; it was a chance he was willing to take. "Selfishly, I kissed you. It wasn't meant to be covetous." He searched her face for any signs of anguish, doubt, or sheer anger. "I just wanted to see if I was *imagining* feeling alive again because of you, if I *was* actually *feeling* again—*at all*. I admit it; completely greedy, and I'm sorry. I've been so numb since we broke up in high school, and hadn't even realized it. Just seeing you sparked something … right at that moment, something I never expected could happen for me again—sadly—ever.

"I never expected to see you again, let alone speak with you. I never thought I'd have the opportunity to apologize for letting you go that night the way I did when we broke up. I was an ass—a terrified and hurting ass.

"I caught myself actually *feeling* something *again* alone in my hotel room after we parted at the check-in desk. I quickly recognized standing there that I was daydreaming. Everything I was fantasizing about, even fleetingly, would complicate my life, would just change everything. I needed to get a grip on my thoughts and emotions, regroup. I regained my balance once isolated behind closed doors; your effect on me was so powerful. Oh, shit! Listen to how I'm just rambling on!!" he moaned. Embarrassed, yet mindful enough, Dane instantly accepted that he had to bare all feelings and emotions, or be trapped in a life that meant nothing. He stared at her dumbfounded after his sudden vast admissions.

Julie was speechless, holding her breath at his every word. She shocked them both when she stood up, crossed the room to where Dane sat, sweetly captured his face with both of her hands, and kissed him—hard. Dane's hands flew up to cover hers. Gentle and tender, his hands drifted to ensnare the back of her neck, deepening their kiss. It was the reunion in reverse. She quickly dismissed the warning in her mind. *I know this is so wrong.* With a highly-charged pull, Julie couldn't pull away from his lips, from him, especially as he drew her into his arms—as if all the lost years might be recovered in one more kiss. *WHAT am I doing!?* she shouted in her head and started whimpering. Though she and Gabe were separated, she was still married. She also hadn't told Dane anything about her marital issues yet; so he probably didn't think much of her at that moment.

Dane tasted Julie's tears as they slipped into their passionate kiss and tenderly stopped. He gently stood, still holding her. Inhaling the fresh scent of her soft hair, they clung to each other, cherishing their warmth until she caught her breath against his muscular chest. He released her only enough to walk toward the front door, standing in her foyer for what seemed like hours, just holding each other. They knew what they were doing was innocent, yet wrong. They had no way to reconcile their circumstances.

Not wanting to move even an inch from their embrace, Julie squeezed her eyes shut tightly. *How did I let this happen?* A sudden internal pull between run as fast and far as possible *from* him, or shockingly, *with* him terrified her. *Well*, she guessed, *my purgatory will be a lifetime without Dane. What true choice do I have?*

She decided then and there. *I'd never leave my kids. Though I honestly don't know if Gabe and I are done, I <u>do</u> know I have to give our marriage at least a final chance. I won't look away from him like this again. After all, we're supposed to be temporarily apart to think and sort things out. Besides, I have to be able to face myself in the mirror daily. Dane's being here didn't help me sort anything; his presence added to the confusion of my marital unhappiness.* Julie accepted that she'd always love Dane and be eternally connected to him for all that he'd brought to her life. She wanted him more than she'd ever wanted any man and knew that alone was wrong.

I won't ever drag either man through my selfish issues. I respect them too much to allow Dane to become a "rebound relationship," or Gabe, a scorned man.

Dane, frozen in their embrace, had similar thoughts, though not for himself, just for Julie. He was heartbreakingly aware that he was too late. Julie had moved on over twenty years ago. *I'd had my chances to be part of her life and never took them. I'd been so determined to move past her that I never took the moment I needed when I'd had it to look back. She had, and I wasn't looking back at her. Had I been, I would've seen then what I see and feel now: a true passion and love that's stood even time's test.* He was sickeningly aware of that. *How hadn't I seen through my own façade at that time?*

As her weeping quieted, he just took in everything about

her and prayed for the strength to let her go. *What was I expecting anyway? I live on the other side of the world. I couldn't leave my children. I already know I couldn't move here until I either finish my overseas assignment, or quit my job and start all over again.* Very painfully, they eased their desperate embrace. Still holding each other with but a fraction of space between them, their foreheads touched, eyes closed. Neither wanted to speak, knowing their tender spell would be broken.

Finally, as each found the other's hands, they sadly took a step back, searching in the other's eyes. Afraid to speak, they completely understood what had to happen next. Their expressions were open books: agonizingly clear, unbearably pained, and excruciatingly soul exposing. Dane quietly backed himself to the door and flipped the deadbolt, searing this moment in his memory.

CHAPTER 44

Gut Space

After their gut-wrenching discussion, Gabe had tempered his request for a divorce to that of his just moving out, giving both he and Julie space to think, distance to cool heated emotions, and time to sort and process what was important to them, both as individuals as well as a married couple. They agreed that they needed to answer a course-altering question: what did they each want from their marriage? The idea of divorce left both sick to their stomachs. Such an extreme step seemed premature, given their admitted love for each other.

Julie shocked Gabe, though, with her composure, even at his initial suggestion of divorce—almost as if she'd been thinking the same way. Gabe wasn't sure what to ascertain from her quiet willingness, but he knew *he* needed to figure out some things. He drove away from their conversation more brooding and thoughtful than he had in years. *Maybe she's right. Maybe I need to get some assistance, some counseling for my own issues. She kept telling me I already knew what to do, and that I was being stubborn. She doesn't understand, though. I really am more immature in our relationship—even after all these years of being married to her—than she wants to believe. I've been so focused on developing our business; I just figured she'd keep us on track. I never thought about my part of "the us."*

In spite of his big 6' 5" frame, Gabe acted like a little kid: impetuous and impulsive when he didn't get his way, brusque and indecisive in his expectations, and indelicately mannered when it suited him. But typical of a Gemini, his cleverness and high energy lent flexibility to those often frustrated in dealing with his wavering commitment skills. Julie hadn't been immune to Gabe's soft-spoken and enthusiastic charms, either, when they'd met.

His easy intelligence captivated her when they'd begun to date, as did his open-mindedness. There was that effortless ability to make even the mundane seem inconsequential. Gabe's gentle brown eyes and strong athletic build enveloped her in warm embraces, and their chemistry was intensely passionate. Surprising all who knew him by getting married, Gabe's attraction to Julie was plainly transparent. Her sheer stamina in all arenas of their relationship was a given; an ability to accommodate his needs to explore life was another "must have" box checked off; and her gracious heart sealed their bond.

Lately, though, Gabe felt restless. *How can our sex life absolutely scintillate, yet I've accepted calls from my ex, whom I've got less than zero interest in? Is it Julie's distracted need to write? Does that threaten me? Am I feeling insecure about her ability to make hardcore decisions, while I'm feeling overwhelmed and erratic in our business? Maybe it was her reunion trip. She was different when she got home. I'm convinced something happened there, but I can't seem to get it out of her.*

Gabe knew a little time and space would help him clear his head—or so he hoped.

CHAPTER 45

Followed?

Julie always seemed to have an effect on people. They, however, had little to no impact on her. In truth, there were only a very few who actually affected Julie at all.

Her children and mother impacted her; her old friends, Aubrey and McKenna, still did, and, much to Julie's surprise, so did Dane—even after decades of silence between them. Someone else had started to touch Julie since she'd accompanied her daughter on retreat, only, verifying his identity hadn't been easy. Somehow, what was on "Waffles" business card didn't match with what he'd shared at the quaint B & B. Gabe had deeply reached Julie for years. His connection was fading and their reciprocity limping, as he seemed to want it, exemplified by his recent move-out.

A few days after that sad incident, Gabe returned to help Julie and the kids with the grill. She invited him to stay for dinner as a thank you for his assistance. The kids were quietly relieved for the current peace between their parents. Gabe accepted the invitation, and then offered to barbeque.

As he walked in from the patio, Julie casually asked, "Gabe," she'd just finished her latest car show update, "why would I have this crazy notion that I was being followed?"

Gabe nearly dropped the plate of freshly-barbecued burgers but regained his composure enough to respond.

"That IS a crazy notion, and a damned good question. Are you sure you're not writing some mystery story instead?" He awkwardly tried on a humorous approach, hoping to mask rising frustration and concern for his estranged wife.

"Nooo. All the question asking's probably going to my head—like a violent late night movie does to me. Kinda creepy. Just sayin'."

"What makes you say that?"

"The tan Nissan Maxima that follows me at various intervals during the day." She tried to be nonchalant.

"Wait, you know the make and model of the car?"

"Yep."

"How can you be sure it's the same one?"

"The license plate number is the same. The driver appears to be the same."

"Male or female?"

"I'm not sure, but I think female."

"When did this start?"

"Um…I think within a few days of my returning from my high school reunion. Weird timing, don't you think?"

Trying to temper his rising anxiety level, Gabe pressed, "It's been that long? A coincidence?"

"Come on. You know me better than that. You know I don't believe in coincidences."

"Well, did you sign up for something somewhere that's shady or questionable?"

Julie tilted her head sideways and looked at Gabe as if he had twelve heads appear on his shoulder all at once. "Did you really ask me that? Seriously?"

"Ok, I—I—don't know what to say, other than maybe we ought to call the police."

"Maybe. I was wondering if *you* had made any weird choices lately that someone would want to know more about *your* personal life."

Julie noted Gabe's uncomfortable shift. She instantly doubted her observation, though, as she thought it. *Ridiculous. Gabe wouldn't hire someone.*

"I don't think so," he tried to recover. *Now I see where she's going with this. WARNING!*

"Ok. Well, if I still feel this way tomorrow, then I'll call the police."

"Good thinkin'," he mumbled absently.

* * *

Julie left the kitchen after that brief discussion and headed to her bathroom feeling uneasy. Every time Julie was so confused about what she thought or felt, she would literally look at herself in the mirror for clarification. She prayed the mirror would speak to her; *just reveal the truth—whatever that truth may be.* She wondered if she saw herself as she really was, or only as she wanted to be. So often, she delivered reality with her funny brand of humor or ironic twist, but Gabe looked at her either as if she was from another planet, or with no expression at all. It had just happened in the kitchen.

TALK TO ME! she silently screamed at her reflection.

She knew she couldn't leave that interaction alone, so she headed back toward the kitchen and ran right into Gabe in the hallway.

"You know, I just left our kitchen feeling very, very uncomfortable. I was somehow hoping that you'd offer some sort of warmth or reassurance."

"Ya gotta admit that what you said would have thrown anyone off. That's why I was coming to find you."

"Of course it's flipping awkward. That's why I figured talking about it with you might actually make it seem less so."

"Sorry," he uttered unemotionally.

"Sorry?"

"Julie, what else did you want me to say? I mean, I've never been through anything like this, either."

"I don't know, but a hug and a few—I don't know—*guy* words of problem-solving or something might have helped more than just looking at me like I'm some sort of whack-job."

"Ok." He gave his distanced wife an awkward, half-hearted hug. "Dinner's ready." He turned and walked away from her, leaving her standing there completely confused.

Muttering to herself, "Now, what do you suppose he expected me to do with that?"

Dinner, she thought. *Ok, well, I'll deal with the strange crap better if I'm not hungry.*

* * *

When the disjointed family had finished dinner together, Gabe kissed the kids goodnight and reassured them that he'd see them during the week. After settling them down from that tearful interaction with their dad, Julie returned to her bathroom while the kids finished homework. Intent on recovering her own emotions, Julie sorted them aloud in the shower.

"Gabe's mental and emotional absence was palpable tonight. What the hell am I supposed to be doing with my life, God? Stay married to someone who doesn't seem to want to get me? I mean, I know that some experiences I don't need to have to know right from wrong. Cheating on my husband, for example, is one I can pass on, but lack of passion or intimate connection is a deal breaker."

Julie not only had a friend who'd knowingly made extremely unwise choices in her life knowingly, Julie had recently made a poor one herself by kissing Dane. She'd learned her lesson and didn't need to multiply it further. She desperately aspired to learn from others' mistakes so as not to experience their pain for herself. *Why reinvent the wheel?* she decided, at that moment, to simplify her life. She knew what she had to do, and pain, unfortunately, was inevitable for this lesson in transitional growth.

* * *

It was a silly conversation to have walking into a grocery store. A stocky, muddle-haired man in his mid-fifties turned, smiled at Julie, and joked, "Hey, lady, I'm outta your way."

Pretty much always playful and good-spirited, Julie chuckled, got a mischievous grin on her face, and teasingly squared off, "I won't run you over in the grocery store. I promised my kids I'd cut back on that. There are *no* guarantees in the parking lot, though; all bets are off there." Julie looked at him with her naughty grin.

He said, "I'm gettin' out of your way, 'cause it definitely looks like you could take me out. What? No kids here with you tonight?"

"No, I was let out for good behavior," Julie said.

"Ah, home with Dad."

"Oh, no. They're old enough to be on their own."

"Have a good night." The man smiled and walked away.

"You, too." But as Julie walked away, the hair on the back of her neck literally stood on its ends. It struck her very hard: she'd said too much. She immediately dialed home to speak with one of her children. "Hey, honey."

"Hey, Mom, what's up?" Maddie sounded less than thrilled to be interrupted.

"Do me a favor, will you? Lock the doors, make sure the doggies are inside with you, and keep the house phone near you. Please also make sure that the front door light is on."

"What's wrong, Mom?" *Crap. This kid misses nothing.*

"Nothing, honey. I just had a very odd conversation with a stranger walking into the grocery store. Well, it wasn't really a conversation; it was more like a brief interaction. He left me feeling uncomfortable—uncomfortable enough to warn you that I'm not expecting anybody. If you hear the doorbell ring, you're to approach it, but only with the house phone in hand, ready to dial out for help, if necessary. I'm sure I'm overreacting and being paranoid. You know me and my overactive imagination—too much crazy TV; but, I'm thinking it's always worthwhile to be cautious."

"Ok. What exactly did he say?"

"Honey, I don't need to go into those details right now. I'd just like you to go and take care of those things, please; *right now.* I'll be efficient in the grocery store and home very shortly. Okay? Love you." Julie tried to sound calm, almost cool.

Sounding bored and aggravated at the idea of having to do anything requested of her by a parent, Maddie said, "Of course, Mom. Love you, too. Bye."

Gotta love teenagers. That intonation of boredom was both a blessing and a curse. It dawned on Julie that he was the same man who'd parked right in front of her moments after she'd pulled into her parking spot earlier in the week. She recalled that conversation with her observant youngest daughter as they parked.

Maddie had wondered aloud, "Why do people do that, Mom?"

"What's that, baby?"

"Pull into a parking spot in front of another car, which is obviously coming all the way through. Then they smirk, as if they'd foiled you with some great move—like raining on a parade."

Julie had noticed but hadn't been terribly fazed by it. He wasn't the first to be in a hurry, was her explanation to her daughter. *He also wouldn't have been the first guy who either smiled or smirked at me in a parking lot, either—but then this odd contact. Afterwards, it was more discomforting to <u>not</u> see him in the grocery store, even just once.* He'd disappeared after that. That now-you-see-me-now-you-don't was what left Julie actually feeling uneasy.

Why had this started, and when was this going to stop?

When she got home, Julie had the kids put the groceries away while she reached for the phone. Several calls to her lawyer friends yielded little information. Most seemed to have only heard about, but not been 'in the know' with, intense issues with few concrete facts. *I'm sure I've left THEM wondering what the hell I'm up to …* Julie's thoughts drifted. Most of the lawyers Julie knew only dealt with domestic issues, child custody challenges, and corporate receivables. There were only a few firms in town that had any international clients, dealt with corporate espionage, or had been involved in any high-level cases.

Strangers tailing her, plus sporadic odd personal dealings sprinkled with paranoia, seemed to be something that may actually have to shift to a higher authority. Julie recognized that her sixth sense had kicked in, but she'd no solid clue as to why. It was time to call her old college friend again. Julie's brain began to work overtime on who to question, how to question them, and how to defend her questions. The thought made her shiver in anxiety about the approaching conflicts. Perhaps Aubrey might reassure her that her imagination was well paid, or else help sort out the limited known facts.

CHAPTER 46

Julie To Aubrey

The lighting after a rare, early morning storm in the desert moved Julie to a level of creativity she hadn't felt in years.

Saguaro cacti and Palo Verde trees glowed, embracing the desert landscape in a soft blanket of warmth. Julie laughed at herself, thinking she ought to be writing poetry instead of car show summaries and novels. *I sound so cliché, even in my own mind.* The desert, the ocean, the mountains always brought that out in her. She was sure it brought the same out in others, until she met someone, usually a local, who didn't appreciate it the same way at all. *The desert has a unique charm often missed by its many inhabitants.*

The light of the morning, however, always seemed to bring a weightlessness to the previous night's heavy issues, a peace perhaps to the volatility, or even a regrowth option filled with new opportunity. Nevertheless, a fresh perspective usually surfaced after one survived a night. Sleep's transformative powers brought renewal. Julie recognized this perception was a gift. She also knew, though, that the incongruity she felt with the stranger at the grocery store had passed—at least for now. She couldn't stop thinking that he was connected to the person following her daily. She hadn't a clue why any of it was happening, however.

Saved by the bell. The phone rang. Caller ID told her it was one of her agency friends. A wonderful benefit about attending a college internship in Washington, D.C. was that she'd made so many different friends with such varying interests over the years. Some she'd stayed in touch with and many she hadn't. However, of those she'd kept up with, there were plenty of interesting contacts and connections around the world. Aubrey—one of those contacts and also her best friend from college—worked for the FBI based out of Seattle.

"Good morning! Long time, no hear!"

"Good morning. Sorry I took so long to get back to you. I know. I'm such a slacker! How are you?"

"Aubrey, I couldn't be better. Life's chaotic with kids, businesses, and my own adventures. I'm not complaining, though," Julie chuckled.

"I know how you feel, girl. It's been crazy ever since *this* job kicked in. You know I got a promotion, right?"

"No! I didn't! Congratulations. What are you doing?"

"Of course, if I told you too much, I'd have to kill you and eat you!" Aubrey's laugh was big and infectious.

"I, of course, wouldn't want you to divulge a single thing that was completely inappropriate. You know that. But you've *got* to give me at least a juicy clue," Julie teased back.

"This is off the record, but I'll guide you as to where you can find related info. Deal?"

"Deal."

"I'm still a special agent in the criminal division, but I'm involved with some crazy white collar crimes with an international reach. It's such a wild adventure. I get to travel all overseas, but the hours are brutal."

"How's hubby dealing with that?"

"He's not. In fact, we got divorced. It was finalized about three weeks ago. It was awful because I haven't been around. The worst thing I could've done was marry a teacher. They just don't have the same schedule. For a while, it seemed to work, because I wasn't as high up. However, as soon as I got this promotion—which was about six months ago—he got sideways almost instantly. We'd talked about what this new position had entailed for weeks prior to my accepting it, so we didn't go into this blindly.

"He told me pretty much right after I started taking on new responsibilities that there was no way he could deal with my career any further. He *completely* caught me off guard. Turned out, it was right about the time that we *started* talking about my promotion that he got involved with another teacher!"

"Oh, Aubrey, I'm so sorry," Julie lamented with her old friend.

"Yeah, me, too. Honestly, Julie, it really sucked. I was totally surprised. I wanted to quit my job, then I wanted us to try counseling, then I thought about confronting that bitch, then reality hit me.

"I shouldn't have been surprised. I really ought to have known when he started pulling away during our discussions. Sex became less important and infrequent. I thought maybe it was a little jealousy, because he'd be very, well, um, almost dismissive, saying things like 'of course' he would be supportive of me.

"Anyway, he was in support of me doing it, but he was in support of me doing it without him. He'd given up without any warning, without even trying. When I'd asked him about it, he'd simply said he saw the writing on the wall. He believed I was going high places that he couldn't relate to. He essentially was intimidated, didn't want to hold me back, and started looking elsewhere for companionship. In all fairness, I couldn't be much support to him, and another teacher would have much more understanding of what was happening in his field. The education industry is taking a beating right now. Ultimately, he simply couldn't relate to me or what I was doing any longer, and—well—frankly, international crimes had my attention."

"Wow. That sucks—the divorce part, that is."

"Yes, it really has, especially because it's still so fresh. I really miss him. I do know that he's been right, and I respect him for that. I guess that's the part that's even harder to swallow."

"What do you mean?"

"We separated very soon after my promotion. My co-workers, immediate boss and his boss, not to mention local friends and family, said they saw a major change in me again—for the better. I'd gone from being almost timid in their eyes while I was still married, to being solidly confident and fully embracing my own power. I don't mean it to sound bitchy. I mean power as in 'I know that I'm capable of so much,' so why not explore that? Does that make sense? I certainly have more time for professional social gatherings now without any guilt. So much of what I do happens over dinner, after-work Frisbee games, or during a golf outing. My, uh—this is still raw to say—my ex didn't play, either, and had little to talk about when we were together for any of my work functions. He didn't really like to socialize with "my" people, as he'd call them. Does this make sense?"

Julie smiled. "Aubrey, it makes more sense than you can imagine. Perhaps that's one of the reasons why I called you."

"Wow, you didn't even know any of this, and I've already brought you to your power? Shit, I'm better than I thought," Aubrey laughed. "Okay, so to what do I owe the pleasure of your calling me? You're not just staying in touch this time."

"I've been having some strange things happen to me here recently, and I was wondering if maybe you could help me figure a few things out."

"Fire away," Aubrey taunted. "You've got my curious ear now."

"I hope you have more than a few minutes. I suspect you might be interested in some of the information I share with you because of your new position. I'd no idea you were in this department. Perhaps *none* of it will be interesting, or even relevant, but I've gotta give it a shot. If nothing else, maybe you could offer me a calming perspective, instead of the uneasy paranoia I'm feeling."

"I'll do my best," Aubrey said.

CHAPTER 47

Deeper Concealments

Last night's news was broadcast like a warning from above: "… new variations to old trends reveal a much more sophisticated approach. There's basic theft, and then there's today's greedy Robin Hood types. They're educated, resourceful, cultured, philanthropic—and angry." The camera shot panned from the reporter to a parking lot full of insanely high-end vehicles. Colorful Ferrari's, Lamborghini's, Bentley's, McLaren's, and Porsche's littered the flat screen TV.

"You realize, this means we've got to be even more neurotic and hyper- thorough: no nicks, no scratches, not even a misplaced hair in the transfer process—a *very* clean room."

"The transfer team is a meticulously-trained group. They've been working together for several years without error or issue. They came highly recommended. They're aware of certain extremely strategic places in these cars to *secure* our investment for safe transport. Frame rails, drive trains, and even engine blocks are solid car parts and have proven to be extremely protective," he reassured her with a sly grin.

"Wouldn't those be among the first parts searched though?"

"Not usually, since those areas are harder to access. Door panels, seat cushions, spare wheel wells, and behind the glove compartment box are typically first. I won't tell you to relax, since that's not going to happen, regardless. How about I make a more proactive request of you?"

"You can make one, but I won't guarantee it'll be granted," she frowned.

"We're in an extremely strong position within our exceedingly-secure organization, but nothing in life is guaranteed, as you well know, except death and taxes. So, my one request, since you clearly need something to do: pray."

CHAPTER 48

Plan/ Try

She sat stunned with her cell phone still in hand. *I hadn't said a single thing to Dane when he was last here. Call me crazy, but maybe it was that impulsive—wrong —WEAK moment when I grabbed him and kissed him before he left here. Ya think???*

"Maybe he wonders why I did that. Hell! *I* wonder why I did that! I've definitely given him the wrong impression. Who am I kidding? *I* have the wrong impression," she moaned to her faithful, four-legged companions lying dutifully at her feet.

Somebody HAD to have told him. Julie jumped out of her desk chair and tried talking through her jumbled thoughts aloud as she paced in her office. "I didn't talk with Bob next door about anything other than cars, so I can't imagine how Dane had found out about Gabe and me. He called *supposedly* out of the blue to say hi, touch base, and to let me know that business may actually bring him back to town. He even chuckled a little as he said it. Chuckled! Dane doesn't chuckle. I know in my gut that he knew something had changed in my marriage. How did he find out, though? There's no such thing as coincidences. I believe everything happens for a reason." She mentally replayed their conversation…

"I don't talk to you for years; now, I keep turning up," Dane noted brightly after Julie had answered her cell. "I've had business on the West Coast on and off for years, but I'd rarely needed to be there. Now, it seems that I might as well buy a house stateside; I've been back so much in the last year. I mean, uh, well, I guess...I don't know where that came from," Dane scowled at himself. *What am I saying?* "Anyway, I wouldn't call this an accident. I'd call it brilliant luck or meant to be. Will you and your family be in town? Maybe available for lunch or dinner or even coffee? I know your schedule is crazy... ." He paused, feeling awkward for his rambling.

"Julie?" He wondered if they still had a phone connection.

"I'm still here," she barely responded, winded from hearing his voice. *He still wants to talk to me?*

"I know we left on a very, shall we say, miserable note between us. Listen, if I can't have just you, I'll take you with your whole package. I just miss you." He hadn't intended to sound as desperate as he was to have her in his life in some way. He simply knew he needed to start somewhere—a first step.

Julie sat very still, mesmerized by his voice, entertaining a dangerous train of thoughts. *He knows something. Men aren't normally willing to share a woman with another man. Why else would he call, though? Why else would Dane want to see me again? And AGAIN, I wonder, how does he know? Well,* she thought to herself, *maybe I've been reading too many romance novels and not enough self-help books. I HAVE to be imagining this. First, I figure out that I'm being followed. That was real.*

A phone call from a man I'd longed for in years past? Can't be real. The myriad of implications that call caused even now? No way. I'm dreaming.

"Well? Will you be in town, or won't you, when I get there next week?" Dane sat holding his breath. *Come on*, he silently begged. *Be there. Be there.*

Julie breathed deeply and quietly. *Holy shit! This is real, too!! What's happening out there in the universe that Dane's surfaced—again?* "Yes. We'll be here. The kids' next varied tournaments are the weekend after you're here, so your timing is perfect." She composed herself and didn't want to sound as scared as she felt. Dane let out the breath he'd been holding very quietly.

"WOW! I wouldn't call this an accident or luck, either. Meant to be... ." *Oh, boy*, Julie thought to herself. *I'm thrilled and terrified by what I'm feeling.* Julie's inner thoughts jumped around like a pinball machine. *Dane's always been my soul mate, but soul mates aren't always meant to be life partners, unfortunately. My marriage to Gabe, who I thought was my life partner, is crumbling. So am I to believe that I'm supposed to be with Dane after all? Has my writing activated all sorts of undreamed-of change? My life is changing at a startling rate.*

Dane smiled broadly at the phone. "My assistant will be working on travel arrangements, so I'll let you know when I know. I wanted to give you fair warning to either escape town while I'm there, or make some time to see each other. Ok?" He laughed nervously.

He knew what was happening in Julie's life and hoped he hadn't given away his excitement at the change of her circumstances. *She's sharp, so I need to be very careful not to push her away by being too aggressive. She's very guarded, yet still vulnerable. I still can't believe I let her go all those years ago.* He also knew, from a selfish perspective, that he'd appear very callous if he just swooped in and pushed her husband aside. *Gabe may very well be on his way out, but I don't need to be the one to finish the job. I wouldn't have wanted to be given a hard shove with the door slammed behind me. Besides, Julie would only resent me then.*

"Ok," she laughed, knowing she'd bend over backwards to make this meeting happen. *He must have missed me. Why else is he coming back? He sounds excited, too. Shit, I sound too smitten,* Julie thought to herself. *I'm dissecting every little word and breath—as if we're still in high school! Ridiculous.* She shook her head. *Well, he MUST want to see me. HE called me. I'm not chasing HIM halfway around the world. I couldn't look at my reflection in the mirror if I was. I still need to try with Gabe. We BOTH made a commitment.*

"I'll talk to you soon then," he closed softly.

As they hung up the phone, Julie realized she was blushing. She and Gabe were separated but still going to counseling. They were trying to work things out, or so Julie hoped—or did she? Gabe struggled with why the marriage needed to stay together. Julie struggled with why it was falling apart. They constantly were at odds with each other. *These aren't good places for a marriage to be. I'm also not willing to just throw it away because I might have another offer, as tempting as that is when issues seem insurmountable. I know they aren't. Is that why I'm ok with Dane's visit? Does he make me feel sexy, strong, and smart enough to fight for my marriage or to walk away, if necessary, say it's been great, and move on to the next round?*

Julie started really believing that there must be someone else in the picture for Gabe. "Why else would he make little to no effort? Is it the sex? I can't imagine that it is. Our connection is unmistakable, right?" she quizzed herself aloud. "Is this about control? I mean, I'm definitely less accessible than I have been in years because of my writing. But I thought loyal men like Gabe were supportive and excited for their wives' contributions and weren't typically going to leave their marriages unless they felt betrayed or out–of–control. Oh shit! Gabe's out of control…and he likely feels betrayed?! That can't be," she argued with herself.

She was completely invested in her marriage. Her willingness to fight for it was solid proof. Gabe hit this "wall," he called it; Julie called it a "stumbling block." He seemed depressed and disconnected. Julie believed it was his work-a-holism drowning what had kept the intrigue in their marriage: little surprises, spontaneity mixed with planned dates, and special time together. Her beliefs and trust were eroding, nonetheless. In their recent counseling session, Gabe blamed Julie for most of their issues.

"I feel that there are still things about Julie I can't seem to connect with. Julie keeps things from me, like details about her reunion trip. Isn't that what you'd call, um, let me get the terminology right, lying by omission? Her oversensitivity has blown everything out of proportion."

"Gabe," Julie interrupted, "those are my feelings and concerns, and I've answered every question you've asked about that trip. You've accepted *zero* responsibility for the distance that's increased between us."

According to their counselor, lack of mutual accountability was a bad sign.

Gabe shook his head in frustration. "Julie's always a bit perplexing, secretive even, since I'm constantly learning new things about her—even after all the years we've been married. That had always been intriguing and exciting about her. Still, I've grown tired of feeling constantly unbalanced and scattered around her. I wanna get rid of all that mystery. For example," Gabe looked Julie directly in the eyes and judgmentally pushed, "why won't you allow me complete access to your writing files or your calendar? And you often leave the room to read and won't connect when we're all watching TV."

Julie, confused and hurt, knew Gabe was grasping at anything to keep the focus off him. She decided it was important to play along for a few moments and tried a firm, but gentle, approach.

"Gabe, if you'd remember, nothing you've just mentioned has changed in all our years of marriage. Sometimes we watch a little TV, but most times, I just don't want anything to do with it. TV's never been my thing! You know this," she'd argued, avoiding the writing files part of his question. "There are other ways to spend time! Have you *just* noticed after all these years?" She felt her frayed nerves unravel more and decided that would be counterproductive.

As she sat in the counselor's office, she resigned herself to feeling detached, as if someone else was actually in her body going through the experience. *Was this really news to him?*

"What made you finally dial in to me? What made

you actually notice that I might not even be in the same room?" Julie kept coming back to the same answer: *there was someone else. That someone must like TV as much as he does. He likely doesn't want that someone to cause the end of his marriage, but she's threatening and changing his perspective on it. Gabe's usually too preoccupied, or perhaps tired, to even notice that there's someone in the same room with him more than 95% of the time. Why the sudden observations?* Julie hoped that Gabe would come clean before he embarrassed himself or her.

She knew that her life suddenly faced some complicated issues. She'd no idea how it had gotten to this point. *I'm just gonna breathe, take it all one day at a time, and pray for peace and resolution. What other options do I have? I have my kids and my budding career to think about. I'm not giving up either. I don't want to give up my marriage, but I'm not the only one making decisions in it. Making rash ones isn't the way to cope.*

CHAPTER 49

Transfer Complete

The meticulous work took longer than usual to complete. Greed drove the decision to hide more gold than usual. *Sure, the car would weigh more*, reasoned the main investor, *but even customs could be persuaded that some older parts cost more and weighed more once upon a time.*

"They just don't make them like they used to," he'd reasoned with them. "Besides," he'd explained to the chief inspector, "when the car sold, then their homeland made more, too."

Dane Michael's paperwork was flawless. He was even better than Victor had led on. He was also setting himself up, and Tate would appear completely innocent. Finally.

It was an easy sell.

CHAPTER 50

Unexpected Intros

Music's universal magic to heal, sooth, inspire, and awaken depended on the listener. For Dane, though he liked most types of music, he particularly enjoyed classical when working. It was also his way to unwind after grueling meetings of negotiations and logistics, and it seemed to shrink the distances he spent far from his children. He made every attempt to attend classical music concerts when travelling on business for more than a few days. His return to Phoenix this time allowed him such a treat. The diversion normally distracted and calmed him, yet Dane found himself still anxious and agitated at the concert's halfway point. *Today was challenging, because I've been concerned about reaching out to Julie. Though we'd spoken about my doing so once my travel plans were known, I didn't want to appear overbearing. I desperately want to see her, nonetheless.*

Instead of the usual soothing effect, without warning, he found himself internally shaken, wondering if he was dreaming. He watched her from a short distance away, shocked at having caught sight of her apparent twin to begin with amidst the mass of people in the spacious concert hall lobby. He turned away, believing he was seeing things.

He rarely got up during intermission when attending concerts, unless he was with someone; then, stretching legs and brief chatter offered a break in the companionship. He preferred to sit and reflect on what he'd heard, and didn't want to break any concentration or relaxation he may have finally reached. For some unknown reason, this time in Phoenix, although alone, he felt the need to head to the brightly-lit lobby. Wading through all of those pretentious people always left him cold, regardless of where he was. One of the lobby bars had a slightly shorter line, so he gravitated toward it, opting for a cocktail.

Standing there taking in the sounds around him, he felt compelled to turn and look back toward his seat's portal, almost as if he needed to be more aware of his surroundings in case he got lost—though that had never happened. As he started to turn back toward the bar, he froze again. Julie was, in fact, standing just outside of the portal next to his with someone, no doubt her husband, and hadn't noticed Dane yet. Dane couldn't look away this time. He was completely mesmerized. Her sloppy elegance was bewitching. He must have been staring hard or intently, because the chatty man behind him almost inaudibly commented, "She has no idea that she's lovely, does she?"

Uncomfortable at having been caught people watching, he tried to play it cool. "I'm sorry. Were you speaking to me?"

Chuckling, the equally handsome man, who spoke quietly so as not to raise attention by his otherwise engaged wife, murmured, "I'm only appreciating your excellent taste, my friend."

"May I help you, sir?" offered the bartender.

Dane was completely annoyed with the disturbance to his apparent hypnotic state. He gruffly responded by asking for a Scotch and water without removing his eyes from her, afraid he would lose sight of her altogether again. Absentmindedly pulling a ten-dollar bill from his pocket, he stuffed it into the tip jar and realized that he'd caught her eye. Julie's recognition of him was shock as well.

"You *know* her?" the man behind Dane asked. "No wonder you're staring… ."

Ignoring the man behind him and watching Julie's husband walk away, Dane knew this was the perfect time to approach her.

"We just keep running into each other," he smiled softly.

She stuttered, "W-wow. You're…back. I mean…you're… *here*. You look amazing. What brings you *here*?"

Dane heard the bartender ask for the next in line and saw the man who'd been standing behind him wink. Dane turned back to Julie, "You look lovely. Do you want a drink?"

"More like, do I need a drink?" She grinned at him, leaned in, and gave him her trademark warm hug and kiss on each cheek, European style, but pressed Dane. "Yes, thank you; I'd love one. Red wine, please. So, what are you doing here?"

"Same thing you are—catching this sublime concert." He guided her back toward the bar line which had shrunk.

"Not the concert; you know what I mean. When did you return to Phoenix? I thought you were going to call me to let me know?"

Ignoring her last question, he answered the first, "Well, when I'm in the same city with a client for more than a few days, I always make a point of picking out some sort of symphonic concert experience, if there's one available. Tonight was the perfect night to attend the symphony, since I'm here for another several days. Music is a way for me to unwind or even get more mentally organized. What about you? You come to the symphony often?"

He's ignoring my questions. Odd. "I don't come nearly as often as I'd like. Our lives are so filled with business events and kids' activities. Don't get me wrong; I love every minute of the kids' part—but those experiences don't always feed my spirit, my soul, if you know what I mean. I *love* to attend the symphony and the theatre, actually. You probably don't remember, but I'd danced for so many years. I still have a tremendous passion for it, especially for attending classical ballets—not so much of the new stuff."

"Now that you're mentioning this, I do remember that about you. How do you marry the differences between classical symphony and basketball, or whatever else your kids play?"

Julie chuckled, "They play all sorts of sports. But I'm happy to shift and have no problem doing so between any one of them. One loves to play classical music, but she doesn't like to listen to it. Go figure. Oh—now you finally get to meet my husband." Blushing, Julie turned to Gabe as he approached and introduced the two men. Having them face-to-face for the first time was quite surreal for Julie. Her stomach had clenched when she first made eye contact with Gabe, who actually seemed quite indifferent to it all. Such apparent indifference put Julie more at ease while upsetting her a little, too. She knew to keep her outward appearance cool as she calmly made their acquaintance. With little in common, including the symphony, the conversation quickly became awkward.

"Nice meeting you." Gabe shook Dane's hand. "I'll see you inside in a minute." He glanced at Julie briefly before returning to observe Dane. "Enjoy the rest of the concert." Gabe dismissed himself.

"Nice guy," Dane commented. "Not much for the symphony, though?"

"Thank you and no. He attends with me because I ask it of him. He's less, um, well, versatile, in his musical tastes than I am," Julie replied quietly. "You ignored my question before."

Briefly forgetting her keen memory, but knowing better than to act stupid with Julie, he deferentially explained, "I didn't think you really wanted to hear from me after our last—'interaction', we'll call it—during my unannounced visit." He searched her face for any indication that he'd been wrong. "I didn't want to upset you, or be pushy and presumptuous, by calling again. Frankly, I had no clue as to how to handle anything between us."

Julie politely looked at him, not having a clue as to what to say to him, since his reminder of their last visit shocked her—their *second* interaction in thirty years.

"We *agreed* that you'd call when you knew your plans. For how much longer are you in town?"

"Another three to four days, depending on how quickly we receive information on the company we're taking over. Will I get to see you again?"

"I'd really like that. Would you be willing to meet my kids?"

"Of course," he smiled. "I've been waiting to meet them for a very long time. Besides, we're likely to be safer around each other then." He paused, looking down at her hands, then just raised his compassionate brown eyes to her luminous green.

Julie struggled to ignore his clear and accurate innuendo. "How do I reach you? Same cell number you've already given me?"

"Assuming you still have it, of course."

"Why wouldn't I have it?"

"I don't know. Again, I didn't want to be overconfident. That sort of thinking gets people into trouble—often," he said with a smirk on his face and a devilish glint in his eye.

"Maybe I *don't* want to see you any more while you're here," she mischievously baited. "You may very well be trouble." It was not a matter of *may*; Julie was well aware of their undeniable chemistry.

"Shall I call you tomorrow?" It was his turn to hug her good-bye—though he didn't want to—for the evening as the concert hall bells began to chime, signaling the end of intermission.

"I'll look forward to it."

Dane smiled and warmly taunted, "Me, too."

CHAPTER 51

Next Step

Julie took a bit of time to explain everything, as she tried to be as succinct as possible giving Aubrey the highlights of what had been going on in her life for the last few months. Aubrey was an excellent listener. *No wonder she got the promotion,* Julie thought to herself in the midst of her story. *Her questions are solid, her concerns are carefully weighed, and her insights are reassuring.*

"Well, Julie, I don't think you're being paranoid at all. There *are* a few things that you've told me that I'm already aware of. Weird, huh? I'm really thankful you called me, in all honesty."

"What? Really?" Julie was calm, but a little startled, nonetheless.

"There are *also* a few things that are *new* to me that I'm going to have to get up to speed with in my department."

"Wow. I didn't think it was *that* interesting, just kind of creepy."

"I'm not certain what my department is and isn't aware of regarding what you're sharing with me. It sounds like you and I are going to be able to help each other here, though. You're going to make me look like a rock star with this 'in the trenches' kind of information, and I'm going to give you great stuff for your book. There *are* a few conditions, however, that I'm going to need to insist upon in order to be able to share information that you may need to know—and perhaps not need to know. I don't want to scare you, but these conditions will be in place to keep us both safe, ok?"

"Oh—kaaaay."

"What's that response about?"

"Kinda freakin' me out here. You're the third person to caution me about my safety lately. *How* am I sharing this information that I'm eliciting this cautionary response?"

"Before we go any further, I'm going to need you to sign a confidentiality statement. I'll explain then. As I've already mentioned, this will protect us both. Nothing's going to compromise my job; however, you need to be source-protected. You kind of understand where I'm going with this?"

"100%, and thank you."

"For what? I haven't given you anything yet."

"Aubrey, just with this conversation, you've given me some peace—some concern, too—but definitely some peace. I couldn't imagine that the hair was standing up on the back of my neck for no reason. I kept thinking that I was paranoid, and *that* was *before* I knew *anything* was happening. When things began happening, *that* was when I *knew* I wasn't paranoid. Got me so far?"

"With you."

"But now, I've got that, um, well, *that* feeling again, so I'm thinking that I'm paranoid again. That frightens me to a great extent, because I'm wondering if it's a premonition that something else is going to happen, or is it already? That's why you're familiar with some of it? I mean, I have kids, Aubrey."

"Your feelings are completely justified. Trust your instincts, Julie. You've a woman's intuition; don't be afraid of it. Respect it. Yours are apparently more acutely developed than many of the agents I have here."

"You're kidding me, right?" Julie was incredulous.

"No, I'm not kidding you. I'm not even sure how some of these agents became agents, to be perfectly honest with you. We've got problems here in the agency because of their lack of common sense, lack of intuition, inability to think, process, or reason, and often even to communicate. There *are* those who are exceptional, of course."

"More who ought to be just the paper processors?"

"Absolutely. Unfortunately, once in our system, they're tough to remove. They get to stick around, sometimes getting shuffled between departments, even getting promoted when they don't deserve it. There *are* those who ought to just, um, say, analyze but are put in leadership positions and have zero clue how to lead—nor are they taught. It's as if they have to be moved within a certain number of years. We look to encourage many to leave or retire early. The really bad agents who screw up, we do move out. Document enough of their messes, they'll get fired—eventually. That's not as easy as many think."

"Sheez, and I thought that was just in the educational system," Julie disparaged.

"Oh, no; it's also big right here in government intelligence work. All the scandal about overpriced items? Overstocked departments full of employees who are useless, clock watching, unmotivated—to name a few? They're all legitimate money-wasting issues."

"I've always known that there's been government waste,

Aubrey. Who doesn't think that? I mean, there's always something in the paper about 'costly red tape' or the vagaries of banking. I just figured that in intelligence work, there was far less of it." Julie was disappointed in this confirmation and wondered what her old classmate could actually share.

"I'll tell you what, Julie; my promotion isn't just about information gathering. My promotion is also about sealing up leaks, tightening up our personnel teams, and improving both the management of those teams as well as the quality of them. There's so much information at the ground level that so many agents feel they're above, but they miss it. Give me a few days to sort out the info you've shared with me, and I'll get back to you, whether it's with good news, bad news, or little-to-no news. At least you won't be sitting in the dark wondering. Meanwhile, I want you to be very careful, and keep an eye on all things that are concerning you—that you're aware of. Keep it in a notebook, keep it in a memo, or send me an email, whatever. Okay?"

"Okay, I can do that," Julie agreed.

CHAPTER 52

Post-Concert

After her conversation with Aubrey, Julie realized that she needed to keep living her life as normally as possible, including getting together with Dane, while Aubrey did some detail checking—in spite of any abnormal feelings and happenings. She found his appearance at the symphony the night before both disconcerting as well as exhilarating.

He'd told her that he'd be in town more due to business, and that he'd call her once his plans had been arranged. *It must've been my imagination that he'd sounded happy, excited even, because he hadn't called me as we'd agreed he would. Was it possible to have a friendship, since nothing further could develop between us?*

Julie thought, *It's best to meet Dane for coffee in broad daylight…safer…to bring order to my jumbled thoughts. I'm not bringing the kids yet.* She decided to get them to their varied activities, run a few errands, and behave far more casually by the time they met. Her "shadow" pulled the usual two car lengths behind her. She wondered if it was a good idea to have the driver know whom she met.

"Good morning." Dane answered his cell with a smile.

"Good morning," Julie replied brightly. "How are you this morning?"

"Better now." He hoped he didn't sound too eager and

relieved.

"Aren't you sweet."

"Sweet? No. Truthful."

"Truthful's nice," she smirked.

"We've talked about that word."

"We have, and you didn't think it could ever apply to you."

"I still don't. Do we still have a plan this morning, or are you calling to cancel on us?"

"Ouch. Why would I cancel?"

"Because you feel wrong about it."

"I don't—yet. Should I?"

"I think you've chosen one of the *least* dangerous places at a *very* innocent time."

"Interesting choice of words, Counselor. Starbuck's at 10 a.m. could be… precarious?" Julie suddenly got a pang of concern.

Dane took his opportunity to tease, "Lunch might have been safest."

"I suppose. You're terrible. Do *you* need to cancel? Now's the time to speak up, or forever hold your peace. I'm en route."

"I'm in…I mean…"

"Very cute. I have to warn you, though, about something odd when I get there. So, please be there in the next few minutes, so we aren't walking in together. Ok?"

"That's a very concerning request, but, of course. You WILL explain."

"Yes, and thank you. See you shortly."

* * *

Julie parked in the busy, uncovered parking lot next to their meeting spot. She approached the Starbuck's counter in the Scottsdale Fashion Square Mall area, trying very hard not to look around at every person and suspect each to have been the one following her. It was, at first, an unnerving undertaking. As soon as she saw Dane seated in an open area, she breathed a little relief, forgetting most of her anxiety. He'd a reassuring effect on her. He looked in control and very much like an attorney in his sharp, medium-gray suit, pressed white button-down shirt, muted royal blue patterned tie, and polished black Bostonian lace-ups—handsome and professional.

He was fully focused on the file in his hands and seemed to not even notice her, as she approached from the counter with her hot latte—or so Julie thought.

"If I'd known you were going to get all dressed up for our get-together, I'd have done the same. Didn't anyone tell you that Arizona is a little more casual than Zurch?"

Dane stood as Julie approached, guided her toward him by her forearm, and kissed her on each cheek as she finished her "hello." He was thankful to have a reason to touch her, take in her scent. *Shit, already I'm thinking this way?* "Good morning to you, too, and don't worry about what you're wearing. It doesn't seem to matter. You look wonderful wearing—" *uh-oh, knock it off, imagination*—"anything." He smiled gently.

"Thank you," Julie accepted softly.

"Now, what's with the concerning request?"

Right down to business. Ok, Julie assumed quickly. "I don't know why yet, but I've got reason to believe I'm being followed, and I didn't want you to be seen with me in case that was bad for you."

"And you think my being in here already will at least not bring as much attention to us together?"

Julie nodded her general agreement, but the weary expression she wore betrayed her unmistakable anxiety.

"Interesting thought, but what about all of the other people in here? Do you think they're also immediately on the suspicious list?"

"You're making fun of me," she sighed cynically. "Just what I needed."

"OK. What makes you think you're being watched?" *Shit, she's sharp, or our team's sloppy.*

"Well, thanks for not getting panicked, at least, when I'd mentioned it. I suppose I'd rather have you mock me than freak out and run off." She sadly shook her head.

"Julie, look at me. I'm still here. I deal with all sorts of clients. I'm not easily run off. Many have been less than quality human beings over the years—unfortunately. In fact, I've one this morning with whom I'll meet after our coffee." She saw Dane's posture change at this reference and noted the sudden formality and care in his word selection.

"By the looks of your expression, he's not one of your favorite people?"

"You're too observant, and no, he's not."

"Why take him on as a client then?" she asked innocently.

"I wasn't given a choice by my boss," Dane replied flatly.

"Oh. Sorry. Look on the bright side: you get the pleasure of coming to Arizona to deal with him. Is he from here?"

"No, he's not, but we've a mutual associate who does live here." Dane didn't share that this mutual associate lived next door to her, hoping she'd forgotten that they'd already spoken of the taciturn Bob Couvey. He thought he might look too much like a stalker if he did.

"I see, and this mutual associate is why you're here this time?"

"Yes." *Uh-oh.*

"What industry do they represent?"

"The auto industry," he resignedly replied. He watched her face very carefully, analyzing her every reaction. He knew what she'd say next. His research rarely failed him.

"Interesting. You clearly refer to my neighbor. Forgot you mentioned him to me during your last fly-by of my house?"

Trying to distract her to change subjects, Dane smiled softly, "Is that what we're calling it now? A fly-by?"

"Close enough. Trying to avoid the subject of cars?"

"You might say that." *Fuck, she's going there.*

"You say that almost disparagingly, as if you know what I write about already."

Apparently, she reads minds, too, he thought. "It's just a challenging topic on which more men write than women typically. That's not to sound sexist, just pointing out a fact. I find it hard to understand why someone with your class and elegance would want to…downgrade their subject material."

"Curious remark from an industry lawyer."

"Touché, Mrs. Archer," Dane conceded. "Now, back to why you think you're being followed."

Julie shifted uncomfortably in her seat, gingerly took a sip from her hot latte, and looked him straight in the eyes. "Every day for months, the same cars show up behind me in traffic, parking lots, and sometimes even pulling out of side streets in my neighborhood. Obviously, they've figured out where I live—disconcerting, but not a secret. So, well, I was hoping you might tell me. Have any light to shed on this unsettling situation?"

Without looking away, he raised his eyebrows and remarked, "What makes you think I have anything to do with that?"

"You're a lawyer. We've parted twice in ways neither of us had anticipated. You've clients here. You like your order and no surprises. And the number one reason: they started very shortly after I returned from the reunion. How far off am I?" The way Julie looked at him made Dane struggle with how to answer.

He decided honesty with this woman was his best strategy, especially given his research about her husband and some of his less-than-honorable meetings. Dane was fairly certain that Julie was either still in the dark about him, or was starting to find out facts that caused their separation. He knew now wasn't the time to encroach on her privacy. Trust didn't need to be *their* issue, too.

"Not very." He waited.

Julie's eyes didn't waver from Dane's. "Alright-y then. I don't know whether to be flattered or pissed. Well, regardless, I appreciate your honesty. Since we're on an honest roll, tell me why you don't trust me."

"This is not about trusting *you*. In my business, some of the clients with whom I work require such regular '*attention*' on my part. This is a safety protocol, because I don't trust them. *You've* nothing to worry about regarding my trust."

"How do we proceed from here, then?" She couldn't help her tone change as she looked down at her purse.

Dane didn't miss it, either. "I'll stop it immediately." He

picked up his phone, touched just one number, and looked Julie directly in the eyes as he spoke. "Please discontinue the tail on Mrs. Archer. Yes. Redirect those teams. Thank you." Dane pressed the disconnect button without taking his eyes off Julie and asked quietly, "Ok?"

"Yes, thank you. It's caused me increasing anxiety on several fronts. I'm not sure whether to hug you for your concern, or hit you for your lack of information."

"You're welcome, and again, you've nothing to worry about."

"Are you sure about that?" Julie and Dane both looked up surprised. "Are you going to introduce me to this beautiful woman or keep her from me?" Tate irritated Dane.

* * *

"Julie Archer, perhaps you remember Tate Parker, my client and a former high school classmate. Tate Parker, Julie Archer." Dane tightly made the introductions.

Yikes, he really doesn't like this guy. I can see why right out of the gate. Mr. Smug and Slick. Julie knew Dane well enough to know not to ask any questions about her observations now. She rose, picked up her purse, and politely, but quite firmly, shook Tate's hand.

"Good morning, Tate Parker." She oozed her charm for Dane's sake. "It's a pleasure to apparently re-meet you. Dane and I were just finishing up." She turned toward Dane, eyes wide, and politely stuck out her hand, knowing he'd understand the look and gesture. "Always good to see you. Thank you so much for your advice, as usual. Invaluable. Please let my husband and me know when you'll be returning. He's disappointed to have missed you this trip."

Her stiffness and formality are such an immediate and harsh contrast to her usually relaxed demeanor. I know why she did it. It's a brilliantly safe move for us both. Such a complete retraction of her warmth left him unexpectedly chilled, forlorn even, knowing he'd feel completely empty and so bereft forever, unless he figured out how to have her in his life.

She turned and left. Dane silently fumed, *the asshole couldn't have been late as usual?* Both men watched Julie leave. Tate broke their silence.

"Sorry to be quite so early. I didn't mean to—intrude," he smirked, egging on Dane. "Who is *she*?"

"Another local client." Dane willed himself to refrain from any comments other than their business.

"She looked familiar. You said she was our…"

Dane interrupted Tate's attempt to make sense of his slip, which Julie thankfully tried to downplay a bit, and refused to take the bait. He decided to firmly manage this infuriating human. "You must be tired from your travels, and we've business to cover."

"Yes, tired with all the traveling I do," Tate replied distractedly. *I wonder why Michaels is acting as if we'd never met. He knows I know who she is. It's understandable that Julie may not remember me.* "That's highly possible. Didn't you say we were former classmates? Of course, it's said that we all have doubles in the world."

"I hope not," Dane sneered under his breath.

"Now, now, Mr. Michaels. Temper, temper."

"Let's get this over with. I have a plane to catch."

CHAPTER 53

Untimely

Tate's excessive earliness for his meeting with Dane and Bob was, of course, deliberate. He hadn't planned to be *that* early, but then Jennifer called reporting on Julie Archer whereabouts. He wanted to arrive for the meeting prior to Julie's leaving. That was, after all, why she was at that particular Starbucks. No coincidence. *Hmmm. I wonder if her husband knows she's meeting with her ex-boyfriend from high school? So tempting to ask, but I have to see if she even recognizes me. Highly unlikely and fabulously juxtaposed to Gabe Archer's ex-girlfriend tailing his current missus.* Tate recognized the delectable paradox.

Tate knew who Julie was to Dane. He'd always known. She was another reason why Tate had come to intensely dislike Dane. In spite of how Dane kept to himself in high school, he'd edged Tate out of too many things: girlfriend, sports, test scores. The fact that Dane didn't even know half of why Tate hated him made it all worse. For most of their high school years, Tate felt virtually invisible to his elementary school friend. Most kids grew in different ways, and that was cool. Tate had taken great offense to such "normal" childhood behavior. Tate's legal issues at an early age were a result of what he termed "emotional abandonment," only it was from his friend more than anyone in his family. Then again, Tate and Dane had been more like brothers all those years than Tate's brothers ever were to him.

Dane and Julie, however, weren't aware of what Tate knew about them. Julie barely even saw Tate in high school. They'd just never moved in the same circles. They'd never even had a class together. Dane had had classes with her, however. Her bright, quick smile invited Dane's closed personality to slowly open. *Then he screwed up with her after graduation by listening to the class bitch spread jealous gossip. Dane had never been a part of that crap—until the very end, which was shocking even then.* His screwing up with a girl Tate would have treated like a queen pissed him off more so. Today, instead of being worshipped for spoiling and caring for someone like Julie, Tate found himself alone or controlled by the female du jour. Currently, it was his highly-jealous boss, though Tate knew better than to be involved with anyone from work.

Dane and Julie hadn't noticed Tate enter the coffee shop, so it was a perfect opportunity to be able to observe them for a while. *Damn, I'd love to just tell all! How can she tolerate him after what he did to her? Did she know, or maybe she isn't that smart? Maybe I've overestimated her? Or, Dane Michaels was a far more formidable opponent than I've calculated. The expression on their faces when I interrupted them, however, was worth leaving the hotel early. Michaels certainly hadn't anticipated me. Julie didn't seem to recognize me at all. I wonder if she might from Bob's that day. Bob was right about how into their kids she and her husband are, though.* Tate's blood turned green at the thought. *My parents just weren't there for me—ever.*

"Let's get this over with. I've a plane to catch." Dane

barely kept his temper intact.

"So anxious to jump into business. I thought you were here for another few days. How fast your mood changed from when you were with *Mrs.* Archer. Note the emphasis on the missus," Tate smugly delivered.

"How very perceptive of you since she had, in fact, mentioned her husband," Dane's tone turned. He boiled just below the surface. *Maintain control. Do not let him get to you,* he ordered himself.

"You sound so…disappointed in her being so. Does she know why you actually broke up so soon that summer?" Tate loved to taunt Dane. *Easy. Don't push too much.*

Dane decided upon a big, deep breath to assist him in holding his tongue. *Do I take the bait? Do I ask how he thinks he knows?* He opted to look disinterested, distracted.

Donning his laser-focused lawyer tone and air, Dane regained his composure. "Bob will be here any minute. I believe the best course of action to swap the vehicles legally and without undue attention… ."

Dane's cell rang. *Victor's ringtone.* "Good morning, Boss."

"Dane, glad I was able to catch you. Where are you now? In the middle of anything?"

"Yes, I'm actually *sitting* with Tate Parker. We're starting to go over some details before Bob arrives. Why?"

"Your ex called me—again."

"Victor, I'm conducting business for our firm right now. Would that call have anything to do with this business at hand?" His animal instincts kicked in; the hair on the back of his neck stood on its ends. *Something's not right about this.*

"Yes, I believe it might." *This is creepy*, Dane thought, as Victor replied so coolly.

"Go on, then."

"She said that she's been receiving regular payments from you from the beginning, but the amount recently doubled. Is there something we need to discuss?"

Play dumb—NOW. "I haven't any idea what you're talking about, and what does that have to do with…" Dane looked up at Tate and saw a hateful gleam in his eyes. *WARNING!!* Dane's mind screamed. *WARNING!!!!*

"Hang up the phone, Michaels."

Dane did as he was instructed. *This isn't going to be good,* he determined.

Tag Along

Another cool start to a day in the beautiful Sonoran desert was a gift to all residents, two-legged and four-legged alike. As Julie drove west on Shea Boulevard to a breakfast meeting with the full moon considering it's early morning descent, she couldn't help but wonder if she'd finally escaped the watchful eye of her latest sunrise shadow. Her relief had been fleeting after Dane had called off his operators. She'd assumed the second car had been following Dane's men, and that finally the bizarre reconnaissance chapter was over—until it showed up behind her mere hours after leaving Dane with Tate Parker at Starbuck's. *Maybe*, Julie thought now, *I've left too early for them to be on me, or they finally "got the memo" to stop.*

Just because she didn't see the tan Nissan Maxima in her rear view mirror didn't mean it wasn't there, or about to be. Somehow, her tag knew what she was up to, so they were always ready for her. The question was how; her schedule changed daily—sometimes even hourly. She'd hoped Dane had had the answers when they'd met earlier in the week for coffee, but only one of the two cars watching her stopped. Now, she prayed that he'd have no idea what she was talking about during a call she planned to make to him later this morning regarding international auto movement.

She decided to turn off her thinking for a few moments and turn up the radio, trusting it to drown out any overly-paranoid thoughts. As she tried to get lost in her music, she saw the tan car slip casually into traffic three cars behind her and one lane over. *Son of a bitch.*

"Hmm. Good morning, stranger. Wonder what you need today? More importantly, I wonder who you are," she tried to calmly speak to herself. "You must've been told to simply follow me," Julie reasoned aloud to herself. "Call me crazy, but I'm guessing any interaction with me must be off-limits. That's a good thing—I think."

She knew, for a fact, that she'd been watched for at least the last three weeks in the mornings, during midday errand running, as well as any afternoon or evenings, especially if she went out. She typically saw them within a mile of leaving home. The shadowing car would slip in behind Julie—usually several cars back, not normally right behind her—and then to the left or right of her lane. Periodically, she'd only *feel* their presence.

She hadn't noticed immediately that the Maxima kept turning up behind Dane's tail. In fact, she'd really thought that her imagination had gone too far initially and began assuming that it was a local who shared her same route. *I need to stop watching all those crime investigation shows,* she decided, chuckling to herself. Then wincing, she thought, *what if it might actually be true? My imagination often works overtime. When Aubrey had reminded me to listen to my intuition, I think I just realized that I haven't been—'cuz it's telling me, quite clearly, what it needs me to know: STAY VIGILANT!! NOW!!*

She tried to go slowly enough to see if it was a male or female driver. The driver wore a baseball cap pulled down low, so the gender was hard to identify. *If I could just ID if male or female, that would at least eliminate a few possibilities. At least I'd have something to tell Dane and/or the police.*

What she *did* know, and clearly, however, was that she *was* being followed; it wasn't an overactive imagination at play, as Bill had questioned. Julie checked the car's clock to see how early she was for her breakfast appointment.

Hmmm. I think it's time to make a little detour before I make this meeting. Time to test my suspicions.

Looking lost, and really straining to see street names and signs, Julie slowed way down—to the point of intentionally causing growing road rage amongst her fellow drivers. She hated when this happened to her on surface streets and felt worse doing it, but the clawing feeling in her gut wouldn't go away. As drivers became frustrated piling up behind her, Julie then made a point of moving over to the far right-hand lane and allowed the traffic in the two left lanes to move past her. Naturally, there was honking, yelling, and glaring. The car that followed her, however, decided to tuck itself just out of a clear observation point. They, too, moved over into the far right lane, but a car or two behind her. The Maxima would then stay put, allowing a shiny, dark-red Pontiac Firebird to continue in its place in the middle lane.

Julie abruptly realized there were *two* of them keeping track of her—again! "What the fu-?!" The hair on the back of her head stood on its ends. "*This* is not a good thing. I now have alternating escorts. It's a freaking convoy! WHAT is going on? I *must* be watching too much TV. This can't be happening. These can't be from Dane. I've no clue who'd want to follow me, or why. My most provocative writing hasn't even been published yet, so it's most certainly not my 'adoring' fans."

She sped up once again and moved back into the center, or even far left lane, looking like she knew where she was going. She alternated looking preoccupied on her cell phone, restarting the same cycle of frustration for different drivers behind her. Each time, Julie moved over a lane or two to the right. Regardless of how often she repeated the cycle, so did her shadows.

Who even HAS a Pontiac Firebird any more? she wondered, shaking from uneasiness.

Instead of messing around any further, she decided to turn around and head toward the nearest police station, forgetting her morning appointment. *She'll figure I'm a no-show,* she rationalized. "This is my last mini-sanity test. Imagination or real event? Final answer?" Julie tried to calm herself with humor. Taking a slow, deep breath, she turned the music from low to off; both cars stayed with her.

No need to pinch myself, Julie said aloud to herself. *Glad I'm wearing sunglasses. They aren't able to see me seeing them, but they're about to realize it.* Julie dialed the police.

"9-1-1, what is your emergency?" the cool, disinterested dispatcher routinely answered.

"I'm being followed and would really appreciate your having an officer or two assist me in figuring out who they are and why. I'm making this easy for you to help me, since I'm heading your way *very* soon."

"Ok, ma'am, what's your name?"

"Julie Archer. What's yours?"

"I'm Officer Johnson. Do you live nearby, Julie?"

"Yes, ma'am. My husband, children, and I live at 13638 North Cargo Trail here in Scottsdale. Please, will you help me?" Julie started to sound anxious.

"I'll do my best, ma'am. Why do you believe you're being followed, Julie?"

"Because I've tried to aggravate drivers to force them around me, but two cars tuck back into traffic *with* me, instead of going around me. They are tag-teaming me. Every turn I take, they're within two or three cars of me. I'm not able to ID whether the drivers and passengers are male or female; but, I do know that one car is a tan Nissan Maxima, and the other car is a shiny, dark-red Pontiac Firebird. Who even still drives those, Officer Johnson?"

"I'm hoping to figure that out. Julie, where are you now?" the operator asked calmly, but was clearly now engaged.

"I'm less than two blocks from the station heading east on Via Linda. Please tell me that as I turn into the station parking lot, you'll have a patrol car watching and ready to follow *them*. I'm sure they'll be caught off guard when I actually pull in, though I doubt they'll follow me into the lot."

"OK. I'll see you on our parking lot cameras."

"Great. I'd be hugely grateful if I knew there was help close by. This sounds crazy, I know. I'm just a local mom. I even thought it was my imagination, or maybe a case of mistaken identity. I think this has been happening for a few weeks, and I'm now worried for my family. Please help me, Ms. Johnson," Julie urged, hoping the stress was evident in her voice.

"Julie, nothing sounds crazy to me these days. There are two patrol cars in position as we are speaking. Please stay on the line with me until I know you're safe. Ok?"

"Ok."

"Where are you now, Julie?"

"I'm just passing the bowling alley on Via Linda. My shadows are three cars behind me. Oh, wow. Wait. One is turning around. Must've finally realized where I was going. They're making an illegal U-turn! Does your officer see them?" She was growing frantic, thinking all her efforts had been for nothing.

"Julie, we see them. Please pull into our parking lot, and stay there until an officer comes out to you. Ok?"

"Yes, ma'am. OK. I'm a little freaked out by this."

"Of course." There was a silence in Julie's ear, followed quickly by a flurry of activity on the blacktop in front of her car about twenty feet. "Wow. You all are fast. Must be the officer. I see tons of unmarked cars in front of me," Julie commentated.

"Julie," the dispatcher said very firmly, "please stay in your car. That's not our officer yet. Do you understand?"

"Yes, ma'am," Julie barely whispered. "What's happening, Officer Johnson?"

"Are you able to lock your vehicle's doors?"

"Yes," she squeaked.

"Good. Please keep them locked until…"

Suddenly, there was yelling, and Julie instinctively slunk down in her driver's seat trying to stay out of the line of any fire. She wasn't sure if she ought to try to move to the back of the car, or even breathe, for that matter. She wasn't feeling clever or strong any longer—especially unarmed.

"Johnson?" she snipped boldly, forgetting her manners in her fear.

"Please remain quiet, Julie, for your sake. I'm still here. Ok?"

"Ok. Should I try to crawl to the back of the car?" she barely whispered, fear throbbing through her veins. Of course, as was typical lately, her cell beeped signaling another call. It was Gabe. She hit the "call later" text option, and hoped it went through. Then she quickly texted him: 'R u and kids ok?' 'Yes,' was the reply.

"Stay still, low, and quiet. This'll be over very soon."

"K."

What's happening? Who's following me and why? Are the kids really ok? Gabe? Our home? Julie shook with concern for her family, angst about the unknown, and suddenly angry that she was left uninformed about the happenings around her now.

"Johnson, please tell me what's happening. This unknown's gotta be more frightening than the actual happenings," she quietly pushed, as her patience and bravery diminished rapidly.

"I promise the reality is worse than you might guess. Stay low. Do you have a jacket or something to cover your head with right now?" Johnson sounded worried now. *Not a good sign. Oh, crap,* Julie thought to herself.

"Yes."

Speaking in a clipped, harsh tone, Dispatcher Johnson calmly, but quickly, commanded, "Grab it fast now; cover your head and as much of yourself as possible. Stay DOWN."

That was when she heard and felt a loud, jarring blast almost simultaneously. *What the f-!!!*

Thrown to the passenger side of her car, Julie was dumbfounded by how quiet it became outside of her Volvo. *Thank God I convinced Gabe that we should buy this S80 model. It's rock solid. Well*, she thought, *at least I think it's rock solid—assuming I'm still alive and not dreaming.* Julie wasn't sure, because it was eerily quiet, dark, and she was definitely not upright.

TO BE CONTINUED ...

ACKNOWLEDGEMENTS

Thank you, everyone! The End. OK!! I'm JUST joking!!!! Are you *kidding* me?

In addition to my Guardian Angels, this book, and the rest of the trilogy coming, *could* not and *would* not have happened without support, encouragement, prodding, pushing, crowbar-prying, and tons of deep breathing exercises from a few amazing folks I *need* and *want* to mention. I just hope two things: 1.) I haven't forgotten anyone, and 2.) of those I've mentioned that they don't get upset that they're mentioned … some of you are mighty bashful!

My husband, Brandon, and our three amazing kids, Jessica, Alexandra, and Jack, you've been my WHY's, cheering me on. Your love, faith, and support to go after something I'm passionate about have meant everything. Humbling to have you give it back to me. You've been right: it feels awesome. I love you and am truly blessed to have you all.

My mom, Joy, thank you for always believing in my writing abilities from the time I was little. You've been encouraging me along the way… even to Portland! You *are* a genius!! Now you're creating, too. Keep going!! I love you!

My dad, Mike, for my sense of humor—clean, and, well, not so clean. Love you.

My sister, Christina, and her husband, Tom; my sister, Toni; and my brother, Ramon, and his wife, Connie, for always loving and uplifting me.

My mother-in-law, Stephanie, for always asking, "Is it ready yet?" I think Mackie would approve.

Daune Thompson, friend and "I Deserve It" Coach, who would NOT let up until she had a book in hand!! You've been a relentless believer "kicking me in the butt" for years. THANK YOU!! P.S. Don't stop now! (P.P.S. Thanks for Carlos's name!)

Charles, fellow writer ("Jump in!"), for introducing me to Nanowrimo years ago (yeah Nano!), and always asking me, "How's it going?"

Niki Roosma, dear friend, confidante, 1st Beta; kismet brought our boys and us together! HOW did you know I needed to meet Cheri??? Thank you so much!!!!!

Cheri, you've become so much to me in such a short time. Niki introducing us was serendipitous, too. Your unwavering generosity with feedback, encouragement, and guidance; unyielding faith in me; straight-up believer in my story and voice; magnanimous with time; and kind heart with my "fragile virgin" writing psyche.

Lois Lee, extraordinary! How you've kept me organized and sane, made my life easier in any way, always a laugh and supportive shoulder with a ready smile, ferociously loyal, AND willing to jump in JUST so I'd keep going!!! Love you lady.

Carlos Avelenda, Daune said to call. SO glad I did! Thanks for sticking with me and for sharing your wonderful in-laws with all of their experience and wisdom. Thanks to your family for putting up with the stop-n-go then GO! GO! GO! Great listener (before you'd even read the book), patient, kind, talented artist, and designer.

Joyce Mochrie, "Saint," her relentless copy editing eyes, attention to detail, and gracious patience with my novice-ness. Thanks for that *second* look!

Lauren Wise, another patient presence in my life and proofreader, even the flu didn't stop you from helping me when I was scrambling. Thank you.

My generous Betas to whom I'm more grateful than I can explain. I was terrified, and your feedback was OUTSTANDING: Leigh Anne Odinet and Monica Wambaugh, understanding friends and carpool gurus, who opted not to strangle me when I would have understood if they had. Kathy Casey-Paulsen, writer, friend, and gifted healer. My children, who indulged me when I asked if they'd listen to me read.

Thank you to Allie and Rob Schulte (for an ear to bend or idea to bounce off of), B2 (golden), Jill McMahon (counseling perspectives), Ashley Epting, for guiding me to Jerry Lee Sadler (Alaskan gold miner insights), Tammy Caputi (accountability, baby!), Lee Wilmeth (all things computer), Katie Mathis (unflappable, talented photographer), Bud (my neighbor and car "educator").

Carla Rice and Rachel Schiavo for keeping me presentable; Elizabeth Prentice and Kendis Browner, healers of hearts, minds, bodies, psyches, and souls. Thank you all for continually asking, always encouraging, amazingly patient.

Dr. Michael Mitchell and his wife, Danette, for helping me heal post head-on.

Julianna Lyddon, coach, mentor and friend with a warm, infectious, beautiful laugh, saw this in me a *LONG* time ago and reminded me to breathe and be open.

Susie and Michael DeMaria, incredible business partners, lifetime friends, always having our backs and laughing with us … even when it wasn't funny lol.

Darren Hardy, *Success* Magazine publisher, advisor, and mentor to so many of us around the world, for his *Insane Productivity Program*, and his assistant, Kat, who tirelessly got all of my questions answered.

Willamette Writers Conference, Portland, Oregon, for allowing me to be brave, educating me, opening my eyes, and introducing new friends. AMAZING weekend!!!!

Reggie Seidel, God rest your soul, the most exceptional high school English teacher I ever knew. Thank you for believing in me, teaching me how to write, sharing your love of writing, and still "red-lining" my work now.

ABOUT THE AUTHOR

Photo by: Katie Mathis

R. JILL MAXWELL graduated from American University with a degree in Journalism. After working in newspapers and radio, she helped her husband start a restaurant/catering business in Arizona where they live with their three awesome kids and two rescue dogs. *G.A.S.P.* is the first book in a trilogy.

Can't believe *G.A.S.P.* ended like that? You're not alone! To learn more go to www.rjillmaxwell.com

Printed in the United States
By Bookmasters